Martin Luther, Machiavelli and Murder
A Mystery of Renaissance Rome
Its Popes, Artists and Future Nemesis

Third Book in the Nicola Machiavelli Series

by
Maryann Philip

Front cover art: Clockwise from upper left: Giulio and Giovanni de' Medici (later Pope Clement VII and Pope Leo X respectively) by Raphael, "La Fornarina" ("bakery girl") by Raphael, Martin Luther as a young monk from the school of Cranach the Elder (from the original by Albrecht Dürer found at Ch. 1), Pope Julius II by Raphael.

Back cover art: Raphael's self portrait from "The School of Athens" and "La Velata," ("the veiled one") his portrait of his mistress, the "bakery girl." Original gammura in white; now in blue.

Color copies of the Renaissance art in this book are here:
https://drive.google.com/file/d/0B_0Hl_jBMWQ9RDhFcmoyZDd4N3M/view

Special thanks to Susan Harrison for her cover design and help with all the art in the book.

Copyright © 2016 Maryann Philip
ALL RIGHTS RESERVED

The History Behind the Mystery

The two months that Martin Luther spent in Rome in 1510 arguably changed the world. By his own account he arrived as a naïve young friar, eager to seize salvation for himself and his family by praying to Rome's holy relics. He left horrified by Rome's corruption, doubting conventional wisdom, and convinced that the pope was "worse than the Sultan of Turkey." (He later compared the pope to the Antichrist.) Seven years later, most of the ninety-five theses he tacked on the door of the Wittenberg Cathedral attacked practices he had witnessed firsthand in Rome.

What happened during that winter in Italy that so changed this devout young man? Read on to find out. As in earlier Nicola Machiavelli mysteries, historical characters appear only where and when they did in real life, doing what they did in real life, with rare exceptions noted in the Afterword.

While the murders that Martin Luther helps solve in this book are fictional, the background murders actually happened.

Cast of Principal Characters

(In order of appearance. Real persons *italicized*.)

Martin Luther: Devout young friar, ordained priest, and university lecturer. Currently an emissary to Rome on behalf of his monastery in Saxony, a German state within the Holy Roman Empire.

Nicola Machiavelli: Bastard daughter of the infamous *Niccolò Machiavelli,* and **of Caterina Biaggi**, publicly known as Nicola's "aunt". Lover of the painter *Raphael,* she has taken on aspects of his real-life mistress, *"La Fornarina,"* ("bakery girl") who reportedly caused Raphael's premature death––from too much sex.

Cardinal Alessandro Beccaria: A murdered cardinal, in life a reform candidate for the papacy.

Leonardo da Vinci: The archetypal "Renaissance man," famous in his own lifetime as the greatest artist, inventor and philosopher in Italy.

Niccolò Machiavelli: Italian diplomat, best known for writing "The Prince" and inspiring the term, "Machiavellian." **Nicola Machiavelli** is his bastard daughter.

Raphael, whose real name was *Rafaello Sanzio:* Artist and architect, most famous for his work for **Pope Julius II** in the Vatican. Ladies' man and lover of **Nicola Machiavelli,** among others.

Francesco Tedesco: Captain of the Swiss Guard, the papal army organized by Pope Julius II. Lover of **Caterina Biaggi, Nicola Machiavelli's** "aunt".

Giulio de' Medici, later Pope Clement VII: Cousin, ward and constant companion of *Cardinal Giovanni de' Medici*, who became *Pope Leo X. Giulio*, as Leo's papal successor, is infamous for hiding in the Castel Sant' Angelo when Rome was sacked and burned by Protestants in 1529.

Caterina Biaggi: Widow of an armorer; armorer herself to *Pope Julius II.* Mistress in their youth to *Niccolò Machiavelli,* and mother to Machiavelli's bastard daughter **Nicola,** who is publicly known as **Caterina's** "niece."

Pope Julius II: Famous in his time as the combative "warrior pope," he is now best known as the patron of Michelangelo and Raphael, among other artists.

Cardinal Francesco Alidosi: Treasurer to the court of **Pope Julius II;** suspected of treasonous dealings with the French. His bloody rule over Bologna at the pope's behest made him enemies.

Prior Piccolimini: Prior of the Augustinian monastery at the Church of Santa Maria del Popolo, where ***Martin Luther,*** as historic fact, stayed during his time in Rome.

Agostino Chigi: Banker to **Pope Julius II** and other wealthy clients, and a patron of the painter ***Raphael.***

Cardinal Giovanni de' Medici, later Pope Leo X. A scion of the Medici family and ***Martin Luther's*** future nemesis. The youngest boy ever made cardinal (at age 13), he was highly educated, a spendthrift and a hedonist.

Bishop (later Cardinal) Pompeo Colonna: Scion of a powerful Roman family who spent decades as a soldier. Led a short–lived Roman rebellion against **Pope Julius II.** Pardoned and made cardinal by **Pope Leo X,** he later helped Protestant troops enter Rome to sack and burn in 1529.

Alfonso Zanna: Notorious henchman who carried out the murders of Bolognese nobility ordered by ***Cardinal Francesco Alidosi.***

Frate Anton: Augustinian friar and member of Martin Luther's monastic order in Erfurt, Saxony. Acted as Luther's confessor during their trip to and from Rome.

Charles d'Amboise, Compte de Chaumont: French governor of Milan, patron of Leonardo da Vinci, and head of the French army that battled Pope Julius II when the pope declared war on France in 1510.

Andrea and Ugo Colonna, cousins and confederates of ***Pompeo Colonna.***

Heinrich von Marberg, brother knight of the Teutonic order.

Giocomo Capretti (*nicknamed **"Salai"** by **Da Vinci)** and **Francesco Melzi** (nicknamed **"Cecco" by Da Vinci):*** Apprentices and either adopted sons or "boy toys" of **Leonardo da Vinci,** depending on which biographer you believe.

Thomas Boleyn and Piers Butler, emissaries from the court of the new king of England, Henry VIII.

TABLE OF CONTENTS

The History Behind the Mystery 2
Cast of Principal Characters 2

TABLE OF CONTENTS 5
Ch. 1 - Death of a Holy Man 7
Ch. 2 – Da Vinci Discovers Another Murder 13
Ch. 3 - Rome's Holiest Place 15
Ch. 4 - The Dying Pope..19
Ch. 5 - The Corpse in the Sistine Chapel 23
Ch. 6 - The Pope's Banker Aids an Escape 31
Ch. 7 - The Gambling Guard..34
Ch. 8 - A Ransacked Room 39
Ch. 9 - A Desperate Ride 44
Ch. 10 - Sex and Money 47
Ch. 11 - Caterina is Followed 51
Ch. 12 - Of Faith, Pasta, and Sacred Pig Knuckles 55
Ch. 13 - A Dead Prostitute 66
Ch. 14 - The Cardinal's Funeral 68
Ch. 15 - Ambush 74
Ch. 16 - A Plan of Action 78
Ch. 17 - Two Smoking Priests..82
Ch. 18 - The Teutonic Knight 86
Ch. 19 - Martin Luther's Confession 91
Ch. 20 - In the Brothel 95

Ch. 21 - The French Count 104
Ch. 22 - The Oarsmen 109
Ch. 23 - A Sinful Past... 112
Ch. 24 - Leonardo is Worried 116
Ch. 25 - The Cardinal's Will 119
Ch. 26 - A Bloody Business.. 122
Ch. 27 - At the Pantheon 125
Ch. 28 - Raphael's Secret 131
Ch. 29 - Mud and Muck 135
Ch. 30 - Of Cannons and Courtesans 137
Ch. 31 - A Christmas Festa 141
Ch. 32 - Recalling a Murder 149
Ch. 33 - A Letter to France 155
Ch. 34 - The Whore and the Future Pope 157
Ch. 35 - Hiding a Message 161
Ch. 36 - Martin Luther Needs More Time... 163
Ch. 37 - Luther Performs His Penance 165
Ch. 38 - An Incriminating Admission... 168
Ch. 39 - At the Court of the French King.. 171
Ch. 40 - Conspiracy at the Medici Palazzo 174
Ch. 41 - A Sensual Interlude 179
Ch. 42 - Hiding from the Swiss Guard 184
Ch. 43 - Martin Luther Has an Epiphany 187
Ch. 44 - A Murderer is Revealed 188
Ch. 45 - Martin Luther Explains All 192
Ch. 46 - Martin Luther Begins His Journey Home 199
Ch. 47 - A Ghost from the Past 201
Ch. 48 - Cardinal Alidosi's Fate 205
Ch. 49 - Henry VIII Makes a Regal Offer.. 207

Author's Biography... 213
Afterword 213
Partial Bibliography 219

Ch. 1 - Death of a Holy Man

Young Martin Luther with tonsure, 1520
by Albrecht Dürer

Rome, Italy
Santa Lucia's Day
Early December, 1510

The naked man landed in front of them on the ancient Roman roadway, knees bent as if felled at prayer, hairy buttocks pointed at Heaven in obscene genuflection. He flopped sideways toward the Tiber River and lay at the inner edge of the road, curled on his side, chin tucked against hands clutched as if in supplication.

Nicola Machiavelli took a breath to calm her racing heart. The man was so close she could see the dust settling around him.

With a strangled cry, Martin Luther rushed forward to cover the man's nakedness with his cloak. "Drunks falling from the sky. The Holy City is Hell. I am in Hell," he shouted in guttural Latin. Skeletally thin in his brown friar's habit, he looked like a lost soul, bending over one of the damned.

He touched the shaved spot on the man's tonsured head. "*Misericordia*. He is a monk."

"A cardinal, *Frate* Martin," Nicola said. "See the ring?"

Luther knelt to stare at the enormous gold ring, set with a sapphire and emblazoned with crosses. Then he stared at the man's face. "I have kissed that ring," he gasped. "I pray God to help me––I only just met him. At the monastery where I am staying. He is Cardinal

Beccaria. The next pope, everyone said. A very holy man, they told me. I cannot believe this."

Luther's naïveté had surprised Nicola when she first met him, earlier that morning. Now, his raw pain sent tears to her eyes. Her mind searched for Latin words she hardly knew. "He may be Cardinal Beccaria but—-I'm sorry to tell you, *Frate* Martin—- he was not a holy man," she said slowly. "He fell from a brothel." Nicola had often hurried past the massive stucco structure, trying to ignore the cries of pleasure that floated over the Tiber River Road from its large second story windows.

"A brothel." Luther crossed himself again and looked at his own chest, as if it were a sin even to see the building looming above them. "God has punished him for his sins, then."

A woman screamed from a window overhead. Swallowing her reluctance, Nicola bent down to feel the cardinal's neck for a sign of life. It was without pulse, and as cold as the winter's day.

"He's not drunk. He's dead," she told Martin Luther, her shocked Latin sounding foreign to her own ears. Moving Luther's cloak, she inspected the wound on the corpse's chest, a stark red triangle against pale, bloodless skin. "And God was not punishing his sins. He has been stabbed in the chest."

"Stabbed? Murdered? This city. Such evil I never imagined." Luther's face was ashen. Then his eyes widened and he crossed himself again. "I must guide his soul towards Heaven, may God help me." Kneeling on the ancient paving stones, he placed a hand on the corpse's forehead and began reciting the last rites for the dead, with the same sincerity Nicola had admired when she watched him recite Mass. The instant he began speaking to God, he seemed lost to the world.

The screaming woman had moved to the brothel's interior, which muffled her agonized shouts. Nicola turned to watch the whores and their customers stumbling from the back of the whorehouse, in apparent response to the screaming. Several prostitutes fled first, their painted faces glancing back at the body as they called to one another in alarm. A papal Swiss Guard whom Nicola recognized followed, buckling on his sword, unmistakable in his colorful striped uniform. Then several merchants emerged and scrambled down the embankment to the river, shouting "Cast off!" to the boatmen moored to the whorehouse dock. The merchants were followed by two raggedly-dressed maidservants. Behind them hurried several more whores in gaudy silks and hooded cloaks. One of them was shoved aside by a Teutonic Knight, followed by a Knight of Saint John, judging from the crosses on their cloaks. Next came a laundress with pendulous breasts carrying a large reed basket of crumpled linens, two priests, and a heavyset matron with a garishly painted face, a colorful turban, and billowing yellow cloak. She stared at the body, mouth agape, then ran after the whores, shouting for them to return.

Nicola memorized what she saw, wishing she had a better view of the faces. All those fleeing disappeared into the first opening leading from the Tiber River Road to the tangle of alleys around the Campo de' Fiori.

Behind Nicola, a crowd was gathering around the body. Another priest bent to anoint the dead man's head, then knelt to join Martin Luther in reciting the rite of extreme unction.

The *bargelli* would surely arrive soon. But could they be trusted to look for what was missing? Unlikely, Nicola decided. Was she about to involve herself in a suspicious death again? Her "Aunt" Caterina would berate her for it, if she found out. But Caterina was in Bologna. On the other hand, Francesco, to whom they both owed favors, would thank her.

She decided to risk it. When she thought the whorehouse was empty, Nicola ducked through its open back door, into a small earthen-floored entryway lined with twig brooms, buckets of dirty water, stacks of stinking chamber pots, and baskets of crumpled sheets redolent of sweat and semen. Hurrying up narrow steps, Nicola went room to room on the upper floor, glancing around.

The two large rooms nearest the back stairs displayed wall-sized frescoes of men with penises as big as their forearms, swiving smiling women with mountainous, pink-tipped breasts. Fresh sheets on the enormous beds smelled of attar of rose, which failed to mask lingering odors of wine, sweat and sex.

These rooms had closets, and Nicola opened them: silk whips, chains, ties, and other instruments whose use she could only imagine hung there neatly. Was the pain a pleasure or a penance? Raphael was so careful not to hurt Nicola that she sometimes wondered if he had hurt other women, and why.

Dismissing these thoughts, she noticed a reddish smear on the windowsill next to the closet. She licked a finger and tasted it: blood. Thrusting her head out, she saw the noisy crowd directly below. Helmeted *bargelli* in brown tunics and chain mail were pushing their way toward the dead cardinal, using the butts of their halberds.

Hurriedly, she looked under the bed. There was nothing––not even dust.

She glanced into the remaining rooms as she hastened down the hall. Small, whitewashed and remarkably clean, each contained a floor mattress and a small table holding flagons of water and wine. A few bore signs of hasty exits: mussed sheets, a forgotten hat, spilled wine.

At the bottom of the front stairs, the parlors where rich men waited for the whores of their choice were garishly furnished, the walls festooned with obscene frescoes of naked figures, coupling in ways that seemed physically impossible. Nicola wished she could stop long enough to study the figures, so she could describe them to Raphael. Too dangerous—she could hear the *bargelli* clattering up the back stairs. She glanced into the back rooms on the ground floor: a kitchen with half-eaten meals on a large table; a tidy office piled with leather-bound account books. Then she pulled her hood around her face and hurried out the entrance door, onto the narrow street abutting the Tiber River Road.

Circling the building, she worked her way through the crowd gathered along the river, to find Martin Luther. Two helmeted *bargelli* stood over the cardinal's body and the kneeling priests, halberds crossed to block the crowd. Nicola could hear Luther's rumbling exchange with the other priest, who was evidently having trouble understanding his guttural Latin.

"There she is," Luther exclaimed when he saw her. "She can understand me. Please tell them what happened, and who this dead man is."

"The friar says this is Cardinal Beccaria," Nicola explained, switching to Italian. "See the cardinal's ring on his finger? He was thrown from the whorehouse window. We saw it happen." She pointed at the window above their heads.

One of *bargelli* knelt to examine the ring, and they glanced at each other. "There is blood on this windowsill," came a voice from above.

As the *bargelli* shouted back and forth between building and street, Nicola moved close enough to speak quietly to Luther. "You lecture at a *collegio*," she said to him. "You must know canon law. What must be done when the body of a cardinal is found on a city street?"

Luther, his face etched with sadness, seemed stunned by her question. Then he bent his head in thought. "In canon law I am no expert, *Fraulein* Machiavelli. But Cardinal Beccaria was a candidate for pope. So, regardless of canon law, I think the Church should handle this. For the sake of the Church.

Nicola envied the straightforward goodness of this simple friar. She had been just as naïve when she left the convent, but years in Florence and Rome and plenty of sin had blurred the lines between right and wrong. She thought of Dietrich, the battle-scarred papal guard she had just seen hurrying away from the whorehouse. She had always sensed violence in him. Had Pope Julius, who was dying, ordered him to commit this murder to eliminate Cardinal Beccaria as his successor? Or had Dietrich been bribed to commit murder, by one of half a dozen cardinals already vying for the papal throne?

On the other hand, maybe the Swiss guardsman had nothing to do with the murder. And maybe Cardinal Beccaria's ambition to become the next pope had nothing to do with his death.

One thing was certain: Francesco, *capitano* of the pope's Swiss Guard, needed to know that a cardinal was just murdered. Nicola saw her chance to pay him back for the many favors she and her "aunt" Caterina owed him. *Frate* Luther's moral compass and her own pragmatic instincts pointed in the same direction.

"This friar is learned in canon law," she told the *bargelli*. "He says you should take this body to the Vatican. I saw every man who fled, and they were almost all monks or priests. One was from the pope's Swiss Guard. Do you really want to question any of them? With the pope dying, and the cardinals fighting over who will succeed him? It's a Church matter. Let the Church handle it."

The *bargelli's* grim–faced leader, a head taller than she, looked as if he wanted to strike her. "Did you see the screaming woman?" he demanded.

"I saw all the whores run away, but I'm not sure which one did the screaming."

"Ask him if he saw her."

She translated for Luther, who nodded. "*Ja,* I saw. At that window, the one the soldier was shouting from."

By now the crowd had dispersed and the remaining *bargelli* had emerged from the empty whorehouse. They all conferred for a few minutes, glancing occasionally at Luther and Nicola. Then one of them walked to the riverside to commandeer a boat. Another tossed Luther's cloak aside as the men discussed how to carry the body.

White as milk, the dead cardinal lay curled like a fetus on his side, hands clutching as if in desperate prayer, narrow face frozen in a grimace of horror. He looked like an emaciated, tortured child. Martin Luther again covered the naked corpse with his cloak. "Tell them to have some respect," he boomed at Nicola, who cringed at his loudness.

"He's stiff. Just pick him up," she told the guards. Nodding, two of them reached under the cloak and grabbed the body wherever handy, heaving it up easily, like a bundle of sticks.

One of the *bargelli* took Nicola and Luther each by the elbow, none too gently. "To the Vatican. *Andiamo.*"

Ch. 2 – Da Vinci Discovers Another Murder

Leonardo da Vinci,
possible self-portrait, c. 1505-1510

Pavia, Italy
The Same Day

Sketchbook on his lap, Leonardo da Vinci peered down at the corpse that *Professore* delle Torre was preparing to dissect. Medical students in university gowns crowded the circular wooden gallery where he sat, their excited chatter echoing in the vaulted space. They called Leonardo "grandfather" and treated him with deference. Was it because of his reputation as the greatest artist and philosopher in Italy? Leonardo wished it were so, but knew his time was past. More likely the students respected him only because their revered professor was preparing an anatomy text with his help.

Leonardo doubted he would produce any useful drawings today, however. The corpse, which stank, was too decayed.

"This is the body of the guardsman killed a few weeks ago when someone ransacked the palazzo of Count Beccaria," delle Torre said. "The guard was Roman, so the City decided he was not a Christian. Therefore we can dissect him."

The students laughed. "Have they found the criminal?" someone asked.

"Not yet. Fortunately it has been very cold, which retards decay. Look here––he has been garroted. When someone has been strangled, the mark on the neck is unmistakable. Here it is a very slender mark––do you see it? Has to be a garrote. The mechanism of death varies, however. See how his head wiggles? I think we will find that the killer actually snapped his neck in the course of strangling him. I am going to begin with his head and neck."

Da Vinci put a sachet of herbs to his nose to prepare for the stink of the first incision. The murdered corpse brought back unpleasant memories. Back when he dissected corpses himself to understand the human body, his friend and patron Niccolò Machiavelli had coerced him into investigating murders, with help from Machiavelli's mistress Caterina and their bastard daughter Nicola.*

Remarkable women, both of them. Da Vinci had been half in love with Caterina since he first saw her, at the Roman convent that raised Nicola as her "niece."** But even with Nicola and Caterina for company, those months in Florence had been unpleasant, haunted by mangled corpses and ghosts from his own past.

"You see?" the professor called out. "His neck is broken. Did he die of strangulation, or when the neck snapped? Let's look at the damage to the windpipe and esophagus."

Machiavelli had written from France recently, to brag that he had told the heir to the French throne all about the famous Leonardo da Vinci. Machiavelli's *braggadocio* always had ulterior motives, of course. And Machiaveli was right: France was winning the battle for Italy, so France was the future. Maybe he, Leonardo, would go there someday. When the armies retreated, and it was once again safe to travel.

"The garrote completely crushed the windpipe, can you see? He could not breathe. Still, he likely died from a broken neck. I'm going to open the abdominal cavity now," delle Torre called out.

The smell nauseated Leonardo, and the nausea made him feel old. Every passing year seemed to make him more sensitive, more vulnerable. Why should he stay in this stinking room? The inside of the guard's body was turning to soup. There was nothing for him to

---

* Read about it is the second Nicola Machiavelli mystery, *Da Vinci Detects.*

** Read about it in the first Nicola Machiavelli mystery, *A Borgia Daughter Dies.*

draw, and no need to prove anything to these striplings in university gowns.

He rose to his feet, and felt lightheaded. "Steady, grandfather," said one of the students, who grabbed his shoulders and sat him down again. "Maybe put your head between your knees, if you are feeling faint."

"I'm fine," da Vinci said. He wasn't, but it would pass.

Ch. 3 - Rome's Holiest Place

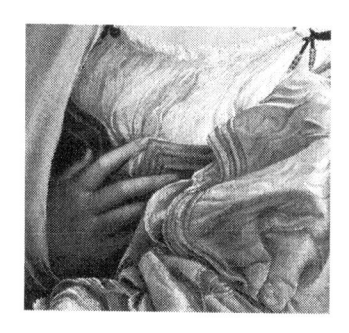

Detail of the blue gammura (beneath the hand)
with underlying white camicia, from
La Velata by Raphael

**Rome,
The Vatican
Later the same day**

Nicola's spirits rose when Raphael, the painter, joined her where she sat watching Martin Luther. Raphael reminded her of a Greek god––a dark, masculine version of a beautiful woman, with delicate features, soulful eyes and a grace of movement that sometimes took her breath away. He had tucked his long dark hair behind ears tinged pink by the cold, despite the wool *beretta* on his head. His elegant black wool tunic and surcoat were dusted with construction grit.

Raphael stared for a moment at Martin Luther, who lay prostrate, hands touching the altar of St. Peter, seemingly oblivious to the cold wind and the sounds of busy workmen. The ancient Basilica of St. Peter had been razed and the new edifice was rising slowly, like a huge set of jagged stone teeth, around the ancient marble altar marking St. Peter's burial site.

Nicola reached for Raphael's hand. "I was on my way to see you."

He sat down beside her and touched her cheek. "To tell me good news?"

"To tell you good news." She smiled at him, knowing there was no need to say more. She could feel that her monthly menses would soon begin. So she was safe from pregnancy, and would not need the abortifacient that had nearly killed her once, terrifying them both. She and Raphael spent less than half each month together, to avoid this happening again.

After so long apart, Nicola longed to be alone with Raphael. He stroked her palm. "One of my apprentices saw you with a foreign friar and Cardinal Beccaria's body. You are always finding bodies. But how did you find the foreign friar? Should I be jealous?"

She squeezed his hand, and smiled her most beautiful smile. "Indeed, you should be very, very jealous. I met him in a church where I stopped to pray for Caterina. He was chanting Mass. He has a beautiful deep singing voice and an odd accent. I thought he sounded like God, so I stopped to listen."

Raphael raised an eyebrow, smiling in the way that quickened her pulse. "Charmed you with his elegant Mass, did he? He is a priest, then? Not a friar?"

She smiled back. "He is both, and lectures in theology. And he did charm me, actually. He was slow and sincere. With that low, beautiful voice."

"Slow. And sincere." Raphael rubbed his forefinger between her middle fingers. "The fastest way to a woman's heart. But should you call him *Frate,* if he is a priest and professor?"

"He prefers *Frate*. Modest."

He moved his hand to her knee. "Now, I really am becoming jealous. Somehow you just happened to start talking?"

She covered his hand with her own. "No. I stopped a chantry priest from attacking him. The priest wanted to recite masses for the dead in the chapel where *Frate* Martin was celebrating Mass. He mocked *Frate* Martin for being slow. I thought they would come to blows, so I put myself between them. And offered to translate."

Raphael chuckled. "Priests coming to blows? I'd like to see that, though not with you in the middle. Your *Frate* Martin must have a bad temper."

"He had words with the chantry priest after he completed the Mass. He only lost patience when he realized the fellow knew no Latin, and therefore didn't understand a word of what he gets paid to recite all day. *Frate* Martin started sputtering in Latin about holy Mass and ignorant priests. The local fellow knew just enough to take offense."

"So he went after *Frate* Martin?"

"He was about to. They were both so stupefied to hear a woman speaking Latin that it stopped them."

Raphael laughed. "Not just any woman. A beautiful woman, dressed in the blue of the Virgin Mary. That would stop any man, priest or no. *Dio*, I wish I had seen that."

"The blue *gammura* is lovely, though a bit immodest. I thank you again for it." She squeezed his hand, which was stroking the top of her thigh.

He turned to stare at the top of the *gammura*, which barely covered her nipples. "It is perfectly modest with that heavy white *camicia* underneath, and those wide sleeves. I like it better without."

Nicola patted the *camicia,* to ensure she was decently covered. "I hurried *Frate* Martin out of there," she continued. "He is such an innocent. He was shocked to see prostitutes everywhere and people urinating in the streets. As he told me at great length. I was showing him the way back to his monastery when the body practically fell on us."

"That must really have shocked him."

"It shocked us both."

He patted her hand. "I'm sure. I didn't mean to sound unfeeling. Are you recovered?"

She smiled at him. "I've seen worse things, nursing the sick and preparing the dead for burial. *Frate* Martin, though. I didn't think anything could stop his talking. But that corpse did. He has done nothing but pray, ever since. He was eager to pray over the bones of St. Peter."

"He looks as if he is trying to sink through the ground to get at them."

"He is very devout. And we have to wait for Francesco anyway, so—"

"So here I am," said Francesco, from behind them. "Nicola, your *Zia* Caterina has sent a note from Bologna. I have it for you."

Nicola turned to face Caterina's lover, the *capitano* of the Swiss Guard. Like Raphael, Francesco had no idea that Caterina was Nicola's mother and not her aunt, as the two women pretended to save their reputations. Dressed in his blue and yellow striped uniform, he was half a head taller than Raphael, with a muscular body and a square, handsome face framed by heavy brows and shoulder–length hair the color of straw. His long yellow moustache drooped almost to his chin.

Stepping over the bench where Nicola and Raphael sat, Francesco turned to face them and bowed, handing Caterina's note to Nicola. She read it quickly.

"She says the pope is still very ill, and Cardinal Alidosi will not give her the money we are owed," she told Francesco.

"When will she give up?" he asked.

"She will never give up. It is a huge sum. And she fears being poor, like when she was young. But she will come home if the pope dies. She thinks it will be soon."

Francesco nodded. "The reports say he is close to death. Is that monk lying beside the altar the one who was with you when you found Cardinal Beccaria's body?"

"That's him."

Francesco ushered Nicola to her feet. "Go get him, and let's go have a look. The body is in the Sistine Chapel. We'd best get there before crowds of clerics show up to pray over it. You both can tell me your story on the way."

"Michelangelo let you into his chapel? He won't let me near the place," Raphael said.

"He's in Bologna, trying to get the pope to pay him. Go fetch your monk, Nicola."

"He's not my monk," she said. But she went anyway.

Ch. 4 - The Dying Pope

Left: *Portrait of Pope Julius II*, by Sir William Rothenstein, after a study by Raphael
Right: *Portrait of Cardinal Alidosi*, by Raphael

Bologna,
The same day

    Caterina smiled at Cardinal Alidosi, the papal treasurer, expecting to be ignored. Instead he glared back as he warmed his hands at the huge stone fireplace next to her, signaling his extreme displeasure that she even existed. His icy stare disconcerted her.

    Frowning down at her sewing, Caterina decided that the needle was her sword, and the embroidery ring her shield. Cardinal Alidosi was one of many hostile churchmen surrounding her stone seat, like an occupying army. Red–robed cardinals, priests in black, and monks in white strolled the brightly tiled floors, stared at the tapestries covering the walls, or clustered in small groups. The low coffered ceilings of the pope's sumptuous new *castello* amplified the quiet cacophony of footfalls and whispered voices that hinted at multiple conspiracies.

    But the clerics surrounding her, however different, were all surely raised amongst women doing needlework by the fire, dressed in widow's black just as she was. And their memories of those women made them as helpless as small boys in her presence.

    She was safer in her widow's weeds, needle in hand, than she would have been in armor, wielding a real sword and shield. These men might never let her into the pope's bedchamber, but they dared not make her leave.

She gave Cardinal Alidosi another sweet smile, and pointed her needle towards his heart every time it emerged from the embroidery hoop. He did not notice.

In previous days, she had periodically approached the clerk's table to request an audience with the pope. Always, the clerk put her off. She had watched Michelangelo appear and be admitted, among others. Now, the clerks were letting no one in, except the doctors who periodically bled the silent pope. She was losing hope.

"Ouch." She had jabbed her finger. The priestly figures around her jumped, then looked at her reproachfully. Renaldo, a tall, black-bearded Swiss guardsman, smiled at her from the iron–studded door to the pope's bedchamber. She smiled back.

He stepped aside as the door opened and doctors streamed out. The clerics formed a processional behind them, led by Cardinal Alidosi and followed by the clerk who usually guarded the bedroom door. Their agitated voices echoed as they swept down the marble stairs.

The anteroom was empty, except for Renaldo. Now was her chance. Nodding at him, Caterina hastened into the pope's bedchamber.

Pope Julius, gaunt and raggedly bearded, was almost as white as the walls and the sheets of his enormous bed. The deserted room, bereft of any decoration, smelled of sweat, urine and the blood left by his doctors in a brass bowl at his bedside. The fireplace was untended. The pope was untended. As much as she disliked the man, Caterina could not help but feel sorry for him.

She laid a hand on his forehead. "You are burning up with fever," she murmured. "Bring me some cool water and a cloth," she told Renaldo, who nodded. The pope's eyelids fluttered. "Caterina," he whispered. When she put the cool cloth on his forehead, his lips twitched into a slight smile.

When she felt the heat of his fever through the cloth, she turned the cool side next to his skin. "I have brought you a *tisana*," she murmured, "a fever remedy from the nuns of San Sisto, made by my niece for you. It has mint and lavender. Smell. Would you like me to brew some for you?"

The smell of the herbs she moved under his nose seemed to revive him a bit. He nodded.

"Put more wood on the fire and bring fresh water," she told Renaldo. "Where are your food tasters, Holiness?"

"The doctors sent the food testers away, two days ago," Renaldo said loudly, his eyes on the pope.

"What? Holiness, were you aware that the doctors sent away your food tasters? Holy Father, I beseech you: bring them back. They are here to protect Your Worship. Your guards will bring your tasters back, if you command them."

The pope's eyes opened wide. "Bring them back," he whispered.

***

Caterina ignored Cardinal Alidosi when he strode into the room later that morning. Flanked by the pope's food tasters and Swiss guardsmen, she concentrated on helping Pope Julius to drink the fragrant *tisana* she had prepared for him. At the fireplace, a cook stirred soup redolent of garlic and rosemary over a crackling blaze. The smell of sickness was disappearing up the chimney.

Alidosi's face turned crimson. "Get her out of here," he roared at the guards.

They looked at the pope. "She stays," Pope Julius murmured. Then he nodded to Caterina, who put the cup to his lips again.

Cardinal Alidosi strode over to the pope's bedside, opposite Caterina and the others. "Your doctors will not allow this," he sputtered.

Caterina moved the cup, so the pope could speak. "Dismiss them," he said, his voice hoarse.

"What?"

"You heard me. Dismiss the doctors. Throw them out," the pope croaked, glaring at Alidosi and the clerk and priest who had joined him. "You. See it done." The Swiss guardsman on Caterina's left came to attention, rapping the floor with the butt of his halberd. Muttering disapproval, Cardinal Alidosi and the others swept from the room, followed by two guardsmen who pointed halberds at their backs.

"More," the pope murmured to Caterina.

She gave him another sip of the *tisana*, which she had fortified with honey. "I know you are thirsty, Holiness, but save some appetite for the soup. You need it."

"It's ready," the cook called to her. She nodded to the food tasters to try it.

"Are you here because you have not yet been paid?" the pope whispered to her, when the servants were busy.

Caterina was grateful the pope had raised the issue himself. "Yes, Holiness."

He closed his eyes. "A woman's touch. The best medicine. Will you stay with me?"

Caterina gave him more of the *tisana* to sip while she spoke. "Alas, Holy Father, I have to leave if I am not paid. Because my funds are at an end–– I cannot afford to stay. Out of love and respect for you I equipped your army, at my own expense. The cannons and *arquebuses* that gave you victory over Venice all came from my armories. I knew you would see to a just payment, as you always do. But then came Bologna and your illness. It is a great hardship, especially to my workers. But I know you regret it, so I have the order—all you need do is sign it."

The pope moved his lips, but no sound emerged at first. "Why didn't Alidosi pay you?" he finally managed.

"He said he needed to consult with you, and you were too sick."

Eyes closed, the pope frowned as the food tasters approached. "The soup is good, Your Holiness. We tasted it again but it's the same as we all ate earlier, and never out of the cook's sight, he says."

Caterina spent the next half hour coaxing soup into the pope, with an audience of cardinals, priests and monks. Color was returning to Pope Julius' cheeks, and his voice sounded better. "Are you strong enough to wield a quill?" she asked him quietly, when he pushed away the bedclothes to help her manipulate the spoon. "Because I need you to sign the payment order."

"You will not leave?"

"Not unless you are asleep." Setting aside the soup, she pulled papers, quill and a corked vial of ink from her reticule. "It's the same as always," she told him, inking the quill and handing it to him.

"What are you doing, Holiness?" Cardinal Alidosi sounded as if he were talking to a small child.

The pope shot him an angry look. "See she is paid, Alidosi," he said as he signed Caterina's document. "Why has this been neglected?"

Alidosi swallowed, glancing around the room. Everyone there had heard the rebuke. "You were too ill, Holiness."

Caterina tucked the pope's order into her reticule, as Cardinal Alidosi glared at her. She had made him an enemy, even knowing he would likely be the next pope. But she'd had little choice. Never again would she extend credit to anyone, even a pope.

"I will sleep now," Pope Julius announced.

Caterina and Renaldo helped the pope to lie flat. "May I ask some of your guardsmen for help with my payment, Your Holiness?" Caterina whispered. "When they aren't busy guarding you?"

The pope nodded at Renaldo, then closed his eyes. "Do as she asks."

Ch. 5 - The Corpse in the Sistine Chapel

Michelangelo, *Noah Fresco,*
Sistine Chapel

**Rome,
The Vatican
The same day**

Nicola hesitated to interrupt Martin Luther at the altar of St. Peter's, though he prayed so much he was probably used to being interrupted. With trepidation, she tiptoed forward and called his name. Her whispered summons brought him to his feet with no sign of resentment, *Dio Grazie.*

Francesco and Raphael awaited them, next to the base of an ancient column from the old St. Peter's that stood incongruously near the middle of the future church. "Nicola, I must go. Find me at home when you are finished," said Raphael, kissing her quickly on the lips. "Pleased to meet you, *Frate*," he added over his shoulder to Martin Luther. Luther stared at him, slack-jawed.

Embarrassed, Nicola wondered whether Luther had ever seen a man kiss a woman before. No matter, she decided, turning to Francesco. "This is *Frate* Martin Luther," she told him. "We will need to speak Latin—he has no Italian. *Frate* Martin, this is Capitan Francesco Tedesco, of the pope's Swiss Guard."

"Swiss?" Luther's deep voice rumbled excitedly in a language Nicola did not understand. Francesco held up a hand to stop him. "I can't understand your dialect. Let's stick to Latin. We'll find the whore who killed Cardinal Beccaria, I promise you. Let's go look at the body."

"This is no ordinary fight between a prostitute and her customer, Francesco," Nicola told Francesco, as they began walking toward the Sistine Chapel. "Cardinal Beccaria was murdered many hours before we found him. The body was already cold and stiff. And there was no blood anywhere—little on the body, and none to be seen in the brothel, except a bit on the windowsill."

"*Ja*, this is what I am trying to tell you," Luther said. "I saw he was long dead."

Francesco absorbed this as they picked their way between piles of bricks and stone blocks littering the basilica construction site. "He was a very small man. Maybe he didn't have much blood in him."

"A wound like that would gush blood," Nicola responded. "It would have been all over his cassock."

Francesco frowned. "But he was naked, wasn't he? And he probably was naked when the whore stabbed him."

"Where is his cassock then? Someone cleaned him, and hid his cassock and his body somewhere, until he became stiff and cold. And did not steal his ring. But I don't understand why the person would throw the body out a window at midday, after hiding everything so carefully."

"To disgrace him!" Luther's voice was almost a shout, as if he were speaking from a pulpit. "He was known as a good man. Someone took his body there and threw it out a window."

"He surely got there on his own two feet, *Frate*," Nicola murmured, keeping her voice quiet. "No one could bring a bloody dead body into a busy whorehouse without people noticing."

"It probably was done to disgrace him," Francesco agreed quietly, as he glanced around as if fearful of eavesdroppers. "They left the ring to identify him. Finding a dead cardinal in a whore's bed is not news. But finding a naked, dead cardinal in the middle of the street under a whore's window will be on everyone's lips for months."

"Finding a dead cardinal in a whore's bed is not news here? *Misericordia*." Luther wrung his hands.

They passed through an unfinished archway into the adjacent courtyard, which was also piled with blocks of stone. Here workmen commingled with many figures wearing the robes of holy orders, hurrying to other parts of the Vatican. On the opposite side of the courtyard stood the Sistine Chapel, a lofty rectangular structure of plain brown stone named for the pope who built it, the present pope's Uncle Sixtus.

Nicola waited until they were away from the crowds to speak again. "This murder was very deliberate," she told Francesco. "The cardinal was killed, cleaned of blood, and hidden. And wait until you see the wound. Making it took some strength. I doubt most women could do it."

Francesco swore. "You mean I can't just arrest the whore and be done with it? You make it sound like an assassination, by a professional." His eyes widened. "*Madre di Dio,* it could be true. Cardinal Beccaria was the only truly holy man who wanted to be the next pope. He had the votes of all the good cardinals who can't be bribed. You make it sound like someone had him killed." Francesco stopped short and stroked his yellow moustache, his face grim. "*Porca Miseria*. That 'someone' could be the next pope himself. Who will be my superior."

"But that is monstrous," Luther boomed. "You are saying that someone murdered a holy man to keep him from becoming pope? That cardinals take bribes and murder their rivals for the pope's throne?"

Francesco stopped abruptly, looked around them, and glared at Luther. "Do you want to get killed yourself? Keep your voice down." He beckoned them away from the Sistine Chapel to a spot near one of its tall buttresses, where they were less likely to be overheard.

Exasperated, Nicola stepped close, to scold the unhappy friar. "You mustn't talk so loudly about things people hardly dare whisper around here, *Frate*. Whoever killed him had plenty of time to steal his ring, but didn't. So it wasn't someone poor. And popes do bribe their way to the papal throne. The Borgia pope did it. Pope Julius did the same when the Borgias' handpicked successor died–– mysteriously, after only a few months as pope. For your own safety, you need to keep your mouth shut."

A new thought occurred to her. "But Francesco, isn't Cardinal Alidosi most likely to succeed Pope Julius? And isn't he in Bologna with the pope?"

"He's in Bologna, yes. But Alidosi has plenty of people working for him, and some of them are killers. When the pope conquered Bologna he put Alidosi in charge. His henchmen systematically killed the supporters of the old ruling family, the Bentivoglio family."

"I remember the scandal," Nicola said. "The Bolognese made strong protest to Pope Julius. But he forgave Alidosi and refused to remove him."

"They say the two of them are lovers," Francesco whispered, looking around.

"The pope and this cardinal are. . ." Luther made a muffled squeak. "The pope?"

"Oh, I doubt that is true," Nicola said. "Pope Julius has three acknowledged daughters, and was always making eyes at Caterina. Alidosi does his dirty work—that's why the pope favors him."

"Daughters? The pope has daughters?" Luther, now whispering, looked stunned.

"Sorry, but it's true. I know one of his daughters personally," Nicola told him. "She was her father's ambassador to Venice when they were at war. And the Borgia pope had nine acknowledged children. I know one of them, too. Lucrezia Borgia, who is married to the Duke of Ferrara."*

---

* Read about it in *A Borgia Daughter Dies*

"A pope with nine children," Luther repeated. "I heard rumors of this when I was at university, but I did not believe them."

"The rumors were true. Nine *acknowledged* children, *Frate*. *Dio* knows how many others. I'm sorry to disillusion you. Truly I am. But it is for your own good. Stop letting every thought in your head come out your mouth. And watch that voice of yours––it's loud. If you can't keep quiet, someone may put a knife in your back."

Luther leaned against the buttress of the Sistine Chapel behind them, swallowing hard. Francesco stood in front of them, hands on his hips, as if to guard their conversation.

Satisfied that she had silenced *Frate* Luther, Nicola moved closer, to speak in Francesco's ear. "I looked through the whole whorehouse before the *bargelli* did, but very quickly. I saw no blood and no cardinal's robes. If you can find where the body was hidden, it may lead you to the killer."

"You went into that place?" Luther said, staring at her. "Have you no shame?"

Francesco laughed, to Nicola's annoyance. "One more thing, Francesco," she said to him. "One of your guardsmen was there."

Francesco turned to stare at her. "Which one?"

"Dietrich, I'm almost sure. I didn't get a good look at the face, though. Just the uniform."

He frowned. "Dietrich? That's not good. He's tight with Alfonso Zanna, Cardinal Alidosi's chief henchman. Zanna is the one who arranged for the murders in Bologna."

"You'll need to talk to Dietrich, obviously. And wait––you need to talk to that Knight of St. John over there, too." Nicola tilted her head towards a figure wearing a cloak emblazoned with a large white cross, who stood across the piazza, talking to a priest. "He was there at the whorehouse today. I saw him. Let's go find out who he is."

She felt Francesco's arm restraining her. "I know who he is. Are you sure he was there?"

"One of the men who fled was a Knight of St. John. That's him, I'm sure of it. Who is he?"

Francesco continued to clutch her arm. "That's Cardinal de' Medici's cousin and ward, Giulio de' Medici," he whispered. "Stay away from him, do you hear? Cardinal de' Medici is a candidate for pope, and one of the most powerful men in Rome. Giulio was at the whorehouse? He must like women. Rumor has it, his cousin prefers boys."

Luther gasped, and reddened. "Boys? A cardinal. . . *boys*?"

"Shhhh," Nicola cautioned him, gesturing.

Francesco took his *beretta* off his head and rubbed his forehead, as if it hurt. "Forget about Cardinal Alidosi and Cardinal de' Medici, for now. Before anything else, I need to look at the body in the Sistine Chapel. Then I need to find out whether His Holiness really wants me to investigate this murder."

"Why wouldn't he?" Luther demanded.

Francesco and Nicola looked at each other. "Because he may have ordered the murder himself," Francesco said, glancing around to be sure no one overheard. "Or he may not object if Alidosi ordered it, because he favors Alidosi to succeed him. For that matter, Pope Julius is a good friend to Cardinal de' Medici, too."

Luther moved closer to them. "You are saying the pope would condone the murder of a saintly man to make a wicked one the next pope," he said, looking Francesco in the eye.

Francesco put his hands on Luther's shoulders, and looked him in the eye. "It's possible, *Frate*. Yes. You are not to repeat that to anyone, do you hear?"

They stood silent for a moment. Nicola felt sorry for Martin Luther, who looked stricken, and ten years older than when she first met him. But at least he was quiet.

Francesco beckoned to them. "Let's go see the body."

*****

Francesco ushered them to the Sistine Chapel, nodding at the Swiss guardsman on either side of the door. "Keep the others out until further order," Francesco told them, ignoring the protests of a small group of clerics who had gathered outside.

Martin Luther gaped at the vast, empty room, its walls frescoed with biblical scenes and ringed with scaffolds that reached to the white plaster ceiling, far above their heads. On the ceiling was only one fresco. Luther frowned at the ceiling, then marched towards the bier near the altar, knelt close to it, and began to pray.

On the bier lay a figure dressed in red cardinal's robes and cap, arms crossed over his chest. Francesco approached it slowly, crossed himself, then moved the corpse's hands and unbuttoned the cassock. "It's Cardinal Beccaria, all right," he reported as Nicola joined him. "Right through the heart. And you were right about the strength needed to make that wound. The hilt of the knife tore into the skin. What are you doing?"

Nicola was pressing a bit of rag into the wound on the cardinal's chest. "Making a tracing, to match the knife if we find it. See how long the wound is? The knife was bigger than most daggers, I think. But not a sword. It didn't penetrate him."

"Are you sure?"

"Francesco, he was on his side. I saw his back. Do you want to turn him over and take off the cassock to see for yourself?"

Francesco backed away. "No. I take your word for it."

Nicola lifted the dead cardinal's hand. "His body is not stiff any more. He was curled up and stiff when we found him, but you and I moved his arms easily. And whoever laid him out was able to straighten him to dress him. It's been cold. He has been dead at least a day, maybe two. And look at his hands. They are clean and unbloodied. Look at his fingernails. No signs that he defended himself. It must have happened fast."

Francesco stared at her. "How do women know these things?"

"Who do you think washes and lays out dead bodies? Not menfolk. I saw some very sad things in the convent, preparing poor women for burial."

Francesco sighed, crossed himself again, then looked at the dead cardinal's hands carefully. "Maybe he was asleep when she stabbed him," he said as he rebuttoned the cassock and repositioned the hands. "Still, this feels more and more like an assassination than a whore's revenge. God only knows who ordered it. Cardinal Alidosi is the pope's handpicked successor, but there are plenty of others who want the papal throne. I'm not sure what the pope would want me to do. Much less, what the future pope––who may have ordered this murder–– would want me to do."

Nicola thought for a moment. "Surely you must at least talk to Dietrich. And those whores. At least the one who was screaming at the window. That much you need to do, to avoid gossip and questions. The pope would expect that much."

"Depends on who is pope. But yes, I must at least talk to Dietrich. Come with me. *Frate* Martin, we are leaving."

Martin Luther stopped near the door, again frowning up at the sole fresco on the ceiling. "The paintings on the side walls are frivolous, but at least the people are clothed," he remarked.

Nicola liked the wall paintings, some done by her old friend Botticelli in his youth. "They are Bible stories. The dancers and dogs are part of the stories," she told Luther.

"My point is, that one on the ceiling is the Devil's work," he rumbled, his voice echoing in the cavernous space. "Look. Noah and the ark are tiny, behind a wall of men and women naked as the day they were born. This is not what is written in the Bible. Noah's nakedness was shameful, when it happened. That painting is nakedness for nakedness' sake. Pure wickedness. Does Pope Julius even know about these paintings?"

Francesco laughed. "He ordered them." He tapped Luther's shoulder. "Let's go, *Frate*."

Ch. 6 - The Pope's Banker Aids an Escape

Detail of Swiss Guards in
The Mass at Bolsena, 1512, by Raphael

Bologna,
Later the same day

When she was sure the pope was asleep, Caterina hurried to the chambers of Agostino Chigi, the papal banker. Making sure no one saw her, she rapped sharply on his door, then entered before he answered it.

Seated at an enormous plank table covered with documents, Chigi looked up in surprise. Graying and heavyset, he was nonetheless handsome, and someone she had flirted with for years.

"Caterina. Why didn't you come see me earlier? I didn't even know you were in Bologna until an hour ago. I hear you have the power to resurrect the dead. The pope's doctors are furious."

She smiled at him. "You're looking well." He looked rich, dressed in fur–trimmed blue brocade and enough gold jewelry to dower every maid in Bologna. His enormous room was also sumptuous: tapestried walls, a marble fireplace with a roaring fire, and a large canopied bed hung with red velvet drapes to ward off winter's chill. The silver cups and wine pitcher on the sideboard, gleaming in the flickering light of two elaborate candelabras, were more elegant than any she had ever seen on a church altar. Had Agostino brought these elegant accoutrements with him, or had Pope Julius favored his personal banker with a room more resplendent than his own? It hardly mattered, Caterina decided. Chigi's power was obvious, and that was what she was seeking.

He smiled back. "You are looking well, also. Where have you been keeping yourself?"

"With the Dominican nuns when I need to sleep, or outside the pope's chamber, waiting for an audience." She seated herself across the table from him, and handed him the pope's payment order. "I need to trade this for a bill of exchange on your bank in Venice, Agostino."

"Venice? Why Venice?"

She had no intention of telling him the real reason. "Venice will be a new customer, now that it is allied with the pope. My armory made the cannons the Duke of Ferrara used to destroy the Venetian fleet, when Venice was the enemy. Now I will be able to offer Venice even better ones."

He raised an eyebrow. "Of course. But are you planning on going to Venice soon? There are rumors you told the pope you would stay with him."

"And I will, but perhaps not for long. It depends on his health. And whether he lives. Sometimes people rally just before death. I question whether he will make it through the night."

Chigi nodded. "He owes you more than money, if he does."

Caterina watched as Chigi drafted the bill of exchange. Signing it with a flourish, he applied three wax seals, imprinting them with his signet ring. "I've given you a bit of a discount, Caterina. But if the pope dies, Cardinal Alidosi may try to countermand the pope's payment order," he warned her.

"But if your agent in Venice has already paid the bill of exchange, it will be too late for that. Alidosi might cheat me, but he wouldn't dare cheat the papal banker."

"I wouldn't let him."

"I know you won't lie for me, Agostino, but please don't tell Cardinal Alidosi about this until you must."

"I can't promise anything, Caterina. My fortunes are tied to the papacy, and Alidosi will likely be the next pope."

"Do what you can, then." Caterina folded the bill of exchange and hid it between her breasts as Chigi watched with a connoisseur's smile. "You didn't hear this from me, Agostino," she said, "but I am very afraid Cardinal Alidosi is poisoning Pope Julius."

Chigi's expression sobered as his eyes moved from her bodice to her face. His congenial expression was gone, replaced by the magisterial mask he displayed as a man of power. "I didn't hear it at all. Just as I didn't hear the rumor that Cardinal Alidosi is a traitor who was bought by the French. As far as I am concerned, he is a great man. That is what Pope Julius thinks. And of course, the pope is always right."

"Agostino, please hear this. I do intend to stay with Pope Julius, just as I promised."

Chigi nodded. "I hear."

"But hear this only in your heart. If you find I am gone, will you find a way to tell His Holiness that fear of Cardinal Alidosi drove me away?"

A servant clattered into the room, stopping short when he saw Caterina. They are looking everywhere for you, *Madonna*. His Holiness is awake."

"*Madonna* Biaggi and I are old friends," Chigi informed the man. "I am giving a dinner party in four days' time, Caterina. Will you honor me with your presence?"

"Unless the pope has need of me, I will certainly be there."

Ch. 7 - The Gambling Guard

Pope Julius II (center) wearing armor,
with the Papal tiara on his head

Rome,
The Vatican,
Late afternoon, the same day

From the surprise on Dietrich's face when they first appeared in the guardroom, Nicola knew he was flummoxed by her presence. He also looked frightened, an oddity for a burly, battle–scarred man whose typical expression was grim enough to curdle milk. Seated on a bench in the guardroom, he kept his eyes on Francesco, who loomed over him. What Dietrich thought of Martin Luther, growling over his rosary by the brazier in the corner, she could not guess.

"I swear, *Capitano*," he said, "I had nothing to do with the cardinal's murder. No one told me to murder him. No one paid me to murder him. I didn't even know he was in the whorehouse, until you told me."

Francesco scowled at him. "Why did you run away, then?"

"Everybody was running away, because of that whore in the hall screaming."

"Did she scream words?"

"Over and over. Murder, murder, murder. Why do you think people were running? I didn't see anything, though."

"Did you see her?" Nicola asked.

"She was in the middle of the hallway, screaming her bloody head off. Yes, I saw her."

"What was she wearing? What did she look like?"

Dietrich gaped at Nicola. "She looked like a whore in a whore's *gammura*. What do you expect?"

Francesco interrupted. "Was she tall? Short? Fat? Thin? What color was her *gammura*? We need to find her."

He nodded, then frowned in concentration. "Tall and a little heavy. Very––" he gestured with his hands to show a buxom figure. "Hair piled on top of her head." He gestured again.

Martin Luther took notice, and interrupted in his native tongue. Dietrich evidently understood him. The two of them spoke for several minutes, sounding like rumbling bears.

"This friar saw her, too," Dietrich explained in Italian, when Luther fell silent. "We were talking about her eyebrows. She'd plucked them almost to nothing. They tilted up, what was left of 'em. And she had a large mouth. Or at least she seemed to, when she was screaming."

"Was she dressed in yellow? And you ran out ahead of her?" Nicola asked.

"She could have been. Yellow, yes. And yes, she was still standing there screaming when I left. It's not like it happened in the Vatican, *Capitano*. It was none of my business."

Nicola remembered the woman, being shoved aside by the Teutonic knight in his hurry to get away. "Did you see anything else? Blood?" she asked.

"Not a thing. I'd paid my whore and was getting dressed when the screaming started. I would have left in a minute or two anyway. I just left a little faster."

"Have you seen Alfonso Zanna lately? Was he there?" Francesco asked.

Dietrich's brows rose in surprise. "No. As far as I know, he is in Bologna with the pope. Why are you asking this, Francesco?"

"You've been free with your money lately. A lot of money. Where did you get it?"

"Gambling. I won it gambling. What are you accusing me of? You know I would never be disloyal to the pope."

Francesco's frown showed his skepticism. "Was anyone you knew there, at the whorehouse?" he asked.

"Evidently Cardinal Beccaria was there, but I never saw him. I didn't know any of the others. Why are you asking about Alfonso Zanna? Are you thinking Cardinal Alidosi is behind this somehow?"

"I think it's a possibility. Keep that quiet, though, understand? You can go now, if you've told us everything you remember."

Dietrich nodded, looking grim. As he rose to go, Luther spoke to him again in the guttural foreign tongue they had used earlier. Dietrich answered with obvious reluctance. After a few moments' discussion, he raised a hand as if in protest, and left.

"What did you say to him?" Nicola asked Luther.

"I asked him if Pope Julius is a good man, and why he is in Bologna. And is it true that he constantly wears armor––which apparently he does. I have a hard time believing everything I have heard about His Holiness," Luther responded.

"The pope went to Bologna to prepare for war with the Duke of Ferrara," Francesco said. "But he fell ill."

"That's what everyone says. I've always assumed there were good and holy reasons for papal wars." Luther responded. "But I don't understand why this duke is an enemy of the Church. They say that the duke was the pope's ally, a year ago."

"The pope and the Duke of Ferrara were allied with the French against Venice," Francesco explained. "But once Venice was beaten, the pope decided France is the greatest threat, and turned against them. But the Duke will not break his allegiance with France, since he took an oath. And French soldiers still surround his lands. So the pope declared war on the Duke of Ferrara."

"The pope is making war on a former ally who is Christian and refuses to break an oath," Luther said slowly, frowning.

"That's correct," Nicola said. "Tell him about the salt, Francesco."

"The Duke of Ferrara won the salt ponds next to the Adriatic Sea in the war with Venice. And unlike Venice, he sells the salt in Italy. The pope has a salt monopoly––or used to––so he is very angry about this."

"The pope is making war on a fellow Christian who used to be his ally, over salt, and because the Duke will not betray a sworn allegiance." Luther repeated, again shaking his head.

Francesco nodded. "That's it."

"He also doesn't like the duke's wife Lucrezia, who is the last pope's youngest daughter. Pope Julius hates the Borgias," Nicola added.

"And he doesn't like the duke's wife. Daughter to a pope," Luther muttered, as he returned to his seat by the brazier.

Nicola approached Francesco, who stood staring out a window at the Tiber River and the darkening sky. Below them, guardsmen were lighting torches along the walkway leading to the Castel Sant' Angelo, atop the Vatican walls.

"It's getting late," she said. "I need to find Raphael and try to get him to take me home."

"Can't you just stay at his house?"

"I hate staying at his house. He is always surrounded by a flock of artists, and busy being gracious to them. They are not always gracious to me."

Francesco gave her a knowing smile, as if to say, "You deserve it." Cheeks burning, Nicola changed the subject. "Do you think Dietrich is telling the truth?" she asked.

"I don't know. I have wondered where he has been getting the money he spends so freely. My men can't really afford that whorehouse the cardinals use. But maybe he did win money gambling. I'll see what I can find out. *Frate* Martin, let's go."

Francesco grabbed a torch and led them down a narrow winding stairwell. "What will you do next?" Nicola asked Francesco.

"I don't know. Maybe take Dietrich to arrest the screaming whore. If I arrest her, it will quiet the outcry. I can let her go if she doesn't know anything. Or keep her, if she knows too much."

"Prostitutes do not belong in the Vatican," Luther said, his voice echoing in the stairwell. "Especially if they are killers. Where would you put her?"

"In one of the cells in the Castel Sant' Angelo. It has housed women before."

"The pope keeps women in his castle dungeon, betrays his allies, and makes wars over salt," Luther repeated, his voice agitated.

Angry, Nicola turned to face him. "Be quiet, *Frate* Martin," she hissed. "These walls have ears." Luther stopped to glance at the wall next to him, his face puzzled. Then his eyes widened and he covered his mouth, gesturing to Nicola to move ahead.

The cobbled courtyard at the base of the steps was deserted. Nicola tugged at Francesco's arm when they reached its middle, where they could not possibly be overheard. "You need to find out whether Cardinal Alidosi's assassins are here or in Bologna," she urged him.

He smiled at her. "Do I? What if word got to Alidosi that I was asking these questions? He is already pope, in all but name. I don't know who to trust."

"You can trust Caterina, and she is in Bologna. Ask her to find out. I'd like to send her a note anyway, Francesco. I am helping run her Roman armory, and I have questions. I can easily ask her about Alidosi and his men."

"Do that, but don't say the question comes from me," he decided. "And do it right now. We have riders leaving for Bologna before dawn."

Ch. 8 - A Ransacked Room

Santa Maria del Popolo, Rome

Rome,
Monastery of Santa Maria del Popolo
Later that evening

From his hearthside chair, Prior Piccolimini of the Augustinian monastery at Santa Maria del Popolo scrutinized Martin Luther, a monastery guest he scarcely knew. He suspected that the dour young friar was starving himself as a penance. *Frate* Martin was too thin, and obviously unhappy. Granted, the body of a dead cardinal had fallen nearly atop him that morning. And *Frate* Martin was still recovering from his long journey on foot, all the way across the Alps. But his traveling companion, *Frate* Anton, claimed that *Frate* Martin constantly confessed the smallest sins, indeed, every time he farted. This young friar had an unholy fear of damnation. No wonder he seemed so despondent.

The young monk had already poured out his story of the day's events, in excruciating detail. Some things are better left unsaid, but Martin Luther had said them anyway. Now he stood with his head bowed, waiting for the prior's reaction.

"The Prior General is still in Bologna with the pope," he told Luther. "I know you are impatient to return home, but you cannot perform your mission here until he returns. In the meantime, are you enjoying the work I gave you, teaching Latin to the kitchen help?"

Luther's broad, bony face was remarkably easy to read. "I am happy to do it," he said, though he plainly was not. "But since most of them don't even know their letters, it is hard going without knowing Italian."

"I had not thought of that. You are getting out to see the sights of Rome, at least?"

Luther's face brightened. "I am praying at all the shrines and relics." Then he frowned. "Some of the other sights are not so pleasant."

The prior sighed. "When did you eat last, *Frate* Martin?"

Luther, his face shadowy in the candlelight, waved a hand dismissively. "Early this morning, with everyone else. Please don't concern yourself. I thought it was more important to inform you of Cardinal Beccaria's death."

"You did right, but now come sit by the fire." The Prior rang a small silver bell. "Bring food for *Frate* Martin," he told the servant who entered. "We can talk as you eat."

"Reverend Father, please, I am unworthy––"

"*Salve, Frate* Martin," said the servant, bowing as he left.

"One of your students, I suppose."

"My best student. Reverend Father, this is not necessary. . ."

"That is for me to judge. Sit, sit." The prior gestured toward the matching carved chair on the other side of his marble fireplace, then rose to tend the fire himself. A few sticks ignited a crackling blaze that danced yellow shadows across the wood-paneled walls.

"Sit and eat," he directed, when the servant entered and presented Luther with a plate of cheese and cold sausage.

"*Grazie*, Roberto," Luther said, as the servant bowed and left. Then he gazed at the food as if God had sent it straight from Heaven. After a quick prayer he wolfed it down, like a starving man.

The prior watched in silence. Surely this was a sign. Martin Luther was a brilliant scholar but his studies and work as a teacher did not satisfy him. He was hungry for something more than food. And his talents were wasted on the kitchen help.

He came to a decision. "God has given you a new task, *Frate* Martin. You must discover who killed our beloved Cardinal Beccaria."

Luther choked, his face turning white as an Easter altar cloth. "The Rule of St. Augustine says I must work, and I will do whatever you order, Reverend Father," he finally managed between coughs. "But I am a stranger here. I speak no Italian. It would take a miracle, for me to succeed at this task."

The prior smiled. "You must work with *Madonna* Machiavelli. God has chosen you both. Surely you do not think it an accident that you and she were both there when Cardinal Beccaria fell from the sky? God will provide the miracle, if one is required." He handed Luther a cup of water.

Luther sipped his water until his coughing stopped. "I will obey you in all things," he finally stammered. "But please do not make me work with the girl. For the sake of my immortal soul. The sin of Rome is eating at me." His face went from pasty white to red. "She is a flagrant and unrepentant sinner, with an artist named Raphael. It brings me——she makes me think impure thoughts, Reverend Father."

The prior resolved to be gentle. "You are afraid she will tempt you into sin?"

"She has already brought me sinful thoughts. And is the most beautiful creature I have ever seen. Why do you want to do this, Reverend Father? Even the Swiss Guard is afraid to seek answers. Are you not also afraid of what you may discover?"

"How can I know that, until I have the answers? You must trust me to use the information in the best interest of our monastery and other Augustinians."

"Of course, of course—"

"Which may mean not using it at all, except in prayer. But at least I would know the right prayer to make. Now—all men have sinful thoughts. That is why we have confession. But do you fear that *Madonna* Machiavelli will tempt you into sin, real sin?"

Luther reddened again. "If you mean, will she seduce me? No. But she is undoubtedly a sinner herself. With that Raphael. I would prefer not to be exposed to her."

"We are friars, not hermits, my son. Right now she is your link with the Swiss Guard. And I would like to speak to her."

"She said she would come to the funeral. Where is it likely to be?"

"It will be here. Cardinal Beccaria was a member of this order and stayed with us whenever he was in Rome. He is to be entombed here––Santa Maria del Popolo was his titular church."

"Did he have a cell here? We should probably see what he left behind. Perhaps there will be a clue to his death."

"The thought never occurred to me. Of course he has a cell here. Unlike most cardinals, he did not use the income from his benefices to pay for a Roman *palazzo* and a host of servants. His cell is near mine, in fact. And I need to go through it for his next–of–kin. Let us go look inside."

The prior's offices and sleeping cell were close to the entrance to the monastery, a long way from the *dormitorium* where the rest of the monks slept. Three stone stairwells accessed a confused labyrinth of short, whitewashed passageways. Torch in hand, the prior led Luther through the maze, and opened one of the doors.

"Not locked," Luther observed.

"We don't do that. Though perhaps we should here, so close to the entrance. But look––see his strongbox? I know he kept that locked. How very strange."

Cardinal Beccaria's cell was three times the size of the tiny spaces allotted to ordinary friars, comfortably equipped with the usual cot, a cushioned window seat, a brazier for warmth, and a chair with an elaborately–carved back, next to a large table scattered with documents. A neat row of books with fine leather bindings was centered against the whitewashed wall at the back of the table. In front of the books a small strongbox lay open, key in lock. Jesus, hanging from the painted crucifix above the table, appeared to be staring at it.

Feeling increasingly alarmed, the prior opened the wooden chest at the foot of the dead cardinal's bed. "I have an uncomfortable feeling this room has been searched," he told Luther. "Cardinal Beccaria was an excessively neat man. I have never seen his papers this disordered. And look here–– these robes and cassocks are tossed about, as if someone was looking for something."

"Did anyone here know he was dead, before I reported to you?"

"The rumors found us midday. Soon after Tierce. I didn't believe any of it, though, until you came to me personally."

They looked inside the unlocked strongbox, finding a few papers, which Luther set aside. "Would he have kept gold or jewels in this box?"

"If he had any."

Luther stooped to pull something out of the brazier, which was filled with ashes. "He has been burning documents. Here is all that is left. The writing is in Italian, I think. What does it mean?"

The prior stared at the corner of a burned paper, aghast. "*Misericordia*. It says 'shame.' 'Disgrace.'"

"Is that Cardinal Beccaria's handwriting?"

"I'm not sure."

Martin Luther frowned at the burnt scrap. "Was there some shame or disgrace in his background?"

The prior took a deep breath while he considered. "As a young man, he was a soldier. In the time of the first French invasion, under the Borgia pope. Something happened to him then, so horrific that he handed his estates over to his younger brother and joined the Augustinians when the war was over. I never asked him what it was. But he confessed and did his penance. And freely admitted he had been a sinner."

"His time as a soldier would explain the handwriting, then. It is not monkish script." Luther pulled a book from the row of them at the back of Cardinal Beccaria's document table. "May I borrow this? I need somewhere to put these papers––particularly this burnt piece of paper–– where they will be safe. And I would like to re-read this book."

"St. Augustine on Grace and Free Will? A good choice. I think we will inherit the cardinal's library, but I have to check his *testamento*. At any rate, it is yours for now."

"The bell is ringing for Compline. I hope you will excuse me for missing the other Holy Offices today, Reverend Father. I am in sore need of prayer, now. Shall I return tomorrow, and have a more thorough look around? I should look through the documents on his table."

"Of course, *Frate* Martin. Let us go to Compline together. When time allows, though, I want you to do everything in your power to learn who is responsible for Cardinal Beccaria's death."

Ch. 9 - A Desperate Ride

16th Century Venetian Galley

Chioggia, Italy
The following evening

Caterina suppressed a groan as Renaldo helped her from the saddle. She nearly stumbled as he set her on her feet.

"Thank you again for letting me join you," she said, her voice shaky. As she brushed off her riding skirt, she gave silent thanks to God for getting her closer to where she could deposit the money the pope had given her, before he could change his mind. Or Cardinal Alidosi could change it for him.

She had promised to keep up with the couriers when they left Bologna before daybreak that morning. And she had. But it had been the hardest ride she had ever endured. Her split skirt had rubbed her inner thighs raw, and her legs quivered with fatigue. They had stopped only once, to change horses. Every muscle in her body ached, and she was simultaneously faint from hunger and queasy from the jarring ride.

Renaldo smiled, without seeming to notice her distress. "It was no problem, *Madonna* Caterina. Our couriers were scheduled anyway. And we are in luck. Our boatman is still in port, waiting for the night tide. The weather is good, so we will be in Venice by dawn. There is even time for a bite to eat. Come."

Stefano, showing no fatigue whatever, handed her saddlebags to Renaldo and took the bridle of her lathered mount. "You did well, *Madonna* Caterina. This was as fast a journey as we ever have made. They probably don't even realize you are gone yet."

She tried to smile, but her jaws ached from clenching her teeth. "I hope not. I left plenty of the *tisana* for Pope Julius, and instructions with the cooks." She had also left behind her maidservant Faustina and most of her possessions, which Faustina would somehow get back to Rome. Except for Renaldo and Stefano, she was utterly alone.

"If the pope gets better he will surely notice your absence," Renaldo said. "But perhaps he will not mind."

He led her to a table overlooking the dock where the galley for Venice was moored. A burly man who seemed to know him brought them a flagon of wine, cups and bread.

Shivering as the damp cold penetrated her cloak, Caterina tried to ignore the smell of salt water and dead fish. Fortunately, the wine had been warmed. She sipped the fruity red and ate a bit of bread while she watched the full moon rise. Busy figures on the galley's upper deck lit oil lamps that reflected off the darkening water. Oars erupted randomly from the portholes below, like the legs of an enormous centipede.

In silence, they watched the glittering triangle made by the full moon on the waters of the dark bay.

"We will need to board soon," Renaldo said.

"Will we freeze to death?"

"There is a brazier of warm coals and plenty of blankets in the passenger cabin. You will sleep like a baby."

*****

The next afternoon, Stefano was on his way back to Bologna at an easy pace, with Caterina's mount in tow. He'd had a good sleep in the portside inn. The dispatches he carried were not urgent––not as urgent as resting the horses, anyway. The day was sunny and unexpectedly warm, the fields green and lush from winter rains. There had been no sign of the French on the hard ride the day before. And anyway he was well armed, big as an ox, and in papal uniform. He had money for a good dinner, at papal expense. What more could a man want?

Then trouble appeared. Three figures galloped toward him, and he recognized them—Cardinal Alidosi's men, the ones no one trusted. Cursing under his breath, he rehearsed in his mind what Renaldo had told him. "Don't volunteer information about Caterina, but don't lie, either. If you must, say we were under orders, from the pope's own mouth. Which is the truth."

They galloped until almost upon him, swords bouncing at their sides, daggers protruding from their boots. Then stopped in unison, in a cloud of dust. Ugly as plague corpses, all of them.

"Where is Renaldo?" Alfonso Zanna demanded. He was the ugliest of all of them, with a long face full of crooked yellow teeth.

Stefano shrugged. "He took the galley last night. Probably in Venice since before dawn."

"And the woman? Caterina Biaggi? Where is she?"

Stefano adjusted his reins while he considered his answer. "I don't know. How is His Holiness?"

The three men looked at each other. "Better. Much better. He swears it is the *tisana* that *Madonna* Caterina made for him. He is roaring for her to come back."

Stefano raised an eyebrow. "Are you claiming he sent you to fetch her, then?"

Zanna frowned. Clearly he did not like being questioned. "Cardinal Alidosi sent us. At the pope's behest, of course. Is she in Venice, or not?"

"I can't say."

Zanna's face reddened with anger. "I know you were ordered to Venice and you took her with her, Stefano. Don't play with me. She is either there or she isn't."

"But I am not, you see," Stefano said ponderously. "So I don't know for sure."

"What *do* you know, then?" Zanna barked. "Tell me what you know."

Stefano saw no way around this question. "She might be gone by now. She went to deposit her money with her bankers there. The pope ordered us to help her."

"He didn't order you to take her to *Venice,* you fool."

"She was no trouble. We were going anyway."

"Do you know where she is staying?"
"No."
"Do you know who her bankers are?"
"No."

Alfonso Zanna, his face contorted with anger, squeezed the hilt of his sword and bit his lower lip, showing long yellow canine teeth like a dog's. Disconcerted, Stefano put a hand on his own weapon. He knew he could not manage the three of them. No need, fortunately. After giving him one last ugly look, they thundered off towards Chioggia.

As he watched them go, Stefano wondered if he should follow them, out of eyesight. In Chioggia he could leave a message for Renaldo, telling him that Alidosi and his men were chasing Caterina. But they would probably miss the night boat, which gave Caterina at least two days' start. And his own orders were to deliver dispatches. He had best follow orders.

Besides, he was looking forward to a good dinner.

Ch. 10 - Sex and Money

Left: *Self-portrait* by Raphael
Right: *La Fornarina* by Raphael

**Rome,
Two days later**

Nicola watched Raphael, who was naked as a newborn, happily eating freshly–baked bread slathered with honey at her table. They had scarce left her bed for two days.

"When I was a little boy, I thought the smell of new–baked bread was the smell of Heaven. It's still what I expect to smell if I ever get there. Now, it is the smell of this place and you, as well as Heaven. You *are* Heaven. I can't pass a bakery without thinking of you."

The scent from the baker's ovens on the ground floor filled Nicola's otherwise spartan *appartaménto*. She had refused the sumptuous silks and paintings Raphael offered her, though she'd let him pin up a few drawings. Botticelli's crucifix, given to her in gratitude,[†] was the only other decoration on the whitewashed walls. The embers from a large fire glowed red in the brick fireplace.

Raphael stood and inhaled deeply, grinning. "That smell makes me hard, I swear. You see? Come here."

Misericordia, she could not help herself. Just as he began to lift her skirts, someone began shouting and banging on the door.

"Ignore it," Raphael said.

"Nicola. Open the door. I know you are there," roared a male voice.

She ran to the window, as Raphael grumbled behind her. "Give me a moment, Francesco. What's the hurry?"

"Papal orders. And a letter from Caterina."

She hesitated at the base of the stairs. Despite the shawl she had grabbed, it was obvious she wore no sleeves or *camicia* under her *gammura*. She covered herself as best she could.

When she opened the door, Francesco looked her up and down, fingering his moustache and smiling broadly. "Where is Raphael?"

"Upstairs," she said, aware she was blushing. "Give me Caterina's letter and come have some bread and honey." As they climbed the narrow stairs, she clutched her shawl and tried to arrange her hair, realizing how she must look. "How is the pope?"

"The pope is better, and wants more of the *tisana* Caterina gave him. And he wants Caterina, who made it and then left. Does her letter say where she is?"

"Give me time to read it." Gesturing to Francesco to take a seat by the fire, she broke the wax seals. "*Dio Grazie.* The pope has finally signed the payment order. We will have money to pay our workmen again."

Francesco poked his sword at the logs he had added to the fire, smiling as the blaze rekindled. "I'm glad to hear it. But where is she?"

---

† Meet Botticelli in *Da Vinci Detects*

"I don't think she got my letter, Francesco. I suppose it is too soon. Because she didn't answer my questions about whether Alidosi's henchmen were in Bologna. The letter is full of complaints about Alidosi, but it doesn't answer my questions."

Francesco pulled a stool close to the fireplace to warm his hands. "Doesn't matter now. *Where is she?*"

"Why does the pope want her, Francesco? Is he angry at her? He isn't threatening to put her in prison, is he?"

"He may be angry at her. But my impression is he wants her to come back to nurse him. Not to put her in prison."

"Nursing the pope would be prison to Caterina."

Francesco glared at her. "Just tell me where she is. Or give me the letter."

She could hardly deny knowing where Caterina was. "She was leaving for Venice when she wrote this, several days ago. She should be there by now. I imagine she is staying in a convent, but I have no idea which one. She says to send letters to the Chigi bank."

"Venice? What is she doing in Venice? The pope has soldiers combing the roadways for her between Bologna and Rome. Why on earth would she go to Venice?"

"So she could deposit our money with our bankers there."

Francesco's surprised face melted into laughter, breaking the tension. "*Porca Madonna!* I miss her. Venice was much closer, of course. It makes sense that she went there. But if she doesn't come back, Pope Julius will never forgive her."

"She doesn't expect to keep the papal account, Francesco. She and Pope Julius have had their differences, and with the pope's new alliance against France, our armory is now on both sides of the war. Our first armory is in Milan, remember."

Raphael walked out of the bedroom, dressed in an old tunic and boots. Both men smiled slightly and sized each other up, like dogs that know each other's scents.

Nicola repositioned her shawl, wishing she weren't naked under her *gammura*. "Why did you say it doesn't matter, Francesco? You said it doesn't matter whether Caterina answered my questions about Alidosi's henchman."

"Because the whore has disappeared. The one who did the screaming. Dietrich and I went to the whorehouse to look for her, and look for blood. Just as you said. She never came back. So she has admitted her guilt."

"She has admitted her fright, is all. Did you find any blood?"

"None."

"What about the cardinal's clothes?"

"She must have burned them, or she took them. They aren't there."

"You need to find her."

"Dietrich is combing the stews for her. He knows what she looks like."

"Is he looking amongst the bodies of the dead?"

"What? No. Why should he?"

"She was screaming because she saw the murderer, which means he saw her. And he will likely kill her."

"He?"

"I think so, yes, because of the strength it took to make the wound. Plus, we think he is a professional assassin. Don't tell me you've forgotten this already."

Francesco frowned at her. "Look, everyone is happy about how the cardinal's murder is being pursued. The world thinks the whore did it, and Dietrich is looking for her. If the whore is dead, good riddance. Finding Caterina and more of her *tisana* is my job now."

He stood, and placed his stool next to her table. "While you put on more clothes-- you really must put on more clothes--I will draft today's dispatches, telling everyone to look for Caterina in Venice instead of on the road to Rome. Then I will take you to that nunnery, to make them give me more of that *tisana* the pope wants."

"Can I write another note to Caterina?"

"Of course. If she is reluctant to return to the pope, your letter will be our bait for her. But be quick about it."

Ch. 11 - Caterina is Followed

Undated image of St. Mark's Plaza, Venice

Venice,
The Same Day

Hand shaking, Caterina began answering Nicola's letter, which the Chigi bank had delivered by messenger:

> Dear Nicola,
> I hope when you get this you will already have the bill of exchange to pay our workers. In case I don't make it back for some reason, you can retrieve the money here at the Fugger bank––I put it also in your name. All is well with me but don't send more letters to Venice. I may not be here much longer.

She did not dare mention where she was going, because the men following her would not hesitate to open her letters. Besides, Nicola knew.

> To answer your question about Alfonso Zanna. As you seem to know, he is a notorious assassin. He was in Bologna when I first arrived, and constantly surrounded by his men. There were five or six of them. The people hate him there, for what he did to the Bentivoglio family and their followers. So he needs constant protection. Even in the pope's new *castello,* it is obvious he did not feel safe.

I am sure Alfonso Zanna was not in Bologna when I left. But I have seen him, here in Venice. His face is fresh in my mind and I am sure I have not seen it in Bologna since November.

Should she tell Nicola that she suspected that Zanna was hunting for her? No—it would only worry her. Besides, maybe these fears were silly.

She had spotted Zanna only an hour before, mounting the marble steps to the Doge's Palace ahead of her. With Zanna was Cardinal Alidosi's henchman Ignacio, and a Teutonic knight, judging by his cloak. Fearful, she had faded to the back of the crowd, entering the *Sala dei Pregadi* only when the trumpets blared to announce the *Doge*.

The audience chamber in the *Doge's* Palace was the largest room she had ever seen, several times the size of the audience chamber Pope Julius used in the Vatican, its walls and distant ceilings adorned with colorful paintings of saints and the history of Venice. She had watched as *Doge* Loredan mounted the dais in his cloth–of–gold robe and matching peaked cap. Then Zanna and his companions strolled in front of the dais, obviously looking for someone in the milling crowd. She melted away, as quickly as she could.

She now sat at the clerk's desk in the Chamber of the Council of Ten, waiting for her meeting to begin. The clerk had lit the tall candelabras in each corner and was centering smaller ones on the mosaic table inlaid with precious stones that was nearly the size of the room. Were the green stones jade from China? Were the candelabras and the Council's ten gilded chairs made with real gold? It was possible. All the riches of the East poured through Venice.

Caterina had spent the previous two days exploring the markets and dockyards of this beautiful city. The Chinese silks fluttering in the Venetian breeze were like none she had ever seen, even in Florence. As a widow she could not wear the bright colors that shimmered like butterfly wings. But she had purchased black *brocado* that glittered subtly with gold thread; translucent black silk for veils that would show her luxuriant dark hair; and silk for sleeves that went from opalescent to grey to silver as it moved, like a fish in a stream.

The clerk gestured, wanting his seat back, so she blotted and folded her unfinished letter to Nicola. "*Grazie* for the loan of your desk and pen," she told him. "Where do you want me to wait?"

He bowed. "At the bench against the wall."

While waiting, she rearranged Leonardo da Vinci's drawings of the weapons manufactured in her armories. She knew from her half day in the dockyards, inspecting the ships, that the Venetian armorers were very skilled. She had surreptitiously sketched the pulley system they had devised to roll heavy cannons inboard so they could be quickly swabbed and reloaded. It allowed them to place guns below decks, behind portholes that could be closed in stormy seas. She would ask Leonardo to duplicate this invention when she saw him.

The Venetians were obviously manufacturing the latest cannons, but she saw many old ones, too. Some of the galleys even had the early versions made of iron rods encased in iron rings, like a barrel. That style exploded. She could help local merchants replace them. Venice undoubtedly had *arquebuses*––probably copied from hers–– but they were small enough that the ships' captains wisely kept them locked out of sight. Her *arquebuses* were famous, and the best. She would emphasize that in her presentation.

The Council of Ten filtered into the room, each man looking at her curiously as he seated himself. Their surcoats, caps and tunics mimicked the bright hues of the table, walls and ceiling. Gray-haired and clean-shaven, their necks and fingers heavy with gold jewelry, they reminded her of peacocks. All that color, some of it moving, made Caterina rub her eyes.

When the head of the Council arrived he bowed to her. "This is *Madonna* Caterina Biaggi, whose cannon destroyed our fleet when we were at war with the pope. Now that we are papal allies, she is eager to show us her wares."

"My lords, you have seen what the Duke or Ferrara did to your fleet with cannons manufactured by my firm. I am pleased to offer you our latest designs, which are even better. We also make the best available arquebuses," she began, gesturing with a flourish at Leonardo da Vinci's drawings.

The Council of Ten seemed startled to be listening to a woman. Fortunately, they were too polite to say so. They admired Leonardo da

Vinci's drawings, particularly the ones of the Duke of Ferrara's cannons. They were also interested in the *arquebuses,* particularly the ones with the wheelock that da Vinci himself had invented, which created a spark without the need of a fuse.

"I can serve you either from my Roman armory, by sea from Rimini, or from the armory in Milan via Pavia and the Po River," she told them.

The head of the Council smiled apologetically. "Alas, *Madonna* Biaggi, our coffers are nearly bare after the prolonged war. We are having trouble even paying our soldiers. But once our trade picks up again, we will want to modernize. And we know how to find you."

Knowing she had been dismissed, Caterina gathered up her drawings. "Are any of you merchants, who need better protection for your fleets? Many of the cannon I saw in the dockyards are outmoded and dangerous––the new, stronger gunpowders will explode them and kill your crews. And you will be no match for pirates or French raiders, either."

One of the older men waved a hand at her. "I'm interested. Come see me tomorrow morning. Mine is the fleet of black and yellow galleys. We often bring goods to and from Pavia, so you could supply us there."

Caterina breathed a sigh of relief. Here, perhaps, was the opportunity she needed.

Ch. 12 - Of Faith, Pasta, and Sacred Pig Knuckles

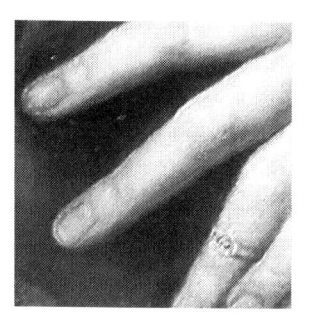

Detail from the painting *La Fornarina* by Raphael
Is this a wedding ring?

Rome,
Later that afternoon

While Francesco waited outside the convent walls, Nicola helped make a new supply of the *tisana* that Pope Julius demanded, enough to last him for many weeks.

"I can't believe I am making my *tisana* for Pope Julius himself," said Sister Beatrice as she stripped dried mint from its stems. "Nor that the request comes from you––almost our only student who was not the daughter of a cardinal or a pope."

Nicola smiled. The mortar and pestle were familiar in her hands, from working with Sister Beatrice as a student. "I had forgotten that Lucrezia Borgia and her sister were here.‡ Do you hear from Lucrezia?"

Sister Beatrice leaned back, looking weary. The flesh of middle age had melted away from her once plump body, leaving her white wimple loose around a face that sagged into wrinkles along her laugh lines. Though now nearly blind, she still looked at Nicola as if she could see through her. "She has made several generous gifts to this convent. Lucrezia was like you–– intelligent and rebellious," she said. "I keep expecting you to be like her––coming back to San Sisto to have a baby in secret so you can still make a good marriage. Lucrezia has done well,

---

‡Read about it in A Borgia Daughter Dies

though, as Duchess of Ferrara. Founding convents and performing all manner of good works. They call her 'the good Duchess.' So maybe you will do well, too."

Nicola patted Sister Beatrice's hand. "I am doing well. And I do good works, too. So stop worrying about me."

Sister Beatrice squeezed Nicola's fingers. "You know we want you back. Your father paid us for your living when he left you here. But we would take you back regardless. We miss you."

Touched, Nicola felt tears in her eyes. "I might come back some day. I miss the quiet here, and the library, and the music. And you, of course! But I visit often enough, don't I? And I think I am doing more good on the outside."

Sister Beatrice raised an eyebrow. "And more mischief, I am sure. We hear the rumors." She let go of Nicola's hands and mixed the *tisana* with her own, sniffed it, then crumbled it back into the bowl, feeling its texture. She crumbled in a bit of lavender and bergamot, smelled the mixture again, and held a handful under Nicola's nose. "There. What do you think?"

Nicola inhaled deeply. The luscious smell masked the faint odor of urine always present in the whitewashed *infermeria,* no matter how thoroughly the nuns scrubbed it. "Heavenly," she said.

"That's as much as we can make for now. We have used all the mint."

"Can you get more? His Holiness may want more."

Sister Beatrice transferred the *tisana* to a small amphora plucked from her shelves of remedies. "Yes, of course. I'll see to it. Other convents and monasteries will supply us. *Dio* knows, we have supplied them often enough." She corked the amphora. "Off you go. Come back and visit again soon."

Francesco snatched the *tisana* from Nicola when she emerged from the convent, then headed up the ancient stone Appian Way at a fast pace, his raised halberd parting the crowds as if by magic. Nicola kept up as best she could. The barrel–domed Bath of Caracalla loomed on one side of them; the long brick wall that surrounded the Convent of San Sisto on the other.

"Well met," a deep voice called to them. It was Martin Luther, rushing up from behind. "*Capitano* Tedesco," he boomed, "Prior

Piccolimini has ordered me to help you find the murderer of Cardinal Beccaria."

Francesco laughed, without even glancing back at Luther. "Tell your prior that I have things well in hand. Dietrich is searching for that whore, who has fled. We will soon have our murderer."

"Excellent," Luther exclaimed as he and Nicola struggled to keep up with Francesco. "The prior hopes to see both of you at Cardinal Beccaria's funeral tomorrow, just after *Nones*. I was going to leave a message for you at the Convent of San Sisto, *Fraulein,* since I did not know how else to reach you. But here you are. Can I tell him to expect you?"

"Probably not," Francesco responded.

"I will be there," Nicola promised.

"Is it necessary to walk so fast?" Martin Luther was beginning to pant. "I have already walked to and from the Christian catacombs this morning, without food."

Francesco responded by walking even faster. "I have to hurry. But you, *Frate* Martin, could escort *Madonna* Nicola to her home. Then you can take all the time you like."

"Can you direct me back to my monastery from there, *Fraulein*?"

"Of course."

Luther wiped the sweat from his face with his sleeve as Francesco disappeared into the crowd. "The prior hopes for your assistance in finding the killer of Cardinal Beccaria, *Fraulein* Machiavelli. He wants to speak to you after the funeral."

Nicola felt glad, and sure that God had answered her prayers. "I am happy to help," she told *Frate* Martin. "I am always looking for good works to perform, and I very much want to help Cardinal Beccaria receive justice." She hesitated when she saw *Frate* Martin's expression. "Why do you look at me so strangely?"

Luther looked as if he had just eaten spoiled fish. He swallowed, and looked away. "I was not sure what you would say. The prior has ordered me to find the killer if I can. An impossible task, without God's help. For which I constantly pray. I just finished praying at the bones of San Sisto, in the convent *basilica*. I hope to pray at all the holy relics of Rome before I leave."

Nicola suppressed a smile. "San Sisto's bones are really pig knuckles."

Luther gasped. "Pig knuckles? How can you say such a thing?"

Nicola amusement turned to irritation. Why did she find this friar so exasperating? "I have an unusually good visual memory, *Frate*," she told him quietly, trying to sound humble. "I remember those bones, and I know a pig knuckle when I see one. The nuns believe in their relic, of course, and it makes money for the convent. But there are many false relics in Rome––that is well known to locals. If you put all the fragments of the True Cross in the city together, you would create a forest. But I'm sure God hears your prayers, even if you aim them at pig bones."

Luther glared at her. "I also have a good visual memory, *Fraulein*." He closed his eyes momentarily, his brow puckered in thought. Then he frowned. "Those bones did look like pig knuckles," he admitted, his face grim. "I have eaten enough of them to know. I would never have noticed if you had not said so. Faith makes me a fool, sometimes."

"Faith does not make us fools, *Frate* Martin. Faith makes us strong, so we can fight our human foolishness."

As they continued their journey, Luther was thoughtful. "Yesterday I climbed the Sacred Steps on my knees. The Holy Church teaches that a prayer on each step means thousands of years less time in Purgatory for a beloved soul. Almost I wished my parents dead, to save them from all those years in Purgatory. But when I reached the top I thought, who knows if it is so? This city is shaking my faith, *Fraulein*."

"If you stop trying to believe in relics, your faith will be stronger for it. I don't remember Jesus saying anything about praying to relics. Do you?"

Luther's brows shot up. "I never thought about that, *Fraulein*. You make a good point. I don't remember Jesus saying anything about praying to relics, either. But still, the teachings of the Church––" He stopped and looked around, his face puzzled. "What is this place? All those arches and columns, supporting nothing."

"This is the Forum, where the ancients met to worship their gods and run their empire. It has fallen into ruin––we use it to graze cattle and sheep. Come, my building is this way."

Emerging from the ancient Roman Forum, they followed narrow, crooked streets that opened into a swampy meadow where more sheep grazed. A jumble of crumbling buildings surrounded it, dominated by a tall stone watchtower blackened with age. A two story brown brick building, newer than most, leaned against the watchtower like a tired child. As they neared it, the smell of baking bread wafted from its open windows, a pleasant relief from the stink of sheep and dung they were trudging through.

Nicola led *Frate* Luther into the bakery, nodded at the baker, and handed Luther a loaf from behind the wooden counter. Luther tried to hand it back to the baker. "I have no coin," he protested.

"It is a gift, *Frate*. I own this bakery. Come."

She led him to the stairs next to the tall brick ovens. Luther looked up, as if something monstrous might be on the upper floors. "I must leave you here, *Fraulein*. Which way to my monastery?"

Nicola smiled at him. Was he afraid of getting lost, or of her? "I will have Raphael take you. He is upstairs. Come."

Raphael, working on a sketch at Nicola's table, wore the soft blue tunic Nicola remembered from their first days together, in Florence.§ As she hung her cloak, he raised a quizzical brow at her.

"You remember *Frate* Martin, Raphael?" Nicola said, glancing at Luther, who peered at them from the top of the stairs.

Raphael always wanted her to himself, but was too well-mannered to object to Luther's presence. "Of course I remember him," he replied, eyes fixed on her. "Delighted to see you again, *Frate* Martin," he murmured.

"*Frate* Martin got the best view of the prostitute who started screaming when Cardinal Beccaria's body fell into the street," Nicola told him. "I only saw her when she was running away. I need you to make a sketch of her from our descriptions, so I can look for her."

Raphael put down his chalk. "Didn't Francesco say he has a man looking for her, who knows her by sight?"

---

§ Read about Nicola and Raphael's early romance in *Da Vinci Detects*.

Nicola nodded. "He is looking in the brothels. And he hasn't found her yet, which is a bad sign. I am going to look in the convents that bury the bodies of poor women, because she may be dead. If she saw the killer, that means the killer could see her, too. He would not want her alive."

"I have worried about that," Luther said. "Do you know which convents to visit?"

"I do."

"She helps them during the fever season," Raphael said. "It is one of her 'good works' that I wish she would stop."

Martin Luther frowned. "The prior would want me to do this. Though I have already missed two of today's Holy Offices. Let us get started."

Raphael opened his sketchbook to a fresh piece of paper. "Tell me what she looked like."

They did. Raphael began making sketches, crossing out early ones as they suggested improvements. Nicola summoned her heavyset maid Maria, who lumbered in with bread, cheese, olives, and watered wine. Martin Luther ate with good appetite, earning a gap-toothed grin from Maria.

After finishing his food, Luther strolled the room while Raphael worked, frowning at the nude sketches the artist had tacked on one of the walls. What is that?" he asked Nicola, pointing to a wood drying rack draped with newly-made pasta.

"*Tagliatelle*– which means 'cuttings'" she told him. "It's a new kind of food, a *maccheroni*, made of unleavened flour. The Chinese invented it–– Marco Polo brought it to Italy. I roll it out at this table, dry it, and sell it at my bakery. You boil it."

"It turns into a porridge, then?"

"No, it keeps that shape, except it's soft."

Luther grimaced at the tangle of dried pasta. Then Nicola's bookshelf caught his eye. "So many books. You own a Bible, *Madonna* Nicola? Do you actually read it?"

She nodded. "As soon as I learned Latin in the convent I read every book I could lay hands on, including the Bible. But since I read it on my own, I had my own ideas. I insisted that Cain was the original sinner, and that God *wanted* Eve to take the apple from the Tree of

Knowledge, because knowledge is good. The nuns were beside themselves."

"I'm sure they were." Luther cradled the Bible and touched its pages as if it were an infant and he the fond father. "They set you straight, I assume."

She smiled at him. "They did their best. I still find the Old Testament difficult, so I concentrate on the Gospels, especially Our Lord's sermons and parables. And the letters of St. Paul. They're more straightforward."

Luther did not seem to be listening. With great care, he turned the pages of the Bible, then nodded. "I am a scholar of the Bible, *Madonna*. I have something to show you."

She glanced at the Bible, and felt her cheeks burning. "First Corinthians, about lust? Yes, I know that one. There is similar text in Paul's letter to the Galatians, and in Matthew, and Mark. I know the New Testament well, *Frate* Luther."

"Why don't you marry him, then?" Luther murmured, nodding toward Raphael, whose back was to them.

Raphael had excellent hearing. "We almost married once, but her father would not release her dowry," he responded, without turning around.

"Then I will speak to your father for you, *Fraulein* Machiavelli," Luther exclaimed. "Where would I find him?"

Nicola bit her lip. Would this monk cause another fight with Raphael, who had proposed marriage when he was poor, but lost interest after becoming rich? Their present truce had been sweet. She did not want it to end.

"You would find my father at the court of the King of France," she told Luther. "He's a high official in the Republic of Florence. So you can't speak to him. And don't assume I want to marry. A married woman is little better than a slave under Roman law. I have my own fortune, and no need of a husband to take it from me, thank you."

"Nicola is richer than I am," Raphael said, his voice amused.

This made Nicola smile. "Only because you spend your money as fast as you make it," she teased. "The way you would spend mine, if you were my husband."

Raphael turned to look at her, and smiled back. "I would spend it on you."

"On me, and other women, and other beautiful things. He cannot resist anything beautiful, *Frate* Martin."

"I can resist all beautiful women except Nicola," Raphael said, his eyes beseeching Nicola to believe him. She did not.

Luther clutched his rosary, his face red, his frown disapproving. "It is obvious that neither of you resists anything. You must marry, or else stop sinning and seek absolution from the Church. For the sake of your immortal souls."

Nicola frowned, and felt herself blushing again. "We break no vows, and harm no one, *Frate* Martin. Remember that Jesus saved the adulteress from being stoned. And forgave Mary Magdalene and the thieves on the crosses beside Him. My sins are small compared to theirs, and I do many good works. So I believe God will forgive me. He did not create us just to send us to Hell when we stumble."

Luther snorted. "You did not simply stumble, *Fraulein*. You are on your back. Sinning, sinning, sinning."

Raphael chuckled. "She is not always on her back, *Frate* Martin."

Speechless, Nicola felt her cheeks go crimson. How dare Raphael, usually so courtly, say such a thing to a priest?

He turned and glanced at her, as if to apologize. "We intend to repent someday, *Frate* Martin," he said. "Like your St. Augustine said—the one who founded your order of monks—'Give me chastity, but not yet.' That is what he said. We agree. We are happy sinners. There is no use trying to reform us now."

Fists clenched, Luther looked at them as if they were both wild animals. He looked a little like one himself. Nicola suppressed an impulse to laugh at him. "I repent occasionally, don't I, Raphael?" she added, as solemnly as she could manage.

Raphael's eyes twinkled. "She does, *Frate* Martin. She does."

Nicola suppressed a smile. "And when I repent, I confess and do what the priest tells me to do, to receive absolution. Except the one who demanded that I prostitute myself to him. I did not do that."

"No, no. She did not do that," Raphael said, grinning. "She told me all about it, though. You see, she is virtuous and wise."

Luther's jaw dropped, reminding Nicola of a gasping fish. "I am sorry, *Fraulein*," he said finally. "The priests here are corrupt. I have seen this."

"Some are," Nicola said. "But I have received absolution from priests who are not corrupt. Plus I bought an indulgence that absolves me, even of future sins. Or so it says."

Martin Luther's eyes widened. "How can an indulgence absolve future sins?"

"That's what I asked the pardoner who sold it to me. I confess, *Frate*, I have never understood the Church teaching that say it can borrow and sell the holiness of the saints as indulgences. How can the Church own the saints' goodness, as if it were trade goods? The sinners are supposed to repent, of course. But if they do, why do they need an indulgence? And how can you repent for something you haven't done yet? I asked the pardoner that."

Luther clutched his rosary. "What did he say?"

"He just kept dropping his price, until it was so cheap I had to buy it. But I have trouble believing in it, *Frate* Martin. Though I believe God forgives me for my confusion on this point."

Raphael chuckled over his sketches. "Nicola drives a hard bargain, even when it comes to salvation."

Nicola grinned at him. "I didn't bargain much. He practically gave it to me."

"I fear you were deceived, *Fraulein*," Luther said.

"So I thought. I decided to do good works of my own, rather than borrow good works from dead saints through the indulgence. If God forgives us, based on saints' good works, He surely will forgive us based on the good things we do ourselves."

She took the Bible from Luther and re-shelved it. "Plus, marriage is just a law, made up by men and very unfair to women. St. Paul says we are justified by our faith, not by law."

Martin Luther stared at her, then began pacing the room, muttering to himself. Nicola looked at Raphael, who was grinning. "Come look at the sketches," he said.

He had made two: in one, the screaming prostitute's mouth was wide open, as Luther had seen her. In the other, her mouth was closed, as Nicola recalled her. "That's her as I remember her," she affirmed, pointing. "Come and see, *Frate* Martin. If you can refrain from lecturing us at the same time."

Looking calmer, Luther joined them, his lips pressed tightly together. He peered at the wide-mouthed sketch. "You have captured her. God has given you a great gift, *Meister* Raphael."

Raphael smiled. "Thank you. I can help you in one other way, *Frate*. Nicola told me that Giulio de' Medici was there, at the brothel. But Francesco, *capitano* of the Swiss Guard, doesn't want you to speak to him."

Raphael paused, examining the chalk in his hand while he considered his next words. "I know both Giulio and his uncle, Cardinal de' Medici, who was one of my first patrons when I came to Rome. Knowing them, here is what I think. They are Medici princes, who wouldn't dirty their hands on something like murder. And if they did, it wouldn't involve stabbing and throwing a naked corpse from a window. That's too crass. It would be something more refined, like a quiet poison. And they'd hire someone to do it. Not go in and do it themselves."

Nicola began gathering Raphael's discarded sketches. "The actual murder must have occurred the day before," she said. "Maybe Giulio de' Medici threw the corpse out the window——"

"He would never do something like that, Nicola," Raphael said. "You need to understand. He is a prince. He probably has the whores undress him because he doesn't know how to do it himself."

Nicola handed him his sketches. "But isn't he a Knight of Saint John?"

Raphael shrugged. "They are the bastards and youngest sons of wealthy families, who play at being knights. Their order hasn't fought a battle in decades. Giulio may not know which end of a sword is sharp. I can't imagine him using one in anger."

"*Meister* Raphael is right," Luther declared. "Even if the Cardinal and his nephew are as corrupt as you say—which I do not for a moment believe—they would not want to weaken the Church. The cardinal's death came from hatred and a violent temperament. That is not the kind of man *Meister* Raphael is describing."

"Exactly," Raphael said. "What are you doing, Nicola?"

She had rolled up his two best sketches of the murdered prostitute, and was tying them with ribbon. "I will take these to the convents that bury the corpses of poor women," she responded. "Right now. If the prostitute is already buried, they will soon forget what she looked like. Can you take the *Frate* back to his monastery on your way to the Vatican? Maria, could you bring our cloaks?"

"You are dismissing me, then?" Raphael said, with the look in his eye that always set her heart fluttering.

"You have work to do, don't you? We will be back before nightfall."

Martin Luther stood muttering to himself as Raphael gathered his belongings.

"Sodom and Gomorrah," Nicola said, overhearing him. "You think Rome is Sodom and Gomorrah."

Luther nodded.

"Well, you are right."

Ch. 13 - A Dead Prostitute

Detail from *Nero with Corpse of Agrippina*
by Antonio Zanchi

The same day

"We have her," Sister Serena said, glancing at Raphael's sketch. "Did you know her, Nicola? Are you coming to claim her body?"

Nicola's heart sank. "Alas, the poor woman. No. I'm coming to determine if she was murdered."

"She was."

"Did you tell the *bargelli*?"

Sister Serena nodded. "Of course. She was a prostitute, so they don't care. Do you want to see the body?"

"Yes."

Wringing her hands, Nicola's maid Maria asked if she could wait in the church. "I will find you when I am finished," Nicola responded, nodding. Maria shuffled away as fast as her heavy legs would carry her.

Nicola turned back to Sister Serena. "Can you tell me where and when her corpse was discovered?"

"Let's make sure we have the right body first, shall we?" she replied. She led Nicola across the gray stone cloister and through a room on the other side, to the convent graveyard, a hillside densely dotted on one side with modest white wooden crosses. A large rectangular area of disturbed soil opposite the nuns' graves showed where poor women were buried until their flesh rotted away. Then their bones were dug up and piled in the brick ossuary dug into the slope, which the nuns also used as a mortuary.

Sister Serena descended its steps and propped open both doors, which released a miasma of rotting flesh. The sun setting behind them lit six female bodies laid out like playing cards on a row of stone slabs, staring sightlessly at the roof. All were clothed except for a heavy, large–breasted figure wrapped in a shroud.

Nicola recognized the corpse in the yellow *gammura* as the woman in Raphael's drawing. She covered her nose with a kerchief, hesitating on the doorstep.

Sister Serena immediately understood. "No contagion in this group. Four died in childbed––one with the babe still in her, as you can see by her stomach. The one in the shroud drowned in the river."

Reassured, Nicola went to look at the prostitute's body. The mark around her neck and her mottled face showed that she had been garroted. Nicola raised her arm and let it drop. "It's chilly in here, but *rigor mortis* has passed off. So she has been dead for several days, at least." She also examined the dead woman's gown. There was a little blood at the shoulders, probably from the garrote, but none elsewhere. "Do you know when she was brought in? And who brought her?

Sister Serena nodded. "I can check our records."

Nicola handed a coin to the sister. "You will need to keep her here for another day or two. I will send someone from the Swiss Guard to identify her. When you bury her, have the priest say an extra Mass for her."

"Why the Swiss Guard?"

"Have you heard about the murder of Cardinal Beccaria? Who fell from the window of a brothel? I think this is the prostitute who was screaming at that window. The Swiss Guard is looking for her."

Sister Serena frowned. "Everyone says the prostitute killed him. But if she was murdered soon after he was. . . ."

"Then she saw the killer, and died for it."

The nun gasped and crossed herself. "The cardinal was assassinated, then. The garrote is an assassin's weapon."

"He likely was. Please keep quiet about it, though. It will only be harder to find the killer, if he knows we have found this second victim. Let's go find out where she died."

While Nicola went to fetch Maria, Sister Serena consulted the convent records. She met them at the front entrance. "She was found at dawn the day after Santa Lucia's Day, outside a brothel near the Campo de Fiori. The other prostitutes denied knowledge of her."

"That's the day after we found Cardinal Beccaria," Nicola said. "The killer must have followed her when she fled the whorehouse. Poor woman, she never stood a chance."

Ch. 14 - The Cardinal's Funeral

A procession of clerics, date unknown

Rome,
The following day

Nicola arrived early for Cardinal Beccaria's funeral. Santa Maria del Popolo was a new church, designed in part by the great Bramante himself in the most modern style, with tall classical columns and a dome. She walked towards the altar to admire the dome—much smaller than the one in Florence—and the first stained glass window in Rome, just unveiled. She had never seen such a thing before: a color picture of Christ and the Virgin with light coming through it. *Magnifico.*

The cardinal's coffin, draped in scarlet cloth and crowned with a cardinal's hat, stood on a bier in front of the main altar. To her surprise, Francesco was there, with two other Swiss guardsmen. They seemed to be performing some kind of inspection, walking among the closest benches, which were also draped in scarlet.

Francesco hastened to her side when he saw her. "You told *Frate* Luther you weren't coming," she said to him.

Francesco motioned her into a side aisle, where they would not be overheard. "I changed my mind this morning, after Raphael gave me your note about the whore's murder. The entire cardinalate will be here today––the ones who are not in Bologna with the pope, anyway. Since the whore was garroted, I have to assume Cardinal Beccaria was assassinated, too. If another cardinal is murdered, Pope Julius will have my head."

"The nuns are expecting Dietrich to identify the body."

"Of course, but from what you said, it must be her. You had Raphael's drawing, and you recognized the *gammura*."

He put a hand on Nicola back, leading her toward the benches at the church entrance. "Here is another note from Caterina for you. Where do you want to sit?"

Nicola broke the seals on Caterina's letter as they walked. She stopped abruptly to stare at a receipt and bill of exchange for a large sum, directed to the Fugger bank in Rome. Her spirits lifted: she had been fretting about this more than she realized.

"Caterina got safely to Venice and deposited the pope's payments," she reported. "Now I can pay the workers in our armory."

"What else does she say? Does she say where she is staying?"

"Let me sit and read it, Francesco."

He took her to a seat near the main door into the church, waiting impatiently while she perused the letter. "This was written in haste, so she could give it to the Swiss guardsmen who escorted her to Venice before they left," she reported. "They took her straight to her bank. No indication where she is staying. I'm sure she's in a convent, but I don't know which one."

"There are a thousand convents in Venice. Some little better than whorehouses."

"So I hear. I'm sure she chose a respectable one. Can I send her another note, Francesco? She will want to know that I received the bill of exchange."

"Of course. Every courier headed for Venice is looking for her. They might as well take your letter."

"*Grazie*. I'll write it now. Oh, here comes *Frate* Martin."

Martin Luther hurried to greet them. "I'm glad you are both here. The prior wants to talk to you after the funeral."

Luther's face fell when Nicola told him about finding the body of the prostitute among the corpses of poor women. He crossed himself. "I was afraid of that. She died with her sins unconfessed, poor soul. I will pray for her." He turned to Francesco. "What will you do next?"

"Now that the pope is better, I have written to him for instructions. Right now, all Rome thinks that Cardinal Beccaria was stabbed by an angry whore because he didn't pay her enough. The pope may want to leave it that way."

Martin Luther scowled at Francesco. "But then a holy man's reputation will continue to be smeared. And the reputation of the Church suffers, too. You cannot-- How can you--"

Nicola stood, putting a finger to her lips. "Keep your voice down, *Frate* Martin," she whispered. "The killer might be here, hoping we have been fooled into believing that the whore is the murderer. Let's observe carefully and talk to the prior. Meanwhile, rest. Kneel. Pray."

Martin Luther gave her an angry look, then sank to his knees beside them. Bowing his head, he began praying, his sonorous murmur sounding like bees in a hive.

Nicola watched him with amusement. "I have never seen anyone lose themselves in prayer the way he does," she told Francesco. "I doubt he hears a word we say."

"Let's speak Italian in case you are wrong. Understand this: I will do nothing until I hear from His Holiness, except to guard the funeral and suggest special vigilance to the bodyguards of the other cardinals. We can't exclude the ordinary people who are crowding the church. Cardinal Beccaria fed the poor, so he was beloved. But we are disarming anyone who comes in."

Nicola could hear an acrimonious dispute about weapons at the door behind her, where a pile of swords and daggers clanked like a bag of coins every time the Swiss guardsmen added another one.

"Who are these people at the back of the church?" she asked.

Francesco glanced at the back row of men, dressed identically in plain brown tunics. "Servants from the monastery."

Nicola looked around her. "What are they pointing at?"

"Probably at you. You are the only woman in the church, other than a couple of old beggars. They probably don't see women very often. Not young pretty ones, anyway."

"It looks to me like they are pointing at *Frate* Martin."

"He was talking to you and now he is praying. Maybe they see a connection."

Nicola suppressed a giggle. "You mustn't mock him, Francesco."

Monks, chanting the Kyrie, emerged into the church in procession, filling the benches behind those draped in red. Cardinals and bishops, escorted by their servants and Swiss guardsmen, were being seated one by one in front of the monks.

After bowing to Nicola and Francesco, Martin Luther moved forward to join his brethren.

"Is there anyone from Cardinal Beccaria's family here?" Nicola whispered.

Francesco cocked his head, considering. "He had a brother in Pavia––Count Beccaria–– but he is not expected. Too far away." Francesco stiffened suddenly, watching as one of his men escorted a bishop to be seated with the cardinals. "*Madre di Dio,* not him," he muttered. "Could he be involved in this?"

"Who? That bishop?" Nicola asked

"That's Pompeo Colonna, bishop of Reiti. Colonna leads a group of influential Romans who talk of armed rebellion against His Holiness. But I can't imagine Beccaria was involved in anything like that."

Nicola gasped. "Francesco, look. Do you see those two priests? The ones sitting down next to Pompeo Colonna? They are the priests I saw fleeing the brothel after the body landed. I'm sure of it. You must find out who they are."

Francesco fingered his moustache. "I know who they are. They are Pompeo Colonna's cousins. They were soldiers together, during the first French invasion. They all took holy orders when Pompeo's brother died––the former bishop of Reiti. The revenues from that bishopric are considerable so the Colonna family wanted to keep them."

He rose to his feet. "The pope would love it if I could pin those murders on the Colonna family. I'll talk to Pompeo's cousins, I promise. But not today." He bowed to Nicola. "Save a place for me. I must speak to Cardinal de' Medici and his bodyguards. It's no secret that he wants to be the next pope, so he could be a target for assassination."

"His cousin is here too––the one I saw at the brothel." Nicola asked, nodding towards Giulio de' Medici, whose tunic bore the white cross of the Knights of St. John. He stood beside a heavyset cardinal, evidently Cardinal de' Medici, who peered around the church with a monocle. "Shall we speak to him?"

Francesco's face reddened. " No. As I already told you, Cardinal de' Medici is not someone I want to offend. We do nothing for now. Excuse me."

Nicola watched as Francesco moved between clusters of scarlet–clad figures, speaking quietly to their attendants. Behind them and the monks, the aisles of the church were filling with ordinary people, some with small children; many raggedly dressed. Nicola was touched to see how many poor citizens had come to pay last respects.

Francesco hurried back to sit beside her, just as the Requiem Mass began.

"*Requiem aeternam dona eis.*" A cardinal whom Nicola did not recognize was officiating. The funeral service she knew all too well. So did the cardinal, who galloped through it like a spurred horse.

The responses were deliberate at first, but soon the audience took their rhythm from the cardinals, who seemed eager to get through the ceremony as quickly as possible. Beside the altar, Nicola could see one distressed face––surely the prior of the monastery, who sat next to the episcopal chair the officiating cardinal had occupied. She felt sorry for the prior. He had no way to force the service to become more respectful.

A murmur arose from the ordinary folk that became louder as the funeral mass progressed. They obviously perceived the unseemly haste. By the time the service ended, the church was buzzing like a nest of angry bees.

"That was certainly prompt," Francesco remarked, as the cardinals' attendants prodded the poor out of the church. When the aisles were clear, the cardinals hurried through the front door as though fleeing the plague.

"It was offensive, doing it so fast." Nicola replied quietly. "It's like they spat on Cardinal Beccaria's coffin. Who was the officiating cardinal?"

"I forget his name," Francesco whispered. "He is the most senior Augustinian presently in Rome. But he was no friend of Cardinal Beccaria. They were on opposite sides of the dispute that brought *Frate* Martin to Rome. Something about the Augustinians becoming lax in observing their rules."

"Whoever he is, he doesn't think much of rules," Nicola whispered back. "Francesco, do you suppose those cardinals were involved with the murder? They certainly seem to have reached an unspoken agreement on the conduct of the funeral. See how angry *Frate* Martin is."

Luther strode towards them, mouth clenched tight, looking as if he wanted to explode. He stopped suddenly, staring at the door of the church, where Bishop Colonna and his cousins were elbowing their way through the monastery's servants.

Francesco rose to his feet. "I don't want to listen to *Frate* Martin. Make excuses to the prior for me, will you? I should help the guard at the door. He has his hands full."

"Here, take my letter for Caterina. Seal it for me, will you?" Nicola could hear two angry men outside the church, shouting about who owned a dagger. She wondered whether they would come to blows over it.

Martin Luther seated himself next to Nicola, keeping his voice low. "The cardinals here are worse than the priests. How could he even speak that fast, much less recite a Requiem Mass? I could not do it if I tried. And does every Roman carry a knife?"

Nicola told him about the officiating cardinal. "He may have been chosen because he was the senior Augustinian in Rome, not because he opposed Cardinal Beccaria. Whatever the case, I agree, he was disrespectful. And yes, most Romans are armed. I myself carry a dagger strapped below my knee."

Luther glanced at her knee, blushed, and looked away. "Come," he said. "The prior is awaiting us."

Ch. 15 - Ambush

Arquebusier, with smoking fuse
by Jacob De Gheyn

On the Po River, Southeast of Milan
The same day

Amazed at her happiness, Caterina watched the wooded banks of the Po River flow by from her seat in the galley's bow. She hadn't felt this elated since falling in love with Niccolò Machiavelli a lifetime ago. Was the fresh air going to her head, after the festering stink in Rome and the salty damp of Venice? Riches had never made her particularly happy, so the pope's payment could not account for her joy. She was going home, finally. Maybe that was it.

Milan was the only real home she had ever known. Florence had not been home since her father put her on the streets, when she was young and pregnant with Niccolò Machiavelli's child. Her recent years in Rome had never felt like home, either, even though Nicola was there. Keeping in Pope Julius' good graces but out of his bed had been a nightmare.

But Caterina had married Ugo Biaggi in Milan after fleeing Florence, and made a good life with him. Though she had missed her "niece" Nicola, she had loved her spacious *appartaménto* above the Biaggi armory, and her work at Ugo's side. She was devastated when he was murdered, when they first arrived in Rome.[**]

[**] Read about it in *"A Borgia Daughter Dies."*

His son Carlo had turned out better than expected. Carlo and his wife ran the armory in Milan now. Caterina had never met her stepson's wife or his children, her grandchildren. She wanted to hold the new baby. She wanted to see old friends and her old *appartaménto*, with the fireplace tiles she had painted and set with her own hands.

And of course, she wanted her share of the profits from the Milan armory. But she wasn't traveling through a war zone in winter just for money. She was trying to get home.

A gunshot echoed around her as the galley rounded a river bend, where she saw a soldier in a French helmet reloading an *arquebus* that her own firm had manufactured. The sight and sound were so familiar that it did not alarm her for an instant. Fear seized her when she saw other French soldiers pushing cannons to the river's edge. The galley, struggling slowly upstream, could not possibly outrun them.

Panicked, she ran from the bow to the cabin, knowing its thin walls offered no real protection.

"What is happening?" *Padre* Antonio cried. Kindly, garrulous, and the only other passenger, he had been confident that priesthood and old age would protect him from warring armies on this journey. Confident, and wrong.

"A French ambush. Come, it is safest in the center."

The captain and crew were all shouting. The oars clattered and she felt the galley slipping backwards downstream, but the lookout screamed that there were cannon there too. More gunshots brought more screams and the familiar smell of gun smoke. They could do nothing but pray.

She knelt beside the elderly priest, who was already prostrate and wailing in the center of the cabin. Trying to make her body small, she stifled an impulse to scream. Instead she beseeched God to spare them from splinters.

The French on shore shouted orders, answered by the boat's captain. From her years in Milan under French occupation, she knew enough to understand the exchange. She felt able to breathe again, though the acrid smoke made her cough. "The *capitano* is taking us to shore," she told the priest, as soon as she could speak. "Our cargo is bound for French buyers in Milan. Maybe it's just an inspection."

Padre Antonio raised his head and looked around, like a mouse peering out of a hole. "At least the guns have stopped." Caterina rose from her knees, feeling relieved. She slapped at her dirty skirt. Her last decent *gammura* and now she'd ruined it, kneeling on a filthy deck.

Fear clutched at her again as the French soldiers thundered on board and into the cargo hold, shouting to each other. "They're looking for food and gold," she told *Padre* Antonio. "So they're thieves, not inspectors."

She untied her coin purse from her waist, holding it in her hand. They were welcome to the little gold she had. Most of the wealth she was carrying was wrapped in a cloth between her breasts, a bill of exchange from her bank in Venice that soldiers would not know how to read. But she feared the worst. They would surely find it there, when they threw it aside with her clothes.

Padre Antonio arose, and rifled through his belongings. "They are welcome to my food. If they insist on stealing from a priest."

The shouts from below were getting angrier. "They might want it, *Padre*. They say the food is 'swill,' fit only for the galley slaves. And you might have to defend my honor. Because now they are shouting for women."

"May God have mercy on you, *Madonna* Caterina. I am no match for the French army."

Caterina pulled her veil and cloak around her body, to hide its curves. Though her heart was pounding she stood tall, hoping that a show of fearlessness and the threat of a struggle would protect her.

Two French soldiers burst in. "There she is," leered one of them, a giant with broken teeth and one blind eye. "A widow. No husband to cuckold."

She smelled their repulsive stink across the cabin. "A widow and a friend of your *Générale*," she said, her voice harsh and strange to her own ears. "So leave me be, because he'll have your head. I wrote to him––he's expecting me."

"Is he now?" the big man jeered.

"Yes. And my firm––my late husband's firm––made your weapons. Look at your halberd. It has a "B" at the base of the head.

That's me. I'm Caterina Biaggi and I own the firm. So you'd best leave me alone."

"It's true," *Padre* Antonio said. "We've been talking about her firm, all the way from Venice. And she does know your *Générale*. She told me so."

He'd said the right thing, *Dio Grazie*. Truth was, she hadn't seen the *Générale* in eight years, and didn't know him well. And she'd received no response to her letter, asking for safe passage.

The French soldiers looked at each other, hesitating. Then a third soldier appeared. "This is all French cargo, and no food," he said. We're leaving."

"We want the woman. But she says she's a friend of the *Générale*."

The newcomer looked her up and down. "Is she, now?"

"She is," *Padre* Antonio affirmed. "And she supplies the French with weapons. She's the widow who owns the Biaggi arms firm."

"Is that so?" The newcomer laughed, and the others joined him. They were looking at her as if she were a haunch of roasted meat. Caterina kept her posture erect, too terrified even to swallow.

A fourth soldier appeared, an officer by his dress and sword. "What's the holdup?"

"We want this woman. But she says she knows the *Générale*. She's his *friend*. And sells him weapons."

Trying not to quake with fear, Caterina allowed herself to hope this man was a gentleman. "I'm Caterina Biaggi. The Biaggi firm made that sword on your hip, as you probably know. Your general has purchased armaments from me for years. I know him well."

"That is what she keeps telling us," one of the soldiers said.

The officer looked surprised. "Since she claims to know him, we'll take her to the *Générale*. He's not three miles from here. Let's go."

"May God go with you, *Madonna* Caterina," *Padre* Antonio said, making the sign of the cross.

The giant soldier and his confederate each grabbed one of her arms, half dragging her from the passenger cabin, complaining loudly to each other that they hadn't had a woman in weeks.

"Silence," the officer who had saved her commanded. "If the *Générale* doesn't want her for himself, maybe he'll give her back to you."

Ch. 16 - A Plan of Action

A Monk
by Antonio Casanova y Estorach

**Rome,
Monastery of Santa Maria del Popolo
The same day**

The luxury of Prior Piccolimini's parlor in the monastery attached to Santa Maria del Popolo surprised Nicola. Though she had been raised in a wealthy convent, the nuns had nothing like this. Tapestries and green velvet drapes adorned the wood–paneled room, which overlooked the monks' cloister and garden. Silver candelabras studded with beeswax candles provided sweetly-scented light, as did the crackling pine logs in the Carrara marble fireplace opposite the window.

The prior himself typified monastics who lived in luxury. Plump, unwrinkled, and benignly self-satisfied, he looked like an aging cherub with a halo of white curls. A good man, perhaps, but only because living a good life had been easy. He gestured for Nicola to sit in the carved, cushioned chair beside the fire, the place for honored guests. Bowing, Martin Luther took a stool nearby.

"*Madonna* Machiavelli, I am happy to make your acquaintance," the prior began, seating himself opposite her at the fire. "May I offer you refreshment?"

Nicola smiled and nodded to a balding servant, who poured her a glass of wine and offered a plate of roasted chestnuts with a bow. The prior took the entire plate with a delighted grin, then waved the servant out the door.

When it was shut, he turned back to Nicola. "I am aware of the good work you do, feeding the poor."

Nicola stiffened, dismayed. She opened her mouth to protest. Seeing her face, the prior raised a hand to ask for silence. "I know you prefer to keep your good works anonymous, *Madonna*. This is between us. Those of us who also feed the poor, we know. Your priest, though, says you refuse to involve him."

Nicola despised her parish priest, who had promised her absolution in exchange for sex. She suspected that he wanted the bread she gave to the poor for his own fat belly and personal profit. "I thought I was here to talk about the murder of Cardinal Beccaria," she said.

"And you are. But I am wondering whether there is some way the Church can work with you—"

Nicola tried to suppress her irritation. "I have already made my position clear to my parish priest. I don't want the Church involved. I don't distribute the bread near the monasteries——like this one——that give out bread themselves. Can we talk about Cardinal Beccaria, please? We need to decide what the next step should be."

"In a way, this *is* about him. Unlike most cardinals, he didn't have an expensive *palazzo* and staff. He stayed with us when he was in Rome, and fed the poor with the money from the Church revenues he received through his benefices. That is why poor folk loved him, and came to his funeral. His successors are not likely to continue this practice. To continue feeding the poor here, we may need your help."

The luxurious furnishings in the room would have bought many loaves of bread, Nicola thought to herself. She was repulsed by this fat, self-satisfied prior. "I will think on this," she promised. "For now can we please attend to the Cardinal's murder?"

She turned to Martin Luther, who was staring at them, a confused expression on his face. He looked calmer than he had a few minutes before, when complaining about the contempt shown to Cardinal Beccaria during his funeral.

"Pardon us for speaking Italian, *Frate* Martin," she said, switching to Latin. "Prior, *Frate* Martin needs to learn as much about Cardinal Beccaria as he can from the monks here. We agree on this point. And I think we need to talk to the people who fled the brothel after the cardinal's body was thrown from the window."

The prior looked startled, as if his dog had started speaking Latin. "A logical suggestion," he said, in the same language. He shifted his focus to Luther. "What have you learned about the cardinal's past, *Frate* Martin?"

"I have spoken to the kitchen help. They all agree that Cardinal Beccaria was practically a saint but they don't seem to know anything about his background. The brethren are reluctant to talk about him, other than to praise his goodness," Luther said. "They are aware that he committed a terrible sin in the past, but they won't talk about it and may not know what it is. His confessor doesn't think he can keep straight what was a confidence and what wasn't. So he will say nothing at all. He doesn't even want to identify the cardinal's closest friends."

The prior nodded. "Tomorrow we have the monastery chapter meeting. I will make clear to all––except his confessor––that they should answer your questions," the prior said. "We discourage gossip and no one wants to speak ill of the dead. But in this instance we need the truth. I will assure them that you will keep their confidences. And I order you to do so. If they are still reluctant to speak to you after that, send them to me."

Martin Luther nodded. "Good," Nicola said. "I also think we need to speak to the other prostitutes in the brothel, particularly since we now know one of them was murdered. And since *Frate* Martin cannot do that––"

"You can't do it either," Luther protested. "What of your reputation, *Fraulein*? It is out of the question."

"Their evil is not contagious," Nicola objected, smiling. "I will not go by myself. Raphael will escort me."

Luther scowled. "*Meister* Raphael doubtless would be comfortable in such a place."

"Precisely why I intend to go with him," Nicola said, feeling herself blushing. How had this naïve friar known about Raphael's weakness for women? And why was he goading her with it?

Luther stared at her as if she had sprouted horns. "I will go with you, but I will not go inside," he countered. "Nor should you."

"Why go at all, Martin?" the prior asked. "It is not seemly, even to be outside such a place."

"I have little memory of the surroundings—— I was with God, giving the cardinal his last rites," Luther responded. "I don't even remember the building. And I want to explore the neighborhood. The murderer might lurk there."

"I also think you should speak to the Teutonic knight, the one who elbowed aside the prostitute who was murdered," Nicola told Luther. "You likely speak his language, and you are both monks."

"How would I find him? I didn't even see him."

"He is a massive man with a long black beard. There can't be many like him. Find out if he went there frequently enough to know the whores and customers. And find out if he knows Giulio de' Medici, the knight from the Order of St. John who left with him."

The prior stiffened. "Cardinal de' Medici's ward was there?"

"He was," Nicola said. "Francesco doesn't want us talking to him. Not yet. He himself will to talk to two priests who were there —— former soldiers, whom he knows."

"There were priests there too? *Misericordia*. Such a scandalous business," the prior said, as he popped a peeled chestnut into his mouth. After swallowing and burping, he focused again on Martin Luther. "Talking with a fellow German speaker would be an appropriate task for you, *Frate* Martin. The Teutonic knights have a palazzo here, in the Via del Mascherone. You will doubtless find him there. What's this about a prostitute being murdered?"

"*Fraulein* Nicola just brought this news," Luther said. "The prostitute who saw the murder of the cardinal was killed the same day. With a garrote."

The prior gasped and crossed himself. "I must pray over this. It had not occurred to me I was placing either of you in any danger. But with two murders—and Cardinal de' Medici's nephew there... *Misericordia*. Have a care, both of you. This may be bigger than we thought."

"Judging from the way those cardinals behaved at the funeral, it is bigger than even I thought," Nicola responded. "And I have always felt it has to do with the papal succession."

The prior and Martin Luther both stared at her. "I hope you are wrong," the prior said.

Nicola rose to leave. "I hope so, too."

Ch. 17 - Two Smoking Priests

Early woodcut of indigenous use of tobacco in the New World

Rome,
The next day

Swallowing his fear because it was unmanly, Francesco wandered through the muddy courtyards of the Colonna family's walled complex on the Quiurnal Hill. Hand on his sword, he bowed his head politely to all who looked quizzically at him. Several men put hands on their own swords, but evidently thought better of taking on a member of the Swiss Guard.

At last he arrived at the imposing *edificio* where Pompeo Colonna and his confederates lived––though by rights they should have lived in Reiti, where Pompeo was bishop. The bricked–in stone columns of its front wall had surely been part of an ancient Roman temple at some point. To Francesco this seemed apt, since his spies reported that Pompeo was constantly spouting off about the glories of ancient Rome and its oldest families--most especially his own family, the Colonna.

    The massive wood door to Pompeo's house was studded with iron spikes, as though its owner expected a siege. In front of it, sitting on a fallen column from ancient times, were the two priests Nicola saw at the whorehouse where Cardinal Beccaria died. Or so she had said when she pointed them out at the funeral. Francesco remembered talking to these two at the Papal Palace the previous year, while they waited for Pompeo. After studying their faces, he remembered their names: Andrea and Ugo Colonna.

    Andrea, tall and thin, held a cylindrical brown object that smoked at one end and smelled abominably. To Francesco's astonishment, he put the opposite end to his mouth, inhaled, then passed the object to his heavyset brother. Who did exactly the same thing. They both exhaled smoke through mouths and noses, as if they were dragons.

    Flabbergasted, Francesco stopped short, stifling an impulse to turn and run. On reflection, he realized this must be a *cigarro* from the New World, something he had heard about but never before seen. *Cigarros* were strange luxuries that few priests could afford.

    "*Buon Giorno*, Andrea. Ugo," he said. "How are you?"

    "We are well, and you?" Ugo responded, his hand moving instinctively for a sword. Since he was a priest, there was none for him to grab.

    Francesco stood tall and touched his own weapon. "I am well. I saw you at Cardinal Beccaria's funeral. Did you know him?"

    "Of course. We were there to pay our respects," Andrea said, as he took the *cigarro* from his brother. "We fought against the French with him, back in the time of the Borgia pope. Pompeo had great reverence for Cardinal Beccaria. We hoped he would be the next pope."

    This was the answer Francesco had expected, which tempted him to turn around and leave. But he knew Nicola would ask him a hundred questions about this encounter. He'd better ask a few more himself.

    "Pompeo was a friend of Cardinal Beccaria?" he said. "That seems surprising. They were very different."

Ugo handed the *cigarro* to Andrea. "They were," he said. "After the cardinal entered a monastery and turned holy, anyway. But not when we were soldiers eighteen years ago, chasing the French back to the Alps."

To Francesco's astonishment, Andrea blew rings of smoke, as if he truly were a dragon. "Beccaria was every Italian's hero, back then," he said, as he watched the rings disappear. "He hunted down and slaughtered the French company that raped and murdered innocent women and children in Fivizzano. The French Disease they got from raping the whores of Naples had already killed most of them. But Beccaria finished them off."

Ugo accepted the *cigarro* from him. "He didn't kill all of the French, Andrea. He left two or three. "

"He left them alive to tell the tale, yes. That is why the world knows it. And he only spared the ones who tried to stop the others, according to the rest of them."

Ugo puffed at the *cigarro*, then coughed. "He had the officers beheaded first, see, for failing to stop their men. He wanted to set an example. Next they beheaded the ones who could not show their innocence. He asked them all, who did it?"

Tired of the smoke's stink, Francesco moved himself upwind.

"To avoid torture they gave each other up easily," Andrea continued, as he took the *cigarro* from his brother. "And the ones accused by their brothers in arms? Of rape and worse? They died hard. Beccaria ordered their balls cut off and thrown in a pile. When we were ready to leave, some of them were still alive. So he ordered a random set of balls be shoved down their throats, until they choked to death. He left them all for the buzzards."

Francesco absorbed this. "Doesn't sound like the man I knew," he said finally.

Andrea exhaled, looking at the *cigarro* as if it were a living thing. "Beccaria became a different man when he entered the Church. Reformed. Very holy. Wouldn't associate with his former comrades in arms. But after Pompeo became a bishop, they worked together occasionally. On Church matters. "

"Like what?"

"Like the Via Giulia, that road Pope Julius made by destroying the homes by the river," Andrea said. "Both of them opposed it. "

"Sad, the way the cardinal died," Francesco responded. "You were there at the whorehouse when it happened, I heard. What did you see?"

They looked at each other, communicating with raised brows and no words, as brothers do. Andrea exhaled more smoke, very slowly, as if protecting his insides from catching fire. "We didn't see anything," he responded, as he handed the *cigarro* back to Ugo. "Not even Cardinal Beccaria, alive or dead. But we were in the whorehouse only briefly--in and out. So to speak."

"In and out, in and out," Ugo repeated, demonstrating with the *cigarro,* which spewed ashes. All of them laughed.

Ugo inhaled, then handed the *cigarro* back to Andrea. "We came together and we *came* together, if you catch my meaning," Ugo said, grinning as smoke passed out between his few remaining teeth, as if his mouth were a fire grate. "We talked afterwards--we were at the same stage with our whores when the screaming started. Andrea was atop his, and mine had me in her mouth. She got restless with the screaming but I made her finish. By the time I was dressed and paid, the screaming had stopped and nearly everyone was gone. Except Andrea, coming out of the room down the hall. We ran after the others, and that was that."

"Did you go there often?" Francesco asked. "Did the Cardinal?"

Andrea puffed on the *cigarro,* and frowned. "We go there occasionally. I never saw Cardinal Beccaria there, but then you don't really see the other men. I'm still surprised by what happened--I didn't think he was the type to stray from his vows. But he once had a wife."

"And was still a man," Ugo added, reaching for the *cigarro.* "We never did see him. We saw the crowd outside after we left, talking about a body. We assumed it was a whore who jumped out a window. Because she was tired of the life, maybe. It's still hard to believe."

"We didn't hear the Cardinal was there until word came about his funeral," Andrea said. "His whore killed him, *si*? That's what we heard. And you have her, right?

"That's what we think," Francesco said. "The whore escaped, but we're looking for her. You didn't see her?"

Both of them shook their heads. "She was gone by the time we left. The thought of a whore with a dagger has softened my dagger, I tell you," Ugo said. They all laughed. "From now on I'm going to have whores strip naked first, to make sure they aren't carrying knives."

"It's better that way, anyway," Francesco said.

Ugo bobbed his head in agreement. "Would you like to try this *cigarro?*" he asked Francesco.

"No, *grazie*," Francesco said. "I must be going." He saluted them, and hurried away.

Ch. 18 - The Teutonic Knight

Death and the Teutonic Knight
by Albrecht Kauw

Rome,
The same day

Heinrich von Marberg, brother knight of the Teutonic order, watched *Frate* Martin Luther enjoy his beer, and wondered why the young friar had sought him out. Luther's German dialect was almost incomprehensible and his loud, rumbling speech and threadbare cowl showed that he came from the lower classes. Heinrich had taken him to the scullery, thinking him entirely unsuited to the formal rooms on the *piano nobile*. The young friar looked at home at the cook's long wooden table, where he sat happily sipping from a kitchen jug.

Unused to servants' quarters, Heinrich remained standing, willing himself to ignore the savory smell of the pig roasting on a spit above the kitchen fireplace. He'd dismissed the cook, who left behind a small boy to turn the spit and tend to their needs.

Martin Luther smacked his lips. "I didn't think Romans could make decent beer."

Heinrich poured more for himself. "They can't. We imported this. Why were you looking for me, *Frate* Martin?"

Luther put down his jug, and stared at Heinrich as if he were Heinrich's superior, rather than the other way around. "The prior of the monastery where I am staying—Cardinal Beccaria's monastery—has asked me to make inquiries concerning the cardinal's death. I'm here because a Teutonic knight of your description left a brothel in a hurry—along with everyone else—when Cardinal Beccaria's body was thrown from its window."

Heinrich felt the hair rise on the back of his neck. Could this emaciated, contemptible monk possibly be a danger? He would speak cautiously. "Everyone fled because one of the whores was screaming about murder. But I didn't see anything. Or know anything about Cardinal Beccaria being there, until days later."

Martin Luther nodded, as if he had expected just such a statement. "Tell me what you saw," he said.

Heinrich paused a moment, to get his story straight in his head. "I chose my whore and was headed upstairs when the screaming began. In the hallway, doors were opening and half-dressed men were spilling out. We stood there, wondering what to do. Then my whore bolted. Everyone was panicking and running away. I didn't want to be the only one left, so I followed."

Luther cocked an eyebrow and stared at him, as though calling him a coward without saying anything. Heinrich felt both enraged and embarrassed, realizing that what he had described *was* cowardly. But it was a whorehouse, not a battlefield. Did it matter?

"You went to the brothel by yourself?" Luther continued.

"Of course."

"You were seen leaving with a Knight of St. John, Giulio dei' Medici. Do you know him?"

Heinrich hesitated, dismayed that they had both been identified. "Only by reputation. We did not come together. If we left together, it was an accident."

"As knights, why didn't you take over and help?"

"As knights, we had no business in a whorehouse. That is not our field of endeavor. We left it to the *bargelli*."

"Did you discuss this with Giulio de' Medici?"

Heinrich bit his lip to keep from shouting at this insolent monk. "Of course not. I told you, we don't know each other."

"Did you know anyone you saw in the brothel?"

"No."

"What about the girl you were with? What was her name?"

Heinrich could feel his face coloring with rage. He clenched his teeth. "I don't remember."

Luther did not seem to notice his anger. He nodded, and took a sip of his beer. "Tell me about the prostitute who was screaming. What was she saying?"

Heinrich took a deep breath, glad that Luther's attention was no longer on him. "She was mostly just screaming. Staring into the door of an open room and screaming."

"Did you look in the door?"

"I did."

"And what did you see?"

"Nothing. I thought perhaps she had lost her mind."

Luther took another sip of his beer. "Did you see anything unusual at all, other than the screaming prostitute?"

Heinrich laughed. "Half–dressed priests and papal guards. One usually dresses before leaving. Other than that, no."

"You saw no one acting strangely, other than the screaming woman?"

"Well, we all fled over nothing. Or so it seemed. Otherwise, no."

"No blood anywhere?"

"None that I saw."

Frate Martin put down his mug, pursed his lips, then frowned at him, like God on Judgment Day. "Do you have any idea who killed Cardinal Beccaria? Or threw his body from the window?"

Heinrich stifled an impulse to slap him. Unwilling to let a mere friar stare him down, he met Luther's glance with a steely one of his own. "Didn't the whore kill him? That's what everyone says. She killed him and screamed 'murder' to throw suspicion away from herself."

Luther looked away, and took another swallow from his jug of beer. "Maybe that is what happened. But what do you think? "

Heinrich smiled, glad he had faced down Luther. "That is what I think."

Luther put his jug down. "You elbowed the screaming woman aside when you fled. Why?"

Heinrich wanted to strike this meddlesome friar. "Did I? I don't remember. But what if I did? She was just a whore. And I was pretty annoyed, I can tell you. I was more than ready for a swiving, and suddenly my whore was gone and I was out the door. I had to resort to a place on the Campo de' Fiori, not nearly as clean."

Luther scowled at him. "You said you didn't know Cardinal Beccaria was there until later? Had you seen him there before?"

"I've never seen any cardinals, though I often see priests and even bishops." He frowned. "But he may have disguised himself as a layman. A cardinal would, I think. I didn't know his face. And despite the screaming whore, I wasn't sure that anyone had died until later. It was the talk of Rome, eventually."

Luther resumed his insolent stare. "What about Giulio de' Medici? Had you seen him there before?"

Heinrich knew that Cardinal de' Medici would want him to protect Giulio. "Not that I remember," he said.

"Did you know anything about Cardinal Beccaria? What did you think of him?"

Heinrich considered feigning ignorance, but why bother? "Very little. I never met him. They say he was a soldier during the first French invasion, but came to despise war and joined the Church. So, I think he was a coward. Why do you ask?"

"I'm just wondering how you and your order felt about him. Who do the Teutonic knights favor as the next pope?"

"Not him, certainly. We are real soldiers, you know. After the Crusades in Jerusalem, we Christianized the godless tribes in Poland and Lithuania. When Constantinople fell we hoped for a new Crusade, to drive the Turks out of the Holy Lands. But the Borgia pope closed our monastery in Sicily and spent the money he raised for a Crusade on wars in Italy. The Turkish threat grows daily, but these Italians are only interested in fighting amongst themselves."

Luther took a sip of his beer. "What do you think of Cardinal Alidosi? These Italians think he is likely to become pope, now that Cardinal Beccaria is dead."

The question surprised Heinrich. What could this ragged friar know about papal politics? Fortunately, Luther was following the wrong scent. Heinrich and many others in Cardinal de' Medici's pay were smoothing his path to become the first Medici pope. Alidosi might have Julius' backing, but he was not well-loved by his fellow cardinals.

"What do I think of Cardinal Alidosi?" Heinrich repeated. "He is owned by the French king, or so people say. But he does not want wars in Italy. And he is pragmatic. He might be a good choice for the next pope."

Luther drained his jug. "There are rumors that Alidosi is a killer," he commented.

"As I said, pragmatic."

Luther's eyes widened and his mouth opened and shut, like a gasping fish. Heinrich smiled, pleased he had flummoxed this irritating monk.

Luther stood to leave. "What about Cardinal de' Medici?" he said. "What do you think of him?"

"I don't think of him at all," Heinrich said. "Not at all."

Ch. 19 - Martin Luther's Confession

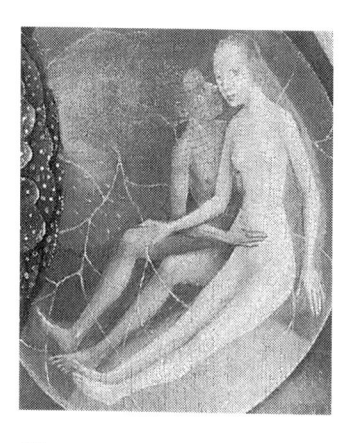

Hieronymus Bosch, The Garden of Earthly Delights, circa 1500

**Rome,
Monastery of Santa Maria del Popolo
Later the same day**

Frate Anton watched Martin Luther hurry towards him down the long corridor of the friars' *dormitorio,* and dreaded what would come next. He had hardly known the young scholar when they started their long walk from Erfurt to Rome. Of necessity, though, they had heard each other's confessions the entire way. Now, he probably knew Martin Luther better than any man on earth.

He found *Frate* Martin a puzzle. A brilliant and erudite young man, yet simultaneously filled with self–doubt and despair. Martin's bouts with *melancholia* worried *Frate* Anton, but he did not know what to do about them.

Luther's agitated face showed that he wanted to confess his sins again––and finally, he had something to confess. His loud, graphic descriptions of the erotic dreams and thoughts he had concerning Nicola Machiavelli had disturbed *Frate* Anton's own equanimity, despite his advanced age. He had been forced to tell Luther to be less explicit, lest Lust reawaken in his own middle-aged soul.

They walked in silence to a small chapel at the end of the *dormitorio,* built for solitary prayer and meditation. It contained a brightly-painted crucifix above a plain wooden altar and a long *prie dieu,* worn in places from the knees of generations of friars.

Luther knelt, crossed himself and recited the introduction to the rite of confession. "I have sinned by thought, word and deed," he said. "I have just spoken to a Teutonic knight who routinely visits prostitutes and thinks that a cardinal who ordered murders can be a good pope."

"How is it a sin to speak to a sinner, Martin?"

Luther shuddered. "I feel soiled by these Romans. As if all the sin here were rubbing off on me. And his talk of prostitutes and visits to whorehouses started my mind to thinking carnal thoughts again."

"You know I don't want the details about your carnal thoughts," *Frate* Anton interrupted. "Just say you are struggling with them. Are there other sins you need to confess?"

Luther's head bobbed. "That damned woman––I am speaking literally here, *Frate* Anton. I am not blaspheming. That damned woman, Nicola Machiavelli, is planning to visit the whorehouse where the cardinal was murdered. She wants to talk to the prostitutes about what happened. She is taking her lover, that artist Raphael, with her as escort. The thought of this fills me with rage. I want to punch Raphael in the nose. I think of this continuously."

Frate Anton was stunned, the more so because he had to suppress a sudden impulse to laugh. "Punch him in the nose? Why?"

"For letting her go to such a place. And for not marrying her. And for not being a better man, so she will marry him and save herself from damnation."

Confused, *Frate* Anton found himself wishing for the days when Luther's sins were small and predictable. "Why won't she marry him?"

Luther waved his arms in the air, as if he were shooing flies. "She says he will spend all her money. And she believes he has other women. And her father refused to dower her."

"Well, her father was certainly right, from everything you have just said."

"But the sin, Anton, the sin! She and that artist are mired in carnal sin. They will surely go to Hell for it, unless they marry."

Frate Anton smiled. "I think you have been hit by Cupid's arrow, Martin. You are in love with this damned woman, and jealous of this fellow Raphael."

Luther's jaw dropped. After a moment, he crossed himself. "May God forgive me, you may be right. Hit by Cupid's arrow? The Devil's pitchfork, more like. My sins mount. How will I ever overcome them?"

"It does you credit, that you want this woman married to a good husband. Your concern for her is noble, Martin. It is not a sin."

"A priest having such feelings for a woman is a sin. Of course it is. Wanting to hurt a man from jealousy, or for any reason, is a sin. I am committing new sins every day." Luther's face was red; his voice growing louder. "When I think I have overcome one sin, I commit a new one. I cannot seem to stop myself."

Frate Anton sighed. "How many times have we had this discussion, Martin? We are all sinners. It is a small sin for a priest to love a woman in a noble way, and to want the best for her. None of us can be perfect. God does not expect it. Is there anything further you need to confess?"

"Yes."

Frate Anton steeled himself for the long litany of minor peccadilloes that followed. Half–listening, he was startled when Luther said, "And that damned woman has me thinking heretical thoughts."

"Heretical thoughts? What do you mean, Martin?"

"She owns a Bible and has read it. She quotes parts of it I haven't thought much about."

Frate Anton gasped. "That's what comes of teaching women to read. Their minds cannot handle these things. You mustn't take your theology from a woman, Martin."

"I don't. I dismiss heretical thoughts as quickly as I can. But I think them first."

Frate Anton smiled at him. "It is human to have occasional doubts and confused thoughts, Martin. All men are thus." He raised the cross on his rosary, and kissed it. "Now I am ready to assign you a penance. And you are not going to insist that the penance is too light, do you understand?"

Luther looked down and nodded, his thin lips pressed together in a straight line, as if he were trapping words behind his teeth.

"First, if at all possible, you will meet this damned woman in public places, preferably churches. Pray then as you did at the funeral. Ask God to protect you from carnal thoughts."

"That is not a penance. That is just common sense," Luther protested.

"Next. This man Raphael, whom you want to punch in the nose. You will speak to him privately and tell him what you have told me—that he should make himself worthy of this woman, and marry her. Dowry or no. You will do so gently and without punching him in the nose. Does her father know that she is this Raphael's mistress?"

Luther shrugged. "I think not. He is in France, she says. At the court of the French king."

"Then you will write to him, tell him what his daughter is doing, and tell him to release her dowry to this man Raphael, so they can marry. So that their immortal souls can be saved. The Church runs couriers from the Vatican to the major cathedrals of Italy and I think also Paris. At any rate, the prior can arrange for delivery of your letter."

Luther nodded. "I am happy to do that. But it is not a penance."

"It is a good work, and that can be part of a penance. But I am not finished assigning your penance yet."

Luther looked down again. "I await your pronouncement."

"Every time you have a carnal thought concerning this damned woman, you must pray the 'Hail Mary' to the Virgin for release and forgiveness. And every time you think an angry thought concerning this man Raphael, you must say the "Our Father," and ask God to release your angry thoughts. When you think a heretical thought, repeat the list of beliefs in the Credo. Finally, you must go into the church and pray for God's forgiveness until the dinner bell."

Luther nodded and rose to his feet. "I will be saying a lot of 'Hail Marys,'" he observed.

"That is a good thing." *Frate* Anton made the sign of the cross. "I absolve you." As he recited the benediction, he felt relieved. At least he would have peace until dinner was over, and Martin Luther found some new sin to confess.

Ch. 20 - In the Brothel

Roman fresco,
2nd century B.C.

**Rome,
The next day**

When Nicola and Raphael entered the brothel where Cardinal Beccaria had been murdered, a half dozen whores stared at them as if they were exotic animals from the papal menagerie. Clinging to Raphael's arm, Nicola watched him look over the women, who obligingly dropped their shawls and preened for him, moving gaudy skirts and cupping half–laced bodices to show thighs and breasts. He smiled, then focused his attention on the obscene frescoes that covered the walls, in colors as garish as the whores' *gammuras*. Nicola felt drab, though she was wearing her brightest silks.

"We don't allow men to bring their own women in here. Except if you take one of my girls too. Then I will let you have one of the large rooms for half price." The madam smiled, displaying yellow teeth. She wore too much rouge, and a multicolored turban over hair too black to be natural. A filigree of wrinkles spilled over her chins like a cascading waterfall, pouring across sagging breasts into a bulging yellow *gammura*.

Raphael smiled at Nicola. "We would like to see those rooms, wouldn't we, *carina?*"

"We would indeed," she agreed. They had discussed how best to get upstairs to take a look around. The madam's offer solved their dilemma.

The large bedrooms, smelling strongly of rosewater, were just as Nicola remembered. She walked to the window that had borne the telltale blood smear and turned to memorize the room layout, while Raphael examined the frescoes of copulating couples on the red walls.

"You can see how clean we keep everything," the madam said. "And our girls are just as clean. And very discreet. Our prices are high but they are worth it."

Nicola paused at the top of the stairs to memorize the hallway layout, then followed Raphael back to the entry parlor, pausing to glance at the kitchen and office, which were just as she remembered them.

They emerged back into the parlor. "Now," the madam said, rubbing her hands together. "Which girls would you like? Violetta and Agrippina have special skill at this kind of thing."

Raphael put his arms around Nicola, and whispered in her ear, "These frescoes are terrible but the artist has an amazing imagination. I'm on fire. Will you quench my thirst?"

Nicola nuzzled against him and whispered back, "With another woman at the same time? No. But as soon as we get back to my *appartaménto.*"

Raphael held her close and kissed her neck. "I will be dying, all the way back. Let's be quick here," he whispered.

Nicola pushed away from Raphael and faced the madam. "We would like to speak to all your girls. About the day that Cardinal Beccaria's body was discovered outside. I was the one who discovered it, you see. And you need to know--if only for your own protection-- that the girl who was screaming is dead. She was murdered the same day that Cardinal Beccaria was."

The whores gasped, the artificial gaiety gone from their faces. "How do you know this?" the madam demanded.

"I saw her body myself, in her yellow *gammura*. She had been garroted. And the Swiss guardsman who was here also identified her."

One of the whores put a hand to her throat. "Dietrich. He's my customer. No wonder he hasn't come back."

They began talking all at once, their voices loud and dismayed. "Get out," the madam shouted. "I am a taxpayer. I run a respectable house. We already talked to the *bargelli*. Why should we talk to you?"

"Because I am going to pay you very, very well." Nicola said, jingling a bag filled with coins. The girls were suddenly silent.

"Why?" the madam demanded. "Why would you pay us?"

"Because important people want to know who killed Cardinal Beccaria."

"The *bargelli* wanted to blame Fiorina, but we knew she didn't do it," one of the girls confided. "When she didn't return, we feared the worst."

"Her name was Fiorina? Do you know where she lived? Did she have any family?"

"She was new, so we didn't know her well," another girl said.

"New to the business, too," said another. "Poor girl. Fresh from the country."

"Where did she live?"

"She lived here," the madam said. "She had run away from her family. Does anyone remember where she came from?"

The girls spoke quietly together for a few moments. "Somewhere out towards Ostia," one of them volunteered.

"Did she have special customers who favored her?" Raphael asked.

"One or two preferred her," the madam said. "But I won't give you their names. My customers expect me to protect their privacy."

"At least tell me they were not present that day," Nicola said.

"They were not. Otherwise, she would have been with them."

Nicola nodded. "Do you serve any cardinals?"

"Several. But not Cardinal Beccaria, as far as I know. He might have come in disguise, I mean. But as far as I know I have never seen the man, nor have any of the rest of us--right girls?" The madam turned to the prostitutes, who nodded.

"What about Pompeo Colonna, the Bishop of Reiti? Do you serve him? And two priests who are his close friends?"

The madam glared at Nicola. "We are not giving you the names of our customers, *Madonna*."

"We see a lot of priests, but only rich ones," one of the prostitutes added. "Either they have money from their families or they are dipping into the poor box. But which ones we saw that particular day? We couldn't tell you if we tried."

Nicola nodded, realizing she was asking the impossible. "Tell me what happened that day. As much as you can remember."

The whores looked to the madam to answer the question. "Fiorina must have seen something," she said. "But we don't know what. I sent her upstairs to inspect the empty rooms, after the maids finished cleaning. As I told you, we pride ourselves on our cleanliness. The maids do the heavy work, but all the girls are expected to help."

"She went up to do her job and just started screaming," one of the whores added. "The rest of us who didn't have customers were eating. We had no idea what was happening. Then we heard people running down the back stairs."

"Who among you was upstairs? What did you see?" Nicola asked.

"I was upstairs," one girl volunteered. "By the time Dietrich had paid me and we dressed, I didn't see anything. Fiorina had already run away. So I ran after her and everybody else."

"Same with me. We knew the *bargelli* would come," another added.

"When people started running, we stopped eating and ran out ourselves," said a third.

"So, no one saw anything unusual?" The whores looked at each other, then shook their heads "no."

"Which of you was with Giulio de' Medici?" Nicola faced the madam, who opened her mouth to object. "I know he was there. I saw him leaving myself," she continued. "Is one of you his favorite?"

A henna–haired whore looked at the madam, then waved a hand. "I am. He was with me since the night before. I was helping him dress when Fiorina started screaming."

"He was never out of your sight? "

She smiled. "Well, we did sleep for at least part of the night. But he never left the room."

"Does he come often?"

"Once or twice a week."

"And asks for you?"

"Always."

"What about Cardinal Alidosi, or his henchman Alfonso Zanna?"

The madam's eyes widened, and several of the whores looked at each other. "Never heard of them," the madam said loudly, glaring at the others.

Nicola could see that she was lying. "It is important that I know whether Alfonso Zanna was here. It is information I will pay you for."

"I know who you are talking about, though I will not say how," the madam responded. "He was not here." Her gaze swept the room and the whores nodded in agreement, their faces frightened.

They were probably lying, Nicola decided. But there was nothing she could do about it. "Now I need you to think about the day before. Did anything unusual happen the day before?"

"Why are you asking that?" the madam demanded.

"Because Cardinal Beccaria had been dead for awhile when he was found. Can you remember the customers from the day before?"

Two whores laughed. "I can't remember the customers from yesterday. You're talking now about a week ago," one said. "Or more."

"There was nothing unusual happening during that time," another said. "The weather has been cold, which brings in extra business. We were busy."

"I wouldn't let them give you the names of customers even if they remembered them," the madam said.

"Do you remember a man carrying a bundle of clothes, perhaps?"

Several of them laughed. "That happens all the time, *Madonna*. They come in the front door dressed as peasants and leave through the back, dressed as priests or monks or bishops. We work hard not to notice. We avert our eyes when we meet a man in the hall. They prefer it that way," said the henna–haired whore. The others nodded.

Nicola was becoming frustrated. "Was Alfonso Zanna here, the day before Cardinal Beccaria was killed?"

"Never heard of him," the madam announced, glaring around the room.

"What about Giulio de' Medici? When did he arrive? You said he came the day before?"

"He came late in the evening and was with me the whole time," the henna–haired whore repeated.

"What about the priests? When did they get there?"

"What priests?" the madam shouted.

Nicola raised a placating hand. "There were two priests. I saw them myself. And there were merchants. . . ."

"What merchants? There were no merchants," the madam shouted again. "No more questions about customers."

Nicola realized she needed to move to a different subject. "Who cleaned the blood off the windowsill?"

The madam's face relaxed. "It was one of the maids, the same day."

"Can I speak to her? To both maids. And there was a laundress, too, who fled with the others."

"The maids I will summon for you. The laundress––we hire that out. I don't know who it would have been."

"A large woman, with big arms and breasts," Nicola told her.

"Ah. Angela, then. If you like I can send her to you, when next I see her. If you will promise her a coin."

"I do promise her a coin. And here are coins for the rest of you," Nicola said as she distributed them. "And I promise another coin to anyone who comes to me with more information that leads to whoever killed Fiorina and Cardinal Beccaria. The better the information, the bigger the coin. You will find me above the bakery in the Campo Sant' Agatha. Now, can we speak to the maidservants?"

The madam motioned Nicola and Raphael into the kitchen area, now scrupulously clean. "Sit," she directed, closing the door that led to the waiting rooms. Opening a second door to the stairs, she roared, "Lucrezia and Cecilia. Come down." Then she left.

They were young girls, both of them thin and tired–looking, who had already been questioned and thoroughly frightened by the *bargelli*. They had finished their cleaning early the morning of the murder and no, they had not seen anything unusual. The blood smear on the window had not been there that morning. Yes, they were sure.

No, they hadn't found any bloody clothing, or any clothing at all that they remembered.

"How often do you clean the large rooms with the red frescoes?" Nicola asked.

"As needed. Sometimes they get little use. We check them every morning, though," said the heavier of the two, a plain girl with stringy hair wrapped in a rag,

"After the cardinal's murder, do you remember noticing any other blood in that room? Besides the smear on the windowsill, I mean."

"There must have been some on the floor," the thinner girl recalled, "you could see it when we damp mopped. But that happens often, *Madonna*. The whips are in there. Some of the monks and priests like to be scourged afterwards. That's why the walls and floors are painted red. If you look carefully, you can see splashes of blood on the frescoes. We don't dare clean them."

"Was there blood under the bed that day?" Nicola asked. The thin girl shrugged. "Hard to know. It was on the mop." Nicola gave them each a coin, and promised them another if they came with more information.

Then she found Raphael in the parlor, flirting with the henna-haired whore––whose name, she learned, was Luisa. Nicola put a coin in her hand. "Come to my shop, where we can talk privately, and there will be another coin for you," she promised.

The whore stared at the coin. "Giulio de' Medici has been generous to me. I'll not betray him."

"Come anyway," Nicola responded, beckoning to Raphael. He looked regretful as he followed her out the front door.

*****

Martin Luther waited for them outside. "What did you do while you waited for us?" Nicola asked him.

"I looked in the back entry you described, with the chamber pots and laundry baskets. Then I walked the neighborhood. Away from the Tiber it is nothing but huts among ancient ruins, and very poor. And I looked down on the riverbank, where the women do their wash."

Luther stopped and pointed. "Now, before we start back, show me the window where the blood stain was, and explain how the building is laid out."

Raphael did so. "I can draw the building for you when we get back, if you like."

"No need. You have been very clear." Luther turned to Nicola. "And you? What did you learn?"

As they walked back toward her home, Nicola described their interviews of the whores and maidservants. "I have an idea about what happened," she concluded. "Someone came up the back stairs and lurked in the large room at the end of the hall, which is not used frequently. When he saw Cardinal Beccaria, he pulled him into the room and stabbed him. He probably used the cardinal's clothing–– which was probably a disguise, not a cardinal's robe–– to staunch and mop up the blood. He stuffed the body under the bed and left the cardinal's ring on his finger, to identify him. And took the bloody clothes down the back stairs."

They sidestepped a cow, grazing next to a solitary ancient column. Ahead of them, Raphael shooed sheep off path and smiled back at them. The smell of animals and their fodder meant they were approaching Nicola's home. She hurried to finish her story.

"But the killer––or whoever employed him––must have gotten nervous," she continued.

"Nervous about what?" Luther asked.

"Nervous that the whores would simply steal the cardinal's ring and throw the body in the river in the dead of night. When you think about it, why wouldn't they? So the killer returned, because he needed the cardinal to be disgraced, not just to disappear."

"Why the need to disgrace him?" Luther said. "That is a key question."

"I can't answer that yet. But I think he stood at the window until he saw us coming, *Frate* Martin," Nicola continued. "He saw a friar and a lady, conversing together, and knew we would not steal the ring or throw the body in the river. That is why the body landed at our feet."

"But the screaming prostitute saw the murderer," Luther said.

"They told us she was upstairs, checking that the rooms were clean. Maybe she saw the murderer go in, or saw him when she was checking the room. Otherwise, he would not have killed her."

Luther frowned. "You think the killer took the cardinal's clothing. Was anyone who fled the brothel carrying a bundle?"

She nodded. "I remember that one of the merchants was. A large one."

They had reached the meadow in front of Nicola's building, muddy from recent rains. Raphael, who had walked ahead, paused to wait for them. He pointed. "Look, Nicola. They're tearing down those hovels. You were wise to buy here. New buildings are sprouting up, now that the popes have begun repairing the ancient aqueducts. The fountain at the Trevi crossing is working again, after a thousand years. And now that there's water, people are moving here. This is starting to look like a real piazza. The problem is, your building leans against that old tower. Pope Julius has a plan for making Rome magnificent again. Those old fortresses will be torn down."

Nicola looked up at the blackened stone tower that loomed over her brick building. "The ancient families of Rome are still powerful," she said. "They will not give up their strongholds without a fight."

As they reached the far edge of the meadow, the odors of wet wool and manure faded, giving way to the smell of baking bread from Nicola's shop. Several dirty beggars, smelling worse than the sheep, sat on the benches outside the open door, eating the small loaves that Nicola gave out as a charity. They nodded a greeting as they chewed.

Once inside the bakery, Raphael waved a greeting to Luigi, the baker, then pulled Nicola into his arms. "I'm still on fire for you," he whispered. "Can you get rid of the monk?"

"Wait for me upstairs," she whispered back.

Martin Luther stood by the door holding his rosary beads, eyes shut tight, reciting the "Our Father," with loud emphasis on, "Lead us not into temptation, but deliver us from evil." Nicola interrupted him when he began the prayer again. "*Frate* Martin, you can find your way back to your monastery from here, can't you? You just follow the river."

Luther's frown deepened and he and opened his eyes. "But we have no plan for what to do next, *Fraulein*."

"I'll think about it, and send you a note," Nicola promised, her mind on Raphael. As she mounted the stairs she called back, "Luigi, give *Frate* Martin a loaf of bread when he is ready to go."

Luther squeezed his eyes shut again, and went back to his prayer.

Ch. 21 - The French Count

Charles d'Amboise
by Andrea Solario, c.1508

North of the Po River and south of Milan
The same day

Caterina's heart sank as she faced Charles, Count of Amboise, alone in his tent. There was no recognition in his eyes, though she remembered him well enough. He had been very young when she first knew him, and was still slender and handsome. But there were deep lines across his forehead, and his eyes looked tired.

"I am Caterina Biaggi," she reminded him. "You sent me and my husband south with Cesare Borgia, when you first ruled Milan.†† We made weapons for you, and for him. And my firm in Milan makes them for you still."

His face brightened. "Of course. I remember now. You will excuse me––I was expecting a younger *Madonna* Biaggi. And

---

†† A Borgia Daughter Dies

wondering what she was doing so far from home. Last I saw, she was obviously expecting a child."

"She is my stepson's wife. When my husband died in Rome, his son returned to run the armory in Milan."

"Of course. I remember now." He gestured at the camp stool opposite him, next to the spindly table serving as his makeshift desk. "Please sit down. And pardon my rudeness, for not recognizing you sooner. May I offer refreshment?"

Caterina sat, glad the table hid her soiled *gammura* and hands. The ride from the river through muddy terrain had been terrifying and tiring. She felt shaky. "Please. Your soldiers took all our food. I am famished."

"Our supply lines are stretched thin at the moment––that is why we stopped your boat. I have men I must feed. But I can still provide for my guests." He rang a small bell. "Andre," he called out. "Food and drink for both of us. Now, why are you here in the middle of nowhere?"

"I am returning home to Milan."

"That's right. You said your husband died in Rome. How long ago was that?"

"Eight years, now."

"So he died soon after you left Milan. Where have you been, all this time?"

Caterina knew she would face this question, sooner or later. "As his widow, I ran the Biaggi armory in Rome, making weapons for Pope Julius."

"Ah. That explains why our soldiers keep capturing Biaggi weapons. I wondered about that. The pope's *arquebuses* are better than ours, Madonna Biaggi. The men are upset about this. I am upset about this."

"When I get to Milan, that will change. The knowledge was with my husband and me, in the south." She tapped her forehead. "Now it is here. Letters and drawings are no substitute for hands–on experience. Plus, I am going to consult Leonardo da Vinci on certain points when I see him in Pavia."

"You know Leonardo, then? Wish him a happy Christmas for me."

Caterina nodded. "I will, Excellency. And I promise that I will never work for the papacy again. Now that France and the papacy are at war, the Biaggi armory must choose sides. We choose Your Excellency. And our home city, Milan."

"You choose wisely. If only because the next pope will not buy weapons."

Caterina smiled. "Is Pope Julius dead? Last I heard, he was dying."

The Count chuckled. "Pope Julius is miraculously revived. Some woman––a former mistress, supposedly––swooped in and gave him a magical *tisana* made by nuns, and then disappeared. He has half his army looking for her. He drinks the *tisana* by the bucket and is back in roaring good health, planning his next battle against the Duke of Ferrara."

"*Madre di Dio*, what an extraordinary story," Caterina said, making no effort to hide her surprise. "And what a pity he survived," she continued, meaning it. "He was one of the most unpleasant men I have ever met."

The count smiled. "So I hear. I have never had the pleasure. I could have killed him when our armies clashed in October, but one hesitates to kill a pope. Directly, anyway. It's a pity he found that *tisana* and discharged his doctors. Things would be much simpler if he died. Do you happen to know Cardinal Alidosi, who will likely succeed him?"

"A little. He is papal treasurer," she responded, choosing her words with care.

"A sound fellow. More of a realist than Julius. And not a soldier, *Dio Grazie*."

Andre entered, replaced the paperwork on the Count's desk with a linen cloth, candles, and wine glasses, and ceremoniously placed two plates before them: pork and lentils cooked with garlic, looking homely but smelling heavenly. "Please eat," the Count said, as the wine was poured.

"Beautiful crystal," she said, raising a glass to him. She promised herself she would not wolf down her food, as much as she longed to.

"I wrote to you some time ago, asking for a safe conduct," she told him as they ate. "I sent it by messenger to Castelfranco, at considerable expense. Did you not receive it?"

"Never saw it. But I am happy to give you a safe conduct, regardless. France obviously needs you in Milan as quickly as possible, to make those excellent new guns for us. You said my men took your food. Otherwise, did they treat you properly?"

Andre brought fruit. "Apples. How lovely," Caterina said, accepting one while she thought about what to say. "Two foot soldiers wanted to rape me, but the *capitano* stopped them. He was civil enough, though he let them steal my purse as well as my food. Would it be possible to return me to the galley where I was captured? All my clothes and belongings are on it."

"Of course. Going upstream the galleys move slowly, and the Po is flowing fast from the winter rains. So you can catch it on horseback, if you can stand another fast ride. You would need to leave as soon as possible. Which may be just as well––it is very awkward, having a woman in camp. I will return whatever my men stole from you."

"Thank you, Excellency, I am happy to do that. I beg one more favor. I am guessing you have contacts in Rome. Could I send a letter to my niece there, telling her that all is well? She will worry otherwise."

The Count rose to his feet. "The person who will carry your letter is outside, about to leave. I need to speak to him anyway." He placed quill, ink and paper beside her on the desk. "Write your note, and be quick about it."

Something made Caterina follow him after he disappeared through the tent flap. She peered through the gap in the canvas. Alfonso Zanna, Cardinal Alidosi's henchman, was conferring with the Count, beside a group of men on horseback. Had they followed her from Venice?

Heart thudding in her chest, Caterina rushed back to her seat, thinking about her letter. Nicola had asked her about Zanna, who would likely unseal and read her response. What did she dare say? She wrote:

Dear Nicola,
    All is well. I am with Charles, Count of Amboise, an old friend. He has given me a safe passage to Milan. His men will

watch out for me. I will write again, once I get there. In the meantime, perhaps the man who brings this letter can answer your questions. His name is Alfonso Zanna.

Your loving aunt,
Caterina

As she melted wax to seal the letter, a shadow fell across the desk. Thinking it was Charles, she looked up with a smile. And froze, when she saw who looked down.

"Madonna Biaggi. I am Alfonso Zanna," he said. An unpleasant, toothy grin spread across his thin, hawk–nosed face. His long, yellow canine teeth gave him a wolfish air that explained the surname he had assumed. It meant "fang."

"I understand you are headed for Milan, via Pavia," he continued. "Pavia happens to be the principal see of my patron, Cardinal Alidosi. If there is anything you need there, do not hesitate to ask at the cardinal's *palazzo*. Should you need another letter delivered, we have regular couriers riding from Pavia to Bologna and Rome. I will be happy to arrange it for you."

"Thank you, that is very helpful," Caterina responded, trying to keep her hands from trembling as she finished sealing her letter. "Should I ask for you personally?"

"Unfortunately, I am on my way to Rome. Where I will deliver your letter," he said. "But perhaps I could escort you part way to Pavia?"

Caterina felt her jaw drop and her heart turn over in her chest. As her mind fumbled for a polite response that would reject this killer as her escort, the Count entered the tent.

"I am sending her a different way, Alfonso," the Count said. "Your men are saddled and waiting. You had best go if you want to make Piacenza by sunset. *Madonna* Biaggi, here is your purse. Count your money, and then you had best go, too. The men are saddling up who will take you.

"I need my safe conduct," she reminded him, gesturing to the writing materials on his desk.

"Of course. Of course."

As he seated himself, Caterina rose from her stool and handed Alfonso Zanna her letter to Nicola. "Thank you for delivering this. May I pay you?"

"No. I am always happy to do a favor for a beautiful lady," he said, with a look and toothy smile that sent a frightened shiver down her spine. "*Adieu*, Your Excellency," he said to the Count. Bowing, he left.

Weak-kneed with relief that her stalker was gone, Caterina sat down again and waited for her racing heart to slow. A new thought occurred to her. She was carrying a large bill of exchange for the remainder of the money she had received from Pope Julius. Would Zanna wait in ambush for her?

Ch. 22 - The Oarsmen

16th Century Oarsman

**Rome,
The Tiber River
The same day**

After walking the river road for most of the day, Nicola found the skiff with the faded red sun cover, its two oarsmen sprawled across the thwarts, napping. On the day of Cardinal Beccaria's murder, she had watched the four merchants who thundered out of the brothel as if pursued by devils escape in this boat.

Nicola picked her way down a narrow, rocky path to the river, swollen from winter rains. The oarsmen, wrapped in identical cloaks, had similar short beards and square faces, though the shorter of the two had the squashed nose of a fighter. Brothers, perhaps. The hawk-nosed man snoring at the bow was a giant, with a neck as wide as his head, and wrists as big as Nicola's ankles. Maybe his fist had done the damage to his smaller brother's face.

"*Buona sera*," she called to them.

Both woke with a start. "You desire a ride, *Madonna*? We will give you a good price," Hawk Nose said.

"I desire information," she said, holding up a coin. "Do you remember Santa Lucia's Day, when you took four merchants in a great hurry from the whorehouse that has its own dock, near the Campo de' Fiori? I need to talk to them. Can you help me find them? I will reward you well."

The two men looked at each other uneasily. "Those men are good customers, *Madonna*. They want to keep their visits to that place a secret," said Hawk Nose.

Nicola frowned. "You know that Cardinal Beccaria was murdered in that whorehouse, don't you? You could be arrested for withholding evidence."

Hawk Nose laughed. "What are you talking about?"

"Was it really Cardinal Beccaria the girl was screaming about?" Squashed Nose asked. "I heard he was a saint. But then he gets himself killed and thrown out the window of a whorehouse."

"You heard her screaming? Did you see anything?"

"Only our customers when they came sliding down the embankment," Hawk Nose said. "See for yourself--we can't see anything here."

Nicola turned around to examine the embankment. He was right-- the river was below the level of the city. She held up a second coin. "Can you tell me who the merchants were?"

The men looked at each other again. "No, *Madonna*. Why are you asking? Are you looking for your husband?"

"I am working with the Swiss Guard and the prior of Augustinian monastery at Santa Maria del Popolo, hoping to find the man who killed Cardinal Beccaria."

"You?" Hawk Nose scoffed. "You are a woman. You expect us to believe that?"

"Would you like me to bring a Swiss guardsman, who could arrest you? Because I can."

The oarsmen looked at each other again. "Those merchants didn't know anything about what happened, *Madonna*. I heard them talking, understand?" Squashed Nose said. "Someone was shouting "murder" -- that's all they knew. They didn't want to be around when the *bargelli* showed up."

"We row them to that whorehouse and back after a guild meeting, every week," Hawk Nose said. "They were just in the wrong place at the wrong time."

"Which guild?"

"Oh, no," he said, shaking his head. "We can't tell you that."

Nicola thought for a moment, then held up four coins. "How about telling me when you next take them to the brothel? I could just happen to be there. I'll give you two coins now, and two coins after I talk to them."

"But why would they talk to a woman?"

Why indeed? Nicola resented it, but the oarsman had a point. "Do you know if they speak Latin?" she asked.

"Well, of course they do," Squashed Nose said. "They are important merchants."

"I will bring a friar to talk to them, then, one who comes from Cardinal Beccaria's monastery. And when you link us with them, I will pay you the other two coins."

"You won't tell them we told you?" Hawk Nose said.

"Absolutely not."

The oarsmen exchanged glances again, then bent their heads together, whispering. Hawk Nose then held out a hand for the two coins, which Nicola gave him. "Their meeting is day after tomorrow. It is usually over just before Nones," he said. "So we should arrive at the whorehouse docks soon after the Nones bells ring. If you and the friar are there, you should be able to speak to them."

Ch. 23 - A Sinful Past

16th Century Swordsman
from a fencing book by Joachim Meyer

Rome,
The same day

Martin Luther hurried into the chapter room of the Augustinian monastery at Santa Maria del Popolo, eager to meet with the friars who had volunteered to tell him about Cardinal Beccaria's early life. Hands in their sleeves, they occupied three of the elaborately–carved seats that hugged the brown brick walls of the circular room, the meeting place of their monastic order.

Luther seated himself where he could see them. Dimly–lit in the early morning light, the room was so cold that he could also see his own breath.

The oldest of the three was *Frate* Domenico, a thin, bent figure with bushy white brows, a beak of a nose and only a few wisps of hair encircling his tonsured skull. His hands, knotted with arthritis, shifted on his cane as he cleared his throat.

"The prior instructed us to tell you what we know of Cardinal Beccaria's past sins." He glanced at his companions, who nodded encouragement. "We were his friends. He was a good man, and what he did was understandable. And God has forgiven him. But he never forgave himself."

Luther nodded. "Tell me his story."

Frate Domenico exhaled, then looked up. "As a young man, Cardinal Beccaria was a soldier. He had been gone for more than a year, fighting the French. Back when they first invaded, in the time of the Borgia pope. When he returned home, his wife presented him with a newborn babe, and said it was his. From when he visited her while she was at her sister's home, she told him. The same thing she had already told the servants."

Frate Domenico grimaced as he used his cane to shift his bony form on the hard seat. "He said to me, 'If I had been the man she knew before the war, I would have gone along with her story, because I loved her. And to save face. But war had changed me. I had never visited her sister. I had not seen her in almost two years." The aged friar hesitated.

With a sinking feeling, Luther said, "What did he do?"

"He pulled out his sword, and killed her on the spot. With as little thought as swatting a fly, he said."

Luther felt his jaw drop. It was one thing to kill as a soldier. But Cardinal Beccaria had also killed his own wife? How could God possibly forgive such a horrific sin?

The dead cardinal's friends seemed alarmed by the look on Luther's face. "It gets worse," *Frate* Domenico said. "Do you want to hear the rest?"

Luther swallowed, with difficulty. "I must."

Frate Domenico clutched his cane, and bowed his head. "After he killed his wife, he chased the nursemaid through the hallways, intending to kill the babe. But God stayed his hand. Praise be to God."

"Praise be," Luther echoed, crossing himself with the others.

Frate Domenico's forehead rested on his cane, as if he were praying, or too sad to continue. Seeing this, *Frate* Marco took up the tale.

"The nursemaid, fleeing with the babe, shut a door in his face. He beat on it with his sword, about to break it down. But suddenly God brought him to his senses. He fell to the floor, filled with remorse and hatred for war. It had made a monster out of him, he told us." The three of them nodded in agreement. "He summoned the bishop, and confessed his sin. Part of his penance was to walk on his knees for miles at a time, stopping often to pray, until his legs bled. Over and over. He was happy to do it. And back then he was a hero, who had fought to free Italy from the French. So his people cheered for him and were proud of their Count. But after he was absolved, he gave his lands and children over to his younger brother, who became the new Count. And he entered the monastery."

The friars sat up and looked at each other, smiling, as if relieved the story was over. Still stunned by it, Luther thought of questions he had intended to ask. "Did he ever talk about the other sins he committed, during the wars?" he said.

"He told us of unspeakable things done by the French," *Frate* Marco said, fingering his rosary beads. "They raped and killed women and children. He said once that he knew what he had become, when he realized he was no better than the French."

"I am sure he killed during the war. Or the soldiers under him did, anyway. It is not something he talked about, though." *Frate* Domingo said.

"What about his wife's family? Were they angry that he killed their daughter?" Luther asked.

"Her parents wouldn't even take his wife's body for burial," said *Frate* Domenico. "They were ashamed of her. They knew the truth of it, you see, from the sister she was staying with when she betrayed her husband."

"What about his children? How did they feel about the death of their mother?"

"His daughters were very young when it happened," Frate Domenico replied. "They were told their mother was dead, but not how she died. Not then. They found out eventually, I suppose. He always saw them and his grandchildren when he was in the north, visiting his benefices there. He felt they had a good relationship."

"He told me once that their mother's fate had ensured his girls' virtue," *Frate* Marco said.

"He was very open about what happened, then?" Luther asked.

They looked at each other. "He was to us," *Frate* Domenico said.

"Was there anyone––can you think of anyone who wanted to kill him?"

They looked at each other, and shook their heads. "We have talked about this endlessly. There is hardly a man alive who wouldn't have done exactly what he did," *Frate* Domenico said. "But very few would have felt so bad about it. He actually asked for a severe penance. He performed it, and was absolved. The world understood and forgave him. Many in his home town praised him. But he never ceased to feel guilty."

Luther understood. He always felt unworthy of absolution, fearing he had forgotten to confess a sin or perform a penance properly. Guilt clung to him like a dirty garment, when he should have felt cleansed. And his own sins were minor, compared to Cardinal Beccaria's. The more he knew of the murdered cardinal, the sadder he felt.

"Did he have any enemies?" Luther asked, hoping to glean something.

The oldest monk spoke up again. "He had rivals. Men who wanted to be pope, who were jealous of his reputation for goodness and common sense. But enemies? None that we know of."

Luther nodded, feeling more and more discouraged. Melancholy, his old nemesis, was creeping into his bones, like a damp fog. "Can you think of any reason that anyone would have wanted to kill him?"

They looked at each other and murmured together. Once again, *Frate* Domenico spoke for the group. "We think that someone wanted to eliminate him as a candidate for the papacy. Someone who stands to benefit if a particular cardinal becomes pope."

"How would I find such a person?"

They whispered together again. "You might be able to identify men who will profit if a particular cardinal becomes pope. But such men would hire an assassin, not dirty their own hands. You couldn't possibly link such men to an assassin, without God's help," the oldest said. "It would take a miracle. We will pray for one."

Ch. 24 - Leonardo is Worried

Leda and the Swan,
Drawing by Leonardo da Vinci

Pavia, Italy
The same day

Leonardo da Vinci unfolded and re-read Caterina's letter, as he had done several times already that day. Where was she? Had she arrived in Pavia, and forgotten her promise to invite his *famiglia* to Christmas dinner? She was supposed to be on the next galley from Venice, but something must have happened.

Huddled by the fire, he looked around the drafty, sparsely-furnished attic that served as his studio, wondering how a female presence might transform it. His adopted sons Salai and Cecco had deserted him for the moment. It was too quiet. It was lonely.

Finally, Salai's hurried footfall sounded from the stairwell, and he burst into the room. "Her things showed up, but she didn't. The housekeeper is still expecting her, though."

Leonardo thrust Caterina's letter under the blanket on his lap. "Where could she be? Do you suppose she needs help?"

Salai hung his hooded cloak on a hook by the door and smoothed his blond curls in front of the mirror. "Her? Not likely. She probably decided to stay in Venice for Christmas. We'll hear from her soon. Count Beccaria has invited us for Christmas dinner, too. We should go there anyway, don't you think?"

Leonardo grimaced. "He invited every prominent person in town. Our absence will not be missed. You said Caterina's baggage arrived? Why would she ship it ahead?"

Salai poured himself a glass of watered wine from the pitcher on the sideboard, and seated himself at the fireplace opposite da Vinci, carefully smoothing his red wool tunic. "Who knows why women do anything? You need to forget about her. Her and La Cremona both. Like you told me to forget about Nicola. Why are you preoccupied with women, all of a sudden? You never used to bother with them."

Da Vinci glared at his adopted son. It was galling to have his own advice thrown back in his face. "Caterina is a business associate, who has paid me well over the years. It would be unwise for me to forget her. And La Cremona is a thing of the past. I wish you would quit talking about her. Did I needle you this way, when you fell for Nicola? Or any of the others?"

Salai laughed. "You just warned me about the wiles of women. Then fell for a courtesan yourself."

"I am a careful man, but still a man, Salai." A fleeting memory of Cremona, modeling naked for *Leda and the Swan,* seized him. He dismissed it. "Enough about her." Cremona had refused to come to Pavia with them. Leonardo ached for her, when he thought about her. Best not to think about her.

Salai gave Leonardo the smile that had long ago inspired his nickname, "Imp." "I'm sorry. About Christmas dinner—the Count will not be here. Apparently his brother died—Cardinal Beccaria. The Count is on his way to Rome to deal with his brother's estate, and may not be back by Christmas. Maybe they will cancel the dinner."

Leonardo rose to put more wood on the fire. "The Count's wife will hold the dinner, even without him. She misses no opportunity to show off her wealth. I don't want to paint her, Salai. She is detestable."

"Francesco and I can paint her."

"She wants a da Vinci." Salai and Francesco both were mediocre painters, unfortunately, as hard as Leonardo had tried to teach them.

Francesco Melzi could now be heard trudging up the stairs. "It's cold out there," he announced as he entered and hung his cloak. "What news?"

"Not much. Caterina Biaggi still has not arrived," Salai said.

"I heard she was captured and sent to the Count d'Amboise, for her own protection," Francesco responded, scratching his prematurely bald head. "Is there cheese left?"

Da Vinci's heart thudded in his chest at Francesco's announcement. After a moment's thought, he decided he felt relieved. "The Count d'Amboise is an honorable man. She is safe with him. I wonder, should I write to him about her?"

"What good would it do?" Francesco said as he helped himself to watered wine. "Would you like some cheese?"

Ch. 25 - The Cardinal's Will

Man wearing beretta with earflaps
(Detail from *Portrait of Matthew Parker* by School of Holbein)

Rome,
Monastery of Santa Maria del Popolo
Later the same day

Martin Luther hurried into the prior's office and placed two leather-bound volumes on the desk. "All the others are in Cardinal Beccaria's cell," he reported, wondering why he had been summoned so abruptly.

The prior sat in front of his marble fireplace, in the ornate carved chair he used to receive powerful guests. Opposite him in the matching chair was a well-dressed man, cradling a silver cup of wine and toasting his booted feet at the hearth.

The prior pointed Luther towards a stool next to the wainscoted wall, beneath the tapestry of Jesus at Cana. "*Frate* Martin, this is Count Beccaria, the cardinal's brother. He is here to claim the cardinal's personal property, which the Cardinal left to his family in his *testamento*. I have explained to the Count that I tasked you with finding his brother's murderer."

A heavyset man with a broad face and thick lips, Count Beccaria wore a black *beretta* with fur earflaps, heavy leather boots, and a fur-lined cloak over a tunic of rich maroon wool. He frowned at the books Luther had brought. "That's it?" he said, his voice brittle with anger. "I came all the way from Pavia for a few religious books and moth-eaten garments?"

"Have you been to the cardinal's cell?" Luther asked. "I can show it to you."

"He has." The prior hesitated, evidently weighing his words. "He has trouble believing that a cardinal could have so few things."

The count looked balefully at Luther. "Did you find nothing of value?"

"He had a fine library of books," Luther said. "Very little else. Shall I go through it with you again?"

The Count tossed back his wine, then belched and grimaced at the cup. "I suppose that is something," he told Luther. "Let's go."

The prior gave them both candles, as daylight was waning. The Count picked up the books on the prior's desk and followed Martin Luther, muttering, "Everyone knows that cardinals are richer than Croesus. How did I get a poor one for a brother?"

"How old are his children now?" Luther asked. "Did he leave them anything?"

"His daughters are adults with children of their own. They will get funds he set aside long ago, yes."

"Did he have any other heirs?"

"None of your business."

Luther swallowed his anger. "The prior asked me to find out who killed him. Do you have any ideas?"

The count looked startled. "Wasn't he knifed by a whore?"

"He was knifed, but probably not by a whore. Did he have any enemies?"

The Count shrugged. "Who doesn't? Who they are, I couldn't tell you."

They reached the cardinal's cell. The Count immediately dumped ecclesiastical robes from his dead brother's trunk and began stacking books in it. Something in his attitude incensed Luther. "Don't you care who killed your brother?" he asked.

"We were never close. I was a boy when he returned from the wars. Here, people seem to revere him, but we were ashamed of him. I haven't seen him in years. He had no gold, no jewelry?"

"None that I have found. His cardinal's ring went back to the Church, I think––you'd have to ask the prior about that. It's possible his cell was robbed after his death––his strongbox was open when the prior and I went to the cell, late the day the body was discovered."

The count stood up and stared at Luther. "They key was in it?"

"The key was in it. And the doors here are never locked."

"*Porca Madonna.* What a fool. Can you hand me those books?"

With great care, Luther handed the count several old manuscripts, including the exquisitely illuminated text of St. Augustine's *Of Grace and Free Will* he had borrowed to read and admire. "I heard the story of Cardinal Beccaria's murder of his wife, Count. Is there anything else in his past that was truly shameful?"

The Count grabbed the books, then stopped to stare at Luther. "*Madre di Dio,* isn't that enough?"

"He was open about it. And did his penance and received absolution. But before his death, he burned a document that contained the word "disgrace." I don't want to pry into family secrets, but I'm wondering if he was hiding anything that a man would kill for. Something that happened during the first French war, for example. You may rely on my discretion."

The Count threw up his hands. "To my knowledge, he was a hero in that war. I spent my whole life, trying to bury the shame our family suffered when he murdered his wife. More bad secrets? I sincerely hope not. I don't know of any. Can you hand me the rest of those books?

"Here. I'm sorry if I offended you. By all accounts, he was a great man. He deserves justice."

Count Beccaria rose and closed the trunk lid. "He killed, and was killed himself. Isn't that justice?"

Ch. 26 - A Bloody Business

A Renaissance era
butcher, detail from a mural

Rome,
The next day

Frate Anton hurried into the monastery kitchen, holding his nose against the stink he had smelled far down the corridor. Its source was obvious: half a skinned pig, suspended from the ceiling, dripped blood into a large cauldron while kitchen workers washed the entrails in an adjacent bucket, minced and chopped pork atop a bloody table, and tended stewpots simmering over both fireplaces, all the while chattering in their foreign tongue.

Martin Luther stood by a corner table, next to a pile of pigskin topped with the pig's head, which seemed to peer up at him through closed eyes. Four kitchen workers, each with a quill poised over blood-spattered paper, sat staring at Luther expectantly. Only one of them, muscular and shirtless under his bloody leather apron, had bothered to wash the offal from his hands.

Frate Anton remained by the door, fearful that the stink would make him vomit. "Martin, that damned woman sent you a note," he called out in German. "Something about meeting her at the Pantheon."

Another voice responded in German, to Anton's surprise. "*Frate* Martin is meeting a damned woman at the Pantheon? Really?" The voice lapsed into excited Italian, and the room erupted in laughter. Luther flushed red.

"The woman from funeral? The pretty woman?" the bare-chested worker at the table asked *Frate* Anton, in slow, awkward Latin.

Flummoxed, *Frate* Anton looked at Luther for guidance, and watched him swallow hard. "Perhaps we should speak outside, Anton," he said.

"How can you bear that stink, Martin?" *Frate* Anton asked him as they walked down the hallway together.

Luther's blush had faded. He shrugged, looking haggard. "I did not grow up wealthy, Anton. We slaughtered pigs next to our house and felt blessed to have them. May I see the note from *Fraulein* Machiavelli?"

Anton handed him the note from Nicola. "I am sorry I referred to 'the damned woman,'" Anton said as Luther perused it. "I had no idea there was a German speaker here."

"Our dialect is different from Adolph's, but 'damned woman' is the same in both, it seems," Luther responded, his voice weary. "And Roberto—the shirtless boy in the bloody apron sitting in the corner—has learned enough Latin to converse a bit. The three of us sometimes carry on a conversation with all the kitchen workers, with one or the other of them translating."

"Which one is Adolph? I couldn't tell."

"Younger fellow with blue eyes and curly hair, tied in a kerchief. Comes from somewhere up in the Alps."

They stopped a short way down the hall. Inside the kitchen, they could hear the workers shout and laugh loudly.

"I am sorry if I caused you embarrassment," *Frate* Anton said.

Martin Luther sighed and shook his head. "No matter. This note summons me to meet that damned woman tomorrow. At someplace called the Pantheon, to share what we have each learned concerning Cardinal Beccaria's murder. And then go talk to the merchants who were at the brothel when the body went out the window. She found them, somehow."

He tucked the note into a pocket. "But now I have to go back in there and explain."

Frate Anton still felt anxious about the trouble he had caused for his friend. "Can I help in any way?"

"I'd like you to be with me."

When they re-entered the kitchen, the worker Luther called Roberto stood at the doorway waiting for them. His neatly-combed auburn hair and angelic young face seemed a strange contrast to his bloody apron and muscular bare arms.

"We want invite pretty damned lady to Christmas *festa*," he announced slowly in Latin. The other workers grinned.

"She is not damned. She is a benefactress of this monastery," Luther responded.

Roberto frowned. "Benefactress? What is?"

"She gives bread to the poor," *Frate* Anton explained, keeping his speech slow. "That is why Martin spoke to her at the funeral."

"Ah. 'Bene' means good. 'Factress' means do. Then why you say she is damned?" Roberto demanded.

Frate Anton considered for a moment. "I think all daughters of Eve are damned. Especially pretty ones," he responded.

Roberto translated for the other kitchen workers, who roared with laughter. "We still want her come to Christmas *festa*," Roberto continued in Latin, looking at Luther. "Here, for Christmas dinner. Special dinner. You invite her, please?"

"I will," Luther promised, much to *Frate* Anton's surprise. "But she may not come."

"Roberto," a voice called out. Evidently the men lowering the remaining half pig from the kitchen ceiling needed assistance.

"You try," Roberto said over his shoulder to Luther, as he hurried to help.

Ch. 27 - At the Pantheon

The Roman Pantheon
Completed by the emperor Hadrian
and probably dedicated about 126 AD

Rome,
The following day

"He was supposed to be such a good man," Nicola exclaimed, when Luther finished relating the story of Cardinal Beccaria's murder of his own wife. "I assumed his great sin was something he did as a soldier. This changes everything, surely. What should we do?"

They stood near the middle of the circular, windowless Pantheon, enveloped in the light from the *oculus* in the center of its coffered dome. The rest of the church was dark, silent and empty. The beam of light from the *oculus* seemed to enlarge *Frate* Martin and his palpable sadness, reminding Nicola of the candlelit crucifix of Jesus in her parish church. She dismissed the thought.

"We still must talk to the merchants, because you arranged it," Luther said. "But what can they possibly tell us?"

"The monks you spoke to are right. The merchants could have ordered the murder to protect their businesses from a reformist pope who would have ended the clergy's lavish parties. I'm not sure what to do after we talk to the merchants, though. I need to think about what it means, that the Cardinal killed his own wife."

Luther bowed his head. "It means he is doomed to Hell. And that makes me very sad."

"You seem very sad. But you need more faith in your God, *Frate* Martin, if you think that."

Luther stiffened. "I have complete faith in our Lord God, *Fraulein.*"

"Cardinal Beccaria performed a heavy penance for his murder, and many good works. So take comfort, *Frate* Martin. He is in Heaven."

"It is hard for me to believe that God ever forgives the murder of a wife. And you forget-- the Cardinal also died with the sin of fornication on his soul. A great sin for any man, but especially a cardinal."

"I don't believe God condemns people to Hell just because they die sudden deaths, without being able to confess their sins." Nicole bit her lip, realizing she had just admitted a heretical belief. Luther showed no reaction, however. "We need to go, *Frate* Martin," she told him.

He followed her toward the door. "While we walk, I need to ask your help," he said. "We need to hear what the servants at the monastery have to say. Which means I need you to translate. You attracted their attention at Cardinal Beccaria's funeral, and they asked me to invite you to their Christmas *festa.* I think it is important to hear their stories, so I said I would ask."

"Why should we talk to the servants at the monastery?"

"The servants had access to Cardinal Beccaria's cell, which may have been ransacked. And remember the burned documents, including the one that said, 'disgrace.' Also I am curious whether the servants knew about Cardinal Beccaria's past sins. If so, what was the 'disgrace' referred to in the burned document? If Cardinal Beccaria didn't keep murdering his wife a secret, what 'disgrace' could he have feared?"

"But you said the Cardinal's cell was close to the monastery entrance which is never locked. Don't we assume that he burned the documents himself, or the assassin did?"

"It could certainly have been the Cardinal or an outsider that burned them, yes. And ransacked the cell. But not necessarily."

"I'll come to the *festa,*" Nicola said as she pulled her cloak tighter to escape the cold wind as they left the church.

"What is this place?" Luther asked, gazing back at the doorway. "I saw the inscription outside. 'Pantheon' means 'house of the gods' in Greek. It is very strange looking, for a church."

"It was a pagan temple to all the gods," Nicola explained. "Raphael says the dome is a marvel of Roman engineering. A kind of miracle. The dome they will build at St. Peter's will be modeled on it."

"Now I know why that domed cathedral in Florence felt godless. In the north we build tall spires to reach for God. Here they worship in pagan temples." Luther shook his head. "Why am I not surprised?"

The sound of men on horseback made them step back. Cardinal and Giulio de'Medici passed without a glance, trotting side-by-side on powerful chargers, each with a falcon on his wrist. Pompeo Colonna, Bishop of Reiti, rode behind them with a quiver of arrows slung over his shoulder. Behind them all, an assembly of noblemen and groomsmen clattered across the cobblestones, on horseback and on foot. Hunting dogs wove between the horses, yipping at their heels.

Frate Martin and Nicola followed the hunting procession for a time, headed for the river. "Where I come from, clergy do not hunt. It is considered too worldly," Luther said, frowning.

"Cardinal de' Medici loves to hunt, and is well-known for his lavish, expensive parties. He is one of the richest men in Christendom, because of the many church benefices he controls."

Luther grimaced. "Who is the bishop? I remember him from the funeral."

"The bishop is Pompeo Colonna. He is cousin to the priests who fled the brothel after Cardinal Beccaria died. Francesco was going to talk to them, but I don't know if he did. He said at the funeral that Pompeo was once a soldier. But his family pressured him into taking his brother's place as Bishop when the brother died, to keep the benefice in the family."

"He went from soldier to bishop? Just like that?" Flushed, his voice indignant, *Frate* Martin looked a little less sad.

Nicola realized she enjoyed baiting this moralistic monk. "Becoming a bishop in Italy is simply a matter of knowing the right people," she assured him, smiling. "Cardinal de' Medici became a monk at eight and a cardinal at thirteen, because he was the second son of Lorenzo 'Il Magnifico' when the Medici ruled Florence. He is still not ordained. Pompeo Colonna may not be ordained, either. Calm yourself, *Frate* Martin."

Martin Luther, red–faced, clutched his rosary. "A monk at eight, a cardinal at thirteen, and not even ordained? Calm myself? How, when I am surrounded by such. . .such. . ."

"Pray for a moment or two, *Frate* Martin. That will calm you."

Luther said a "Hail Mary," then dropped his rosary beads. "Even if Cardinal de' Medici and his cousin are as corrupt as you say, I still cannot picture them stabbing and stripping another cardinal and then throwing him from the window of a brothel," he said. "Nor could *Meister* Raphael, and he knows them."

"But Giulio was there," Nicola reminded him, "He had motive and opportunity. Cardinal de' Medici wants to be pope, and that means power and wealth for Giulio, too. I'm not saying they are the guilty ones. But it is a possibility."

Frate Martin grunted, then resumed working his rosary. They walked through Rome's twisted, stinking alleys in silence, soon reaching the Tiber River. "I see the boat coming upriver with the merchants," Nicola said. "You'll need to question them before they go into the brothel. I'll stay here to pay the oarsman what I promised them, then join you."

Martin Luther looked up, as if startled to see his surroundings. Nicola shooed him ahead of her, then waved at the boatmen and ducked into an alley.

After the boat docked, the merchants climbed the wooden stairs to the Tiber River Road and headed upstream toward the brothel, with Martin Luther bustling after them. The boatmen headed for the alley where Nicola stood waiting, received their coins and whispered their thanks.

When she reached Luther's side, the merchants were backing away from him, and shaking their heads. The tallest of them motioned to the others to follow, turning towards the whorehouse entrance.

Nicola intercepted them. "*Maestro* Flavio. I'm so pleased to see you. It has been a long time. Soon I will give a dinner party, and will need some excellent wine. What is best? I am planning to make a *porchetta*. These are your colleagues? Are any of you near the Campo Sant' Agatha? I don't live near the Vatican any more, now that my father is in France. Which is why you haven't seen me."

Maestro Flavio nodded politely. "I am overjoyed to see you, *Madonna*," he said, without enthusiasm. "And to know the reason your father stopped coming to my shop. In France, is he? They have some fine wines there. He knows how to pick them."

"My shop is not far from the Trevi crossing," the shortest one said. " I am at your service."

Nicola gave the group her best smile. "I see you have met *Frate* Martin. Did he tell you that the body of Cardinal Beccaria fell almost at our feet, right here? Such a terrible thing. "

They agreed it was a terrible thing, and murmured wishes for her speedy recovery from such a shock.

Nicola switched to Latin. "And you were there, I know, because we saw you. It must have been terribly shocking for you, too. Did you see it happen?"

They looked at each other, and at Martin Luther. "As we already told this monk, we saw nothing," *Maestro* Flavio answered.

"Wasn't there blood everywhere?" she asked, wide-eyed.

They looked at each other again. "We were in the public rooms, Madonna," *Maestro* Flavio said. "The–events—occurred upstairs. Truly, we saw nothing."

Nicola turned to the shortest merchant. "You were carrying a bundle when you fled. What was in it?"

He flushed. "I was not carrying a bundle."

"You were carrying your cloak, Lorenzo. Don't you remember?" one of the others said.

"That's true. I was carrying my cloak."

"We heard the screaming, and fled before the *bargelli* arrived," a third merchant said. "Who wants to be mixed up with them?"

"Exactly," Nicola said. "You didn't see anyone suspicious? The *bargelli* are still looking for the killer. I am very frightened."

Talking all at once, they assured her that she should not be frightened. "Everything seemed normal. But for the screaming," one of them said. "Nothing to threaten a respectable woman like yourself."

"If you pardon us, we must be going," *Maestro* Flavio said. "I have a beautiful red wine from *Sicilia* that would go well with your *porchetta*. Shall I set some aside for you?"

"I will sell you the same for less, and I am closer to you," said another. His friends laughed.

"I will visit your shop soon, *Maestro* Flavio," Nicola promised him. *"Buon giorno."* The merchants took turns bowing to her, like birds pecking at crumbs, while ignoring *Frate* Martin. They stood expectantly as Nicola turned her back on them and walked down the river road, away from the whorehouse entrance, sensing Martin Luther behind her.

She paused a short way down the road. "Did you see how guilty they looked? Like dogs caught with their faces in the master's plate, all of them."

Luther shrugged. "They were caught about to enter a whorehouse, by a priest and a lady who is one of their customers. How were they supposed to look?"

Nicola laughed. "That's true; I had not considered that. And I remember now––the one carrying the bundle was not wearing a cloak when I saw him after the murder. So perhaps the bundle was his cloak. But he could have hid the cardinal's missing clothing inside his cloak."

"It's lucky you knew one of them. They would not even tell me which guild they belonged to."

"The wine merchants are a powerful guild––one of the most powerful in Rome. And of all the guilds, the one that would be most hurt by a reformist pope. So maybe the cardinal's friends at the monastery were right. Maybe the merchants did murder Cardinal Beccaria."

Ch. 28 - Raphael's Secret

Cupid and the Three Graces,
by Raphael, at the Chigi villa,
now known as Villa Farnesina

**Rome,
Later the same day**

Clutching her shawl around her, Nicola sat in front of the massive brick forge of Caterina's armory, missing its usual warmth. She cradled a sack of freshly-baked holiday loaves, studded with lemon peel and dried fruit. The familiar yeasty odor, redolent of anise, overwhelmed the usual smells of sweat and hot metal.

This evening, there was no fire in the forge and no clanging of hammer on anvil. Dressed in their best tunics, the workers stood in line, grinning. Nicola had cashed the bill of exchange Caterina sent, to pay long overdue wages. Along with a fragrant loaf of *pannetone* from her bakery, she handed each armorer a bag of coins, which he counted carefully before putting his "X" next to his name in the wage book.

When all had received their due, Rodolfo, Caterina's business partner, passed around a jug of strong red wine. The men's joy was building, and infectious. The money had come in time for Christmas. They talked excitedly of *festas* for their families and gifts to celebrate Befana, the witch who helped the Wise Men find the Christ Child, and brought Him gifts of her own. Soon the room was roaring with raucous laughter and songs accompanied by the tinny rhythms of tools banging on half-made armaments. Even Nicola's maid Maria took a little wine, which inspired her to dance with Giuseppe, the foreman.

Nicola drank little. "It is getting dark, Rodolfo," she said, finally. "Maria and I need to get home. Who here can be trusted to escort us?"

Rodolfo grinned, his cheeks red from the wine. "Have no fear. I will do it myself." He splashed more wine into his cup, spilling a little, then frowned. "Caterina said when she left that she may not come back, anytime soon. Is it true, Nicola?"

"I'm not sure what she plans."

As Maria and Nicola donned cloaks, Francesco appeared at the door. "I have been looking for you everywhere," he told Nicola. "I have another letter from Caterina for you. And we still can't find her. Do you know where she is?"

Nicola took the letter, glancing at the seal. "It looks like you opened it, Francesco. You know as much as I do."

"She says nothing about where she was. We have combed Venice, looking for her."

Nicola scanned Caterina's letter. "Francesco, this is important. Let me think a moment." Frowning, she counted days in her head. "She told me Alfonso Zanna was not in Bologna after November. But when she wrote this letter, she had just seen Zanna in Venice, three days after she left Bologna. So Zanna could have murdered the cardinal in Rome, if he went directly to Venice afterwards."

Francesco waved a hand dismissively. "Doesn't matter now. the pope has ordered me to do nothing further—the whore killed him, as far as we are concerned."

"And then she garroted herself? Francesco, how can you? And you promised you would talk to those two priests."

"I did. They knew about the Cardinal's time as a soldier, but nothing else, Nicola. And I have orders. Aren't you worried about where Caterina is?"

"Isn't she in Milan?" Rodolfo's voice was puzzled.

"Milan? Milan?" Francesco's shout was loud enough to bring the entire room to silence. He glared at Nicola. "You never said anything about Milan."

Nicola swallowed, and gave him a weak smile. "You didn't ask. You know we own an armory there, Francesco. Why shouldn't she go there?"

"She has gone over to the French?" He sat down abruptly on the bench by the forge, his face miserable. "I will never see her again. And Pope Julius will have my head, for losing track of her."

"Why tell him, then? Isn't he busy planning his war on the Duke or Ferrara? Surely he has forgotten all about her."

Francesco shook his head. "I have orders to find her."

"Then tell him she went to Milan to see her grandchildren and help with the birth of the third one. That's partly true."

Francesco looked startled. "Grandchildren? Ah, her stepson. I had forgotten about him. I thought she didn't like him."

"Nor does she trust him. But she still wants to meet her grandchildren and hold the new baby."

"And get her share of profits from her Milan armory," Rodolfo added, lurching towards them with a cup of wine for Francesco. "Maybe the next pope will be French. Then she will come back. Have a drink."

"Yes, drink!" shouted another armorer, to universal, loud agreement. Rodolfo poured more wine in outstretched cups, belching. Francesco drained his cup and declined a second one. Then he stood. "I'll tell the pope she went to Milan to see her grandchildren and family. Let's hope he doesn't remember that her armory there makes weapons for the enemy. I need to go."

Nicola could see he was angry, but she needed his help. "Can you walk Maria and me home, Francesco? These men are drunk."

"*Senz'altro.* Let's hurry, though. I need to issue new orders telling the men to look for her on the way to Milan––though it is probably too late." He ushered them out the door. "You knew she was going to Milan, didn't you? Why didn't you tell me?"

"I didn't know for sure, and still don't. It's a possibility, is all. She was still in Venice when she wrote this, and says nothing about her plans. I'll feel better when we hear from her again."

She stopped Francesco so that Maria could catch up with them. "Tell me about Cardinal Beccaria's time as a soldier," she said.

The dark streets were deserted. Francesco guided Nicola and Maria past a pile of horse dung, his face angry. "Beccaria was a famous soldier and a hero, in the time of the Borgia pope. He slaughtered the French company that committed the atrocities at Fivizzano. First he had the officers beheaded, then had those accused of the worst atrocities put to torture before they died."

Nicola felt stunned. "Why didn't you tell me earlier, Francesco? The Cardinal had a whole set of enemies *Frate* Martin and I didn't even know about."

Francesco took her arm, to guide her around a dead dog. "He had enemies in France, yes. So what?"

"Isn't Cardinal Alidosi supposed to be a minion of the French? If Cardinal Beccaria was notorious for killing an entire French company, it gave Alidosi an additional reason to kill him."

Francesco halted and looked at her, his face still angry. "You are chiding me for keeping secrets, when you never told me Caterina was headed for Milan? Do you think I want to hear this, Nicola? You keep harping on Alidosi, who will probably be the next pope. There is nothing I can do about him. There is nothing I *dare* do about him."

They reached Nicola's bakery, where Luigi was still at work despite the late hour. As Nicola opened the door, the sweet, yeasty smell of *pannetone* greeted them.

Francesco ushered Maria inside, but held Nicola back. "I'm going to tell you something that I was going to keep secret," he said, when Maria was out of earshot. "But right now, I am angry about secrets. Do you have any idea what Raphael is up to, when he isn't with you?"

Nicola's heart sank. "No. And perhaps I don't want to."

Francesco's smile had malice in it. "Agostino Chigi, the pope's banker, has hired him to paint the most beautiful women in Rome for the walls of the villa Chigi is building across the river. Nude women, of course. So, since the pope is gone, Raphael is staying there, visited by the most beautiful courtesans in Rome, who are eager to be his models."

Nicola swallowed hard, resisting the impulse to cry. "I know he sees courtesans, Francesco. He lies about it, but I know."

"That's not the worst of it for you, Nicola. He says he takes different features from each courtesan––the breasts of one; the legs of another–– to make the ideal woman. But he has always told the men that you are the most beautiful woman in Rome. And he knows what you look like. So when he paints those courtesans, he may actually be painting *you*. And every man in Rome will soon know it. "

Ch. 29 - Mud and Muck

Detail from *Susana and the Elders*
By Guido Cagnacci

Pavia, Italy
The same day

"Would you like more hot water?"

Half asleep in the tub, her hair slathered in olive oil, Caterina looked up gratefully. "Please. You are a godsend, Daniela. Have you found a lice comb?"

The plump, elderly housekeeper poured a flagon of hot water into Caterina's bath from the cauldron heating over the nearby fireplace. "I have. I'll attend to your hair as soon as I finish soaping those clothes of yours."

"They are rags. I don't know why you are bothering."

Daniela stirred the wash pot, her good humor shining on her broad–cheeked face. "You may not wear them again, but a poor woman will be grateful for them."

Caterina sighed with happiness in the newly-warmed water. She had just spent three days as cold and filthy as she had ever been in her life. The French count had been wrong in believing that horses could catch the river galley from which she had been snatched as a hostage. The winter muck on the Po River road was so deep and the surrounding lands so marshy that the horses often had to be walked and sometimes swum, with Caterina and her escorts stumbling and slithering along in the mud behind them.

Besides being cold, wet and filthy, she had been anxious the first day, fearing both her French escorts and Alfonso Zanna, whom she expected around every bend, waiting to steal the bills of exchange hidden between her breasts. But Zanna never appeared, and her escorts had been perfect gentlemen, thanks to the safe passage granted to her by their *Générale*. They had shared their scant provisions, and graciously yielded her their driest tent.

"Here, lean on this and I'll take care of those lice," Daniela said, placing a pillow behind Caterina's head. She was gentle with the comb.

The soaking brought back bittersweet memories of a time long ago, when she and Niccolò Machiavelli had shared a warm bath after making love, while baby Nicola slept in the next room. Niccolò had recited Petrarch's most sensual love sonnets from memory, and they had made love again while slick with soap.

After all these years, she still missed Niccolò. She and her husband had never bathed together––*Dio grazie*, since he always stank from the heat of the forge. And Francesco—she could picture him jumping in, scrubbing off, leaping out to dry himself and gesturing at her with the blanket, saying, "You come out now, *ja*?" Neither Ugo nor Francesco had one whit of imagination, much less a sense of humor. Perhaps bathing alone was not so bad.

As Daniela worked the comb through Caterina's hair, Caterina tried to clean her fingernails. "Daniela, I am so grateful to you."

"Glad to have something to do. The *capitano* is hardly ever here. I like to have something to keep me occupied."

"He told me the *appartaménto* would be spotless, and he was right."

"We'll make it extra nice for Christmas."

Though small, the *appartaménto* was richly-furnished, its walls hung with paintings and colorful hangings from Turkey and other Venetian ports of call. The Venetian merchant had promised it to Caterina as part payment for the cannons he ordered from her armory. She intended to stay a fortnight or more––long enough to rest, confer with Leonardo da Vinci, and have some of the elegant Venetian fabrics she purchased there made into *gammuras,* in the latest style. When she rode into Milan, finally, she wanted to look like a queen. A regal presence would help her take back what belonged to her.

Daniela combed her hair until her scalp tingled, wiping the comb repeatedly on a rag that she then threw in the fire. "Now, I'll skim the dead lice off this water. Then we're going to have to get the oil out of your hair. Use this strong soap first. Then I'll go get you some nice perfumed soap to wash your hair again. Use it all over your body if you like. It's made special in France."

Caterina sighed. "I need to hire a new maidservant. Can you help me find a girl who would be willing to go to Milan with me?"

"There are plenty of girls who would love to see Milan. I'll see what I can do."

An hour later, wrapped in a blanket and wearing only a *camicia,* Caterina wrote a note to Leonardo da Vinci, to remind him that he was invited for Christmas dinner.

"Daniela, can you take this note to *Maestro* da Vinci for me? And fetch back that tailor you told me about? I'm going to sleep until he comes. And maybe into next week."

Ch. 30 - Of Cannons and Courtesans

"The beautiful boy" in the Stanze di Raffaello;
The Vatican, Rome

Rome,
The following day

Nicola sat in the tiny alcove that Caterina used as an office, balancing the armory's books for the year 1510. The task had come at the busiest time for her bakery, unfortunately, but it had to be done. Rodolfo needed his share of the profits and Caterina had to have the information to reconcile the books in Milan.

At least the task kept Nicola's mind off Raphael, who was probably painting beautiful prostitutes in the Chigi villa across the river.

The armory workmen were hard at work putting edges on new swords as they shouted cheerfully at each other over the din of the anvils. It was deafening, but Nicola was used to it.

"Rodolfo," she shouted, "There is something I don't understand. Could you come here, please?"

He arrived, wiping his hands with a rag. She pointed at an entry in his handwriting. "This is an enormous sum. What is it for?"

Rodolfo beamed at her. "Part payment for an enormous order. From Pompeo Colonna. Swords, *arquebuses* and cannons. We are just finishing up the swords now."

Nicola was astounded. "Swords I understand. Everyone has a sword. But *arquebuses* and cannons? Why would Pompeo Colonna want those? How many did he order?"

"Thirty swords, a dozen *arquebuses* and three cannons. As to why he wants them–– who can say? I assume it has to do with the feud between the Colonna and Orsini families."

"With that many weapons? That's not for a feud, Rodolfo. That's for a war! And where is the payment for all this? This is a large amount but it wouldn't cover––"

"That's the deposit you are looking at. He pays the rest on delivery. A thousand gold ducats. You would know this if you were ever around, Nicola."

"A thousand gold ducats! When is Pompeo Colonna taking delivery?"

"The day after Christmas. That's why the men are so busy."

"*Madre di Dio!* We need to tell Francesco about this right away, Rodolfo."

"Tell Francesco? Why?"

"Because he suspects Pompeo Colonna of conspiring against Pope Julius, that's why. He told me that at Cardinal Beccaria's funeral.

It's bad enough that we've lost the pope's favor. But to make an enemy of him? That would be dangerous."

Rodolfo shuddered. "Make an enemy of the pope? Are you serious?"

"Of course I am serious. We are already in trouble if the pope decides to believe that Caterina has gone over to the French. Don't you want to keep your head on your shoulders?"

Rodolfo's eyes popped wide open and he grabbed his neck. "I swear, Nicola, on all that is holy. This never occurred to me. I never heard anything about Pompeo Colonna rebelling against Pope Julius. *Dio Mio.*" His hands jumped from his neck to his head and he swayed back and forth, as though it hurt. "What should we do?"

"I'm headed over to the Vatican after I finish here. I'll let Francesco know immediately. Don't worry, Rodolfo. He can send spies to follow Pompeo's men to where they will store those weapons. We are in time. It will be fine."

*****

"Who is she, Raphael? That face there? And there? And there?"

Three women stared at Nicola from walls bearing line drawings for frescoes that Raphael had begun for Pope Julius. Nicola had stared at them long enough to see that they were really the same beautiful face, from three different angles. Several other bodiless faces peered at her as well–Leonardo da Vinci, for one. Raphael himself, for another. And Michelangelo, sprawled on the ground at the center of an enormous array of outlined figures. Evidently Raphael liked to paint the faces first, and the bodies later.

Raphael did not look pleased to see her. "What are you doing here, Nicola?"

"I had information to deliver to Francesco, and he brought me here afterwards. To look for you. I wanted to see what you are working on. Who is she?"

He shrugged. "That's a boy."

"I see from the *cartone* of the clothes that it will be a boy. But that is a woman's face and hair, Raphael. No boy has ever looked like that. Her name is Imperia, isn't it?"

Raphael winced. "Imperia?" He paused, as if at a loss for words. "Where did you hear that name?"

Nicola's cheeks were burning. She put her hands on her hips. "From your apprentices, who were pointing at her portraits. You painted her three times. Three times! She's a courtesan, isn't she? Isn't she?"

Raphael's apprentices were staring at them, she realized. Raphael took her arm and led her to the side of the room. Then he took both her hands, exhaled deeply, and looked down.

"She is a courtesan who models for me."

Nicola wrestled her hands free. "And does other things for you too, doesn't she? In the weeks we are apart to avoid pregnancy, you spend your time with her. Don't you?"

"No, Nicola. I don't. I work. She models for me, yes––"

"You are obsessed with her, Raphael. Her face is on three sides of this room! All the time you pretend to love me––"

"I do love you, Nicola. I would have put your face on three sides of this room, but I know you wouldn't like it."

Nicola was struggling to keep back tears. "No, I wouldn't. But that doesn't mean I like you spending all your time with courtesans. I'm going home, and you aren't invited."

Raphael's apprentices were listening and grinning, Nicola realized. Raphael bent toward her. "Nicola, I can explain," he murmured. "Please let me come with you. Aren't you past your dangerous time of the month?"

Nicola felt as if she were about to explode. "That's all you care about, isn't it? My time of the month? Is that because you can't wait to get back to Imperia? Leave me alone."

Nicola choked back a sob, and hurried from the room.

Ch. 31 - A Christmas Festa

Lute Player,
by Antonio Carracci,
late 1500's

**Rome,
Christmas Day, 1510**

After Nicola and her servant attended Christmas Mass at Santa Maria del Popolo, *Frate* Martin appeared to escort them to the monastery kitchen for the Christmas *festa* she had promised to attend. Christ's Mass should have left her feeling joyous and festive. But she had prayed about Raphael's betrayals and lies, which left her feeling jealous and sad instead.

To match the solemn surroundings and her own mood, Nicola wore her best black *gammura* and a starched white veil. "What is this?" Luther asked her, gesturing towards the sack she held. "May I carry it for you?"

Forcing a smile, she handed it to him. "Christmas bread, for the *festa*. A gift from my bakery." The sack also held a packet addressed to her from Raphael, which had been delivered the night before. She had not had the heart to open it.

"Francesco told me something about Cardinal Beccaria that will make you very sad, *Frate* Luther," she told him as they left the church. She then related the story of Beccaria's methodical execution of the French soldiers who raped and murdered women and children in Fivizzano, back when he was a soldier himself.

"It's odd he didn't tell this story to his friends here in the monastery," she concluded. "Maybe he was ashamed. Or maybe he thought he was simply doing his duty as a soldier."

Luther's face had sagged into shock. "At least he tried to separate the guilty from the innocent. Still, he is surely doomed to Hell."

Nicola raised an eyebrow. "Why do you think so? I am sure he confessed and received absolution."

"Ah, but did he confess every single sin, and truly repent? And perform his penance exactly? And execute only the guilty? It is hard for me to believe that anyone with that much blood on his hands can be forgiven," Luther said.

Nicola thought for a moment. "God knows we are imperfect because He made us so. Surely He forgives imperfect confessions. And surely the French think twice now, before they rape and slaughter innocent women and children. The Cardinal might have believed he was God's instrument. And he may have been. Who are we to say?"

Luther stopped and stared at her for a moment. Then he descended stone steps that led into the bowels of the monastery, reciting the Hail Mary. Nicola and Maria trailed behind.

"I'm sorry *Meister* Raphael could not attend with you," Luther said stiffly, when they reached the passageway at the bottom. Nicola made an involuntary noise, causing him to stop at the base of the steps and stare at her. "What is wrong? Has he done something to you?"

She forced a smile. "Nothing of consequence. Please, I don't want to talk about it. Let's just enjoy the *festa*."

Luther grimaced. "As you wish," he said. Marching ahead, he began reciting the Our Father, his sonorous voice loud in the torch-lit brick tunnel beneath the monastery.

Feeling like she had just joined a church processional, Nicola hurried to keep up with him, gesturing to Maria to follow.

The huge monastery kitchen had leaded glass windows that admitted fading daylight from the monks' herb garden, a half–story above them. Under the windows, a long wood table spanned the room, ending at two brown brick fireplaces on opposite walls that bristled with spits, cauldrons and utensils. Floor–to–ceiling ovens flanked the fireplaces, hung with huge wooden paddles used to turn and remove breads, roasts, and other baked savories.

The center table held dishes already prepared for the monks' Christmas dinner: eels, cod and other fish, prepared seven different ways as customary at Christmas; pies, both sweet and savory; stewed fruit, and a variety of breads.

The household staff turned to stare at Nicola and Maria as they entered, grinning as if the women were part of the feast. There were twelve men and boys of various ages, all dressed in plain brown tunics reminiscent of monks' robes. Several gestured towards a small table on one side of the room, which held platters of food evidently reserved for the kitchen staff's *festa*. Next to the food stood several jugs of wine.

Martin Luther introduced Nicola to everyone. "This is Adolf, who speaks German. And this little one is Angelino, who I taught to spell his name. And the one in the leather apron is Roberto, who is learning Latin, an excellent student. Over here is Alfonso. . . ."

Nicola nodded to them all, memorizing names and faces. The cook was Antonio; his bald assistant Ricardo. "May I?" she said to *Frate* Luther as she took her sack from him, adding her breads to the offerings on the side table. She pocketed the package from Raphael.

"Let's eat, before we have to serve the monks," the cook said. "Will you bless the food, *Frate* Martin?"

Luther offered a short blessing in Latin, smiling as the men crossed themselves. They said their "Amens," and looked expectantly at Antonio.

"There is enough for everyone to have a little of each dish, and for all to have plenty," he said. He gestured for Nicola and Maria to go first, helping their brown crockery plates himself with small amounts of every kind of fish and savory.

"Let me cut the bread for you," Roberto offered, pulling a butcher's knife from his belt to splay a loaf into thin pieces with astonishing quickness, as though it were made of air.

"And let me pour you some wine. It isn't the best, but it is good," said Ricardo, the bald fellow who hovered next to the wine. Nicola suspected he was the monks' wine steward. He poured generously.

Nicola and Maria were given places of honor on benches near the window. The kitchen help seated themselves on the floor around them, or leaned on the center table staring at them. Between surreptitious glances the men began wolfing down their food and slurping wine. No one spoke.

Luther seated himself on the bench next to Nicola. She murmured in Latin, "Tell me what to ask them."

He cleared his throat, leaning closer to her to speak. "Say you were with me when the body of Cardinal Beccaria fell in front of us. Ask if they heard about this."

"None of them speaks Latin?"

"Only Roberto, and only a little."

Shifting to Italian, Nicola did as Luther asked. The men offered loud sympathy for her terrible experience. It was obvious they had already heard the story.

"I'll ask them if they knew Cardinal Beccaria and what he was like," she told Luther, who nodded.

He was a saintly man, they all agreed. Kinder and more generous than the other friars.

"But I heard he had been a very wicked man in his past," Nicola responded. "Have you heard those stories?"

"He killed his wife," an older man offered.

"The mother of his children, in front of their eyes," another said.

"She cuckolded him while he was at the wars," Antonio explained. "Had a baby that was not his."

"I heard the boy was his," Roberto offered.

"Why would he kill his wife, then?" the cook scoffed.

The youth shrugged. "Maybe I heard wrong."

"The point is, he had children. And he was a friar," a tall, stooped man wearing a bloody apron said.

"He wasn't a friar when he had the children," a bald, heavyset fellow in a pristine white apron responded.

"Didn't he kill them, too? I heard he did," Angelino said.

"No. But he did kill a bunch of Frenchmen," said another boy. "But he was nice, for a man who killed people."

Luther nodded at Nicola, signaling to her that he had understood at least part of what was said. It was obvious that the dead cardinal's sins against his wife were known to the kitchen staff.

"I suppose he killed other soldiers during the wars," Nicola added. "Wasn't he a soldier before he was a monk?"

"A great one," Antonio declared. "He avenged the rape and murder of innocents by the French at Fivizzano." Several of the men nodded as they ate. Evidently this was old news to them.

Nicola looked at Martin Luther for guidance. "Ask what Cardinal Beccaria kept in his cell," he murmured to her in Latin.

She nodded. "I never heard of a cardinal who lived in a monastery," she said. "They are usually rich. Did he keep pretty things in his cell?"

"Not that we heard," Giorgio said.

"We weren't allowed up there, *Madonna*," one of the young boys told her. "The prior's personal servants cleaned that part of the monastery."

"The prior is richer than he was," the cook asserted.

"I don't believe it. How can that be so?" Maria said. Nicola looked at her in astonishment—Maria rarely said anything. "He was a cardinal. That just doesn't happen," Maria insisted.

"All I know is, the prior's treasure room is full of money. And the cardinal had a little tiny strongbox that was full of nothing," the bald man insisted.

"How can you know that?" the youth in the leather apron scoffed.

"*Frate* Domenico told me. He's the treasurer. He knows."

The bell overhead rang. Several men jumped to their feet and disappeared with platters laden with food.

"Maria and I must go," Nicola said.

"Wait. *Frate* Luther wants us to sing a song for you," one of the boys said to Nicola. "He wrote it."

Astonished, Nicola looked at Martin Luther, who blushed and looked down. Someone brought him a lute, which he quickly tuned. "It's a *hymnus,* an ode to the gods. Except I wrote it to the one true God and his holy Son, for Christmas. It's in German, but the men have learned the chorus. "

Frate Luther had a beautiful bass voice, and played well. Not knowing the words, the men sang "Christmas, Christmas, Christmas" during the chorus. When the cook signaled frantically that it was time to end the song and get back to work, Luther increased the tempo for one last verse, strumming loudly during the final "Christmas." Laughing, several of the men rushed out with the remaining dishes for the monks' table. Martin Luther looked pleased with himself.

"Where did you learn to write music and play the lute?" Nicola asked him.

"My father wanted me to be a lawyer. So I had the usual education, and did the usual things that young men at university do." He smiled sheepishly.

"What changed your mind? About being a lawyer?"

"An experience. During a storm." He stood suddenly. "Stay here. I will fetch other brothers, to help me escort you home."

While she waited, Nicola decided to open the package that Raphael had sent her. In it was a heavy gold and emerald necklace, and a note:

My darling Nicola,

I wish I could spend Christmas with you. I wish I could spend every Christmas with you. I wish I could feel your neck and the top of your breasts, the way this necklace will when you put it on.

You know I could never truly love any woman but you. Please let me show you. I swear, I have not seen Imperia in a long time. I painted her face because I remember it. Who could forget it?

I have a request I want you to think about. Agostino Chigi is paying me to stay in his villa across the Tiber, to paint beautiful women on his walls. He has chosen the models and they are indeed beautiful, though not as beautiful as you. They are courtesans and are tempting me sorely. I am resisting them, but it is hard.

When your safe time of the month comes, would you consider staying here with me, to keep me from temptation? You needn't model for me. It is a beautiful place. The gardens are exquisite. The food is excellent. We would have a wonderful time together.

This invitation comes from Agostino Chigi himself, who is concerned that I am distracted by my longing for you. You will receive a warm welcome from the staff and from him, when he is around.

Happy Christmas. Think about it, and let me know soon, soon, soon, that we can be together again,

Your loving helpless slave,
Raphael

Nicola stared at the page, not knowing whether to laugh or cry. Was Raphael actually being honest with her? He loved beauty, and it was possible he painted Imperia's face from memory. Should she still be angry that he was secretly painting her as well, or happy that he wanted her instead of the most beautiful courtesans in Rome? Or both?

She folded the note and thrust it in a pocket, realizing that Martin Luther and Ricardo the cook, both in cloaks, were waiting to escort her and her maid home.

Luther stared at her. "Is something wrong?" he asked.

She looked down, fighting a temptation to cry. "I don't know. Help me put this necklace on, Maria, *per favore*. I might as well wear it."

The four of them crossed Rome through darkening streets and alleys, largely deserted except for clusters of folk in their best clothes, hurrying home from Mass. Ricardo and Maria struck up an animated conversation about cooking, the best street markets, and the best seasons and times to frequent them.

Behind them, Luther walked next to Nicola, muttering the "Our Father" over and over again. Grateful to be ignored, Nicola clutched her new necklace, and struggled to calm herself.

After they passed through the ancient Forum, Martin Luther stopped praying and cleared his throat. "We have spoken to everyone I can think of concerning these murders," he said quietly in Latin. "What is our next step?"

"We have not spoken to Giulio de' Medici or his brother the cardinal," Nicola responded. "I would like to hear what they have to say."

"But *Herr* Raphael said they cannot possibly be involved," Luther responded. "It is not in their character, he said. And even if it were—which I do not for a moment believe—it is unthinkable that they would take actions that would undermine the Holy Mother Church."

"*Herr* Raphael says a lot of things that are not true," Nicola responded, surprised by the bitterness in her own voice. "And it seems obvious that this murder has to do with the papal succession. Cardinal Alidosi is Pope Julius' likely successor, so one of his men could be responsible. But everyone says Cardinal de' Medici wants badly to be pope. And his cousin was there when we found the body. I saw him. I am just not sure how to approach him."

"I agree with *Herr* Raphael on this point," Luther said. "I am not at all sure that Cardinal Beccaria's murder had anything to do with the papal succession. And even if it did, you are not going to get any information out of the cardinal or his cousin. Do you think *Herr* Raphael is a bad judge of character?"

"He is a bad judge of my character," Nicola said, making no effort to control the bitterness in her voice.

"I think he knows you all too well, *Fraulein*," Luther murmured.

Nicola choked back a sob, her shoulders heaving. Fortunately, they were nearing the door to her bakery.

Luther gasped, as if stung by a bee. "I am sorry if I made you cry," he responded, his voice agitated. "But you two need to repent, for the sake of your immortal souls."

"I am sick of your sermons," she managed through her tears. "Leave me alone."

He sighed. "Maybe that is best, since we see things so differently. I cannot stop you from sinning and have no wish to cause you pain. I will pursue ideas about the murders that do not require me to know Italian or speak with cardinals. Please promise that you will send me a note if you learn any new facts."

As she entered her bakery, Nicola wiped the tears from her eyes before turning to face Martin Luther. She nodded agreement, then slammed the door in his face.

Ch. 32 - Recalling a Murder

Palazzo Beccaria, Pavia, c 1503

**Pavia,
The same day,
Christmas Day, 1510**

Caterina swept into the *sala grande* of her rented *appartaménto* to greet her guests, knowing that she looked well in her new *gammura* of black *brocado* shot with gold. She had chosen a translucent black veil that did not hide her hair, hoping to appear both respectable and memorable. And rich. Finally, she really was rich—— and looked it, against the backdrop of Venetian paintings and dark wood furnishings ornamenting her temporary home.

The three men rose to greet her. She was shocked at how gaunt and frail Leonardo da Vinci looked. He now used a cane, his hands shaking as he pushed himself to his feet. The black velvet *beretta* crowning his long white hair and his rose-colored tunic were uncharacteristically splendid. It was unsettling, as if she were making new acquaintance with an elderly nobleman rather than greeting an artisan and old friend. She was glad to see recognition and delight in his eyes.

Da Vinci leaned over his cane to bow. "*Madonna* Biaggi. It has been too long. You are as lovely as ever. You remember Salai? And this is my new secretary and assistant, Francesco Melzi."

The two young men bowed to her, doffing their hats. Salai, in a bright yellow tunic and shoulder–length blond curls, was less coltish than she remembered him, back when he was in love with Nicola.‡‡ Francesco Melzi, not as handsome as Salai and prematurely bald, wore an ornate maroon tunic and moved with a graceful confidence that suggested a privileged upbringing.

"Please, sit," she said to them. "I would have been glad to serve Christmas dinner to you. But I am even happier to attend Count Beccaria's dinner––thank you for getting me the invitation. And tell me about the family, so I do not embarrass myself. The Count is brother to Cardinal Beccaria, who was just murdered in Rome?"

Leonardo looked up at Salai, who was helping him into a seat by the fire. "Salai has made it his business to know everything about everyone in Pavia. Tell *Madonna* Biaggi what is needful."

Salai smiled as he settled himself into a nearby chair and crossed his legs. "Count Beccaria is indeed brother to the murdered cardinal. Best not to mention the murder, of course. We may not see the Count because he went to Rome to fetch his inheritance. But the Cardinal's married daughters will be here."

Caterina nearly spilled the wine she was handing to him. "Cardinal Beccaria had daughters?"

Salai smiled and raised his glass to her. "He had daughters because he was married before he became a monk. He took to religion as a penance for murdering his wife, who cuckolded him. And one of the Count's guards was murdered in November. Someone broke in and ransacked the Count's strong room and killed the guard, but nothing was taken."

He settled back in his chair, plainly pleased with himself. He wasn't much of a painter, to Caterina's recollection––but he was obviously an accomplished gossip.

"It's not likely those things are connected, Salai," da Vinci commented.

---

‡‡ Read about it in *A Borgia Daughter Dies*

"True. Except they are murders. Everyone knows the Cardinal was killed by an angry Roman prostitute. He cheated her of her fee, they say."

Having served the men, Caterina poured herself a glass of wine and sat opposite Leonardo in front of the crackling fire, spreading her new skirt carefully. "Actually, Nicola thinks it was a political murder," she said. "Cardinal Beccaria was a reform candidate for the papacy. She suspects that one of his rivals was involved in the killing."

Salai uncrossed his legs and sat forward. "Nicola thinks that? Really? Cardinal Alidosi is supposed to be the next pope. Does she suspect him?"

"Not in particular. This city is his principal See, isn't it? It's best not to talk about such things here," Caterina responded, wishing she had not mentioned Nicola's suspicions.

Salai nodded, his curls bouncing. "I'll just say people in Rome suspect that Cardinal Beccaria was killed so he could not become pope."

Caterina shook her head. "That would point a finger at me as the source of your information. Since I am Roman, and someone new here. Please don't, Salai. I don't want Cardinal Alidosi or his men thinking I have started rumors about them. He and I have a history."

Salai raised an eyebrow. "You have a history with Cardinal Alidosi? What kind of history?"

Caterina waved a hand, irritated that she'd given Salai more fodder for gossip. "He is papal treasurer. That means I had to apply to him to receive payment from Pope Julius. It was never easy to get money from him, is all."

"For a lovely lady like you? Surely--"

"Enough, Salai," Leonardo said. "That is no way to speak to our patroness. Shall we go? We don't want to be late."

Salai murmured apologies as he helped Caterina into her cloak, then helped Leonardo down the steps. On cobbled streets dusted with snow, they wound their way from her appartaménto near the covered bridge, past the brick basilica of San Teodoro and the Palazzo Folperti, to the Beccaria family's new palazzo. Rectangular and proportional in the latest classical style, it reminded Caterina of every other new palazzo she had seen. Unusual, though, was its gleaming red brick, embellished with terra cotta botanical reliefs in the same color.

They entered the enormous front door, then mounted the marble staircase to the *piano nobile*. A servant took their wraps and announced them to the clusters of clerics and well-dressed nobles who sipped mulled wine while they listened to groups of singers and lute players strolling the room. Bright new frescoes of mythical figures looked down on the crowd from a high ceiling. The space glittered with sweet-smelling beeswax candles, their odor mingling with fainter smells of cinnamon and perfume.

The receiving line was long, giving Caterina an opportunity to study the Beccaria family before being introduced to them. All had dark hair, aristocratic noses, and an obvious family resemblance. The bejeweled *contessa* was too heavyset to wear red *brocado* with any grace, but she seemed good-humored. Her eldest son, splendidly dressed in gold and red, played host with obvious pride. The middle son, in a rich brown tunic, had the air of a soldier. The most youthful, in a black cassock, was obviously a priest. The two middle-aged couples beside them also wore black: Cardinal Beccaria's daughters and their husbands, probably; dressed in mourning for him. From their accoutrements, Caterina guessed that the cardinal's daughters had married merchants rather than landed gentry.

Leonardo introduced Caterina with a grace that bespoke his years as courtier to the court of Il Moro, the Duke of Milan. "*Piacere*, a pleasure; *benevenuto*, welcome," the Beccaria family murmured as she passed down the line.

"When are you going to paint my portrait?" the *Contessa* demanded of da Vinci, when they reached her.

He reddened. "I am still very busy," he told her, bowing with elaborate deference and then retreating with remarkable speed, for a man who walked with a cane.

"Is he painting you?" she asked Caterina, a frown on her face.

"No, although he is doing some engineering work for me, something he agreed to long ago. We have worked together for many years. He has many commitments." Caterina curtseyed deeply, and made her own escape.

When dinner was called, the assemblage moved into a long dining room frescoed with scenes of harvest and hunting. The table was covered with a white damask cloth, and decorated with figures of the Holy Family made of sugar and colored icing, lit by huge silver candelabras.

Caterina was seated next to a merchant, who knew all about travel and commerce between Pavia and Milano. "There is a merchant convoy going soon," he told her. "It will provide you with an appropriate escort. There is a convent with a fine guest house at the halfway point. A very respectable place for you and your maid."

"Are there brigands on the roads?" she responded. "I just heard a shocking story, that one of the Count's guards was murdered and the Count's strong room ransacked. Did they catch the killer?"

"You needn't worry," he assured her. "The robber rummaged through deeds and suchlike, so perhaps the crime had something to do with property. The Count owns vast estates and handles many land disputes. There are brigands on the roads, of course. Some of them are French deserters, since we are at war. But they don't dare bother groups of merchants, escorted by armed guards."

The banquet went on for hours, while musicians, dancers and acrobats took turns performing. Since it was a holy day, and Christmas, the Contessa served the customary seven kinds of fish instead of meat. A swarm of servants first delivered platters of big and small white fish, eels, sardines and calamari, all pan–fried and sprinkled with cinnamon, sugar, and juice from Sicilian oranges. Then came glistening red crayfish, and something Caterina had never seen before: fish eggs from Po River sturgeon, called "caviar." She tried everything gingerly, and found it good. Despite the weather, the cook had managed a few vegetables: cabbage, fava beans and parsnips, all cooked until soft in oil, salt and herbs. Later came candied oranges, lemons, cucumbers and almonds.

Caterina took dainty portions and very little wine, befitting a lady. The merchant's wife on her left talked of nothing but her own children, her physical ailments, and how they were related. Caterina longed to escape, wishing that Leonardo was her banquet partner. Knowing that he did not eat animal flesh of any kind, she was happy to see him consuming *maccheroni,* swimming in a sugary sauce, as well as egg and cheese pie. He drank little and looked very bored.

Salai and Francesco were happy, however. They sat near Leonardo, drinking wine and flirting with several of the *Contessa's* young female attendants. Salai, his cheeks red, glanced at Caterina frequently and once pointed to her with a smile on his face.

He was gossiping about her, obviously. She feared that everyone in Pavia would soon know that Romans suspected Cardinal Beccaria had been murdered by a rival—perhaps by Cardinal Alidosi—to keep him from becoming pope. And they all would know that she was the source of this rumor.

So much for enjoying a few weeks' luxury in Pavia. As soon as her tailor finished her new wardrobe, she would leave, to escape awkward questions. And Cardinal Alidosi's men.

If she could, though, she would use Alfonso Zanna's offer of help, to send one last letter to Nicola.

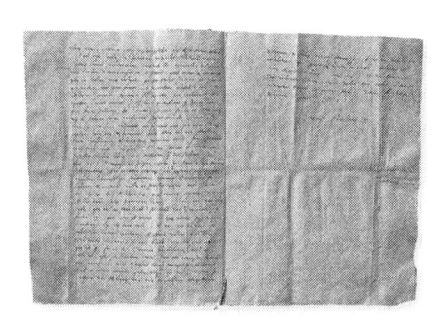

Ch. 33 - A Letter to France

Martin Luther's letter to
Emperor Charles V, 1521

Rome, the following day

"We missed you at Christmas dinner, *Frate* Martin," said the prior, as Martin Luther entered his office, clutching something in one hand. "How was your time with the kitchen staff and *Madonna* Machiavelli? Did you learn anything?"

"One thing I think you should know," Luther responded, his face solemn. Then he told the story of Cardinal Beccaria's execution of the French who had raped and murdered the innocents at Fivizzano.

The prior was shocked. "I had no idea. The Cardinal had enemies in France, then. This is the first I have known of anyone who might have wished him harm. Let's keep this information to ourselves, *Frate* Martin. There is no reason to speak ill of the dead."

"Agreed," Luther responded. "I also learned some other useful things. The kitchen workers know that Cardinal Beccaria murdered his wife. They seemed certain he had no riches. And they said they have no occasion to come into this part of the monastery––your servants see to the cleaning here. Is that so?"

The prior seated himself at his desk, pleased that Martin Luther's face no longer wore the gaunt, haunted look it had when he first arrived. The task of finding Cardinal Beccaria's murderer seemed to energize him.

"The kitchen staff do not clean the monks' cells, true. As you know, that is each monk's task. Though in my case—and Cardinal Beccaria's case—my own servants take care of this. They were family servants before I became a monk and I would trust them with my life. The kitchen help do not frequent that area. But they are constantly here, at my offices, because they bring food and drink to me and my guests."

"I've seen them," Luther affirmed. "But the two areas are connected. So surely—"

"The kitchen help could easily be in Cardinal Beccaria's cell, yes. But so could anyone else. And outsiders, too, if they were careful."

Luther nodded. "I will speak to your servants, if I may? And where is your Treasury? They gossiped about that."

"You may speak to anyone, *Frate* Martin. The Treasury is under lock and key, in the sacristy of the Church. Only *Frate* Domenico and I have keys. What's this?"

Luther was clutching a sealed letter and another piece of paper. "Letters. *Frate* Anton says you can pass them to Vatican couriers. One of them has to go to the Augustinian monastery in Pavia, privately. That is, I am particularly concerned that it not come to the attention of Cardinal Alidosi or his people up there. Is it possible to do that?"

"Address it to *Frate* Giorgio. He's an old friend of mine, who has been there for many years. Tell him you act at my request."

Luther smiled. "Just what I was hoping for."

As Luther worked on his second letter, the prior examined the other one, frowning. "You are writing to *Madonna* Machiavelli's father? At the royal palace in France? Why, if I may ask?"

"It's a part of a penance, assigned by *Frate* Anton."

The prior raised an eyebrow. "Extraordinary. But if it is a penance, I will ask no more questions."

"Ask whatever you want, Reverend Father. I have no secrets. How long before these letters are received?"

"Depends on when the couriers leave. The letter to France will likely take weeks. To Pavia? That's Cardinal Alidosi's principal See. Probably much faster."

He stood, as Luther handed him the letter going to Pavia. "You were careful what you said?" he asked Luther. "In case it is opened?"

"Very careful. Very careful indeed."

Ch. 34 - The Whore and the Future Pope

Left: A Courtesan by Paris Bordone, mid 1500's
Right: Giulio de' Medici by Sebastiano del Piombo, 1526

**Rome,
The day after Christmas, 1510**

Still pondering what to do about Raphael, Nicola spent the day after Christmas running errands. In the Piazza Navona, she passed the small wine shop belonging to Flavio Biondi. The grapes and cup on its painted sign had faded during the years since she visited the shop with her father. Otherwise, it was just as she remembered.

Giulio de' Medici stood in front of Biondi's shop, in the same cross–emblazoned cape he wore when fleeing the whorehouse where Cardinal Beccaria died. Nicola watched him send his servants in different directions before entering the shop alone.

Though she knew Francesco would not approve, she decided to follow Giulio. She entered to see him handing a bag of coins to Biondi, who smiled and bowed repeatedly. Both seemed startled to see her.

"*Madonna* Machiavelli, I'm happy you have come, finally," Biondi said, though his face did not seem happy at all. "How is your father?"

"Still in France. I have not heard from him. I came to buy that wine you told me about. But please don't let me interrupt Signor de' Medici," she responded. "I can wait."

De' Medici looked her up and down. Tall, swarthy and gracefully built, he would have been handsome but for the frown etched on his face and the scowl line between his brows. "Your father is not, by chance, Niccolò Machiavelli?" he asked, raising an eyebrow.

"That's right," Biondi said, when Nicola hesitated. "A good customer, when he was here in Rome. You know him?"

"I know *of* him. He came to power in Florence when my family was forced into exile. How does he have a daughter in Rome?"

Nicola gave him her best smile, wishing Biondi had not called her by name. "That is a long story. Please don't let me interrupt your business here."

Giulio frowned at her intently, as if he were trying to remember her. Then he turned and began to negotiate the purchase of several tuns of fine wine. Apparently his cousin, Cardinal de' Medici, was throwing a *festa* for the Feast of Epiphany.

When he and Flavio Biondi had agreed on a price, de' Medici turned abruptly to Nicola and asked, "Would you like to come? To the *festa*? It will be a masked ball "

"My father is not here to escort me. It would not be seemly," Nicola replied, startled.

"Raphael the painter can escort you. I've seen him with you, have I not? The cardinal would be happy to welcome him, as well."

Nicola felt her face color. Did all of Rome know of her relationship with Raphael? "If I see him, I will tell him of your kind invitation," she said finally, with a curtsey.

He smiled and bowed to her. "See that he brings you, if he comes. Flavio, get the wine delivered by Wednesday," he called as he left.

The wine merchant's ingratiating smile turned sour as soon as the door closed behind his exalted customer. He uncorked one of the tuns stacked behind him, filling a small crockery pitcher. "This is the red wine I told you about, *Madonna* Machiavelli. You said you are making a *porchetta* roast? This would be excellent with it. Try it. I'm going to have some myself," he added. After pouring Nicola a sample, he filled a larger cup for himself and took a huge swallow.

"You are lucky to have such a prominent customer," she remarked as she sipped the fruity wine.

"I'm lucky when he pays the bill. Huge sums flow to Cardinal de' Medici from benefices all over Italy. But sometimes the money comes slowly. He is always behind with his payments. Sometimes, he pawns his silver plate to fund his *festas*."

"Does your guild favor him for the next pope?"

Biondi chuckled. "I favor him. If he is next pope he will have more money. Then maybe he will pay his bills on time."

"What about Cardinal Beccaria? What did the wine merchants think of him?"

Biondi sipped his wine, and stared at her. "As I told you the last time we met, we don't get into church politics, Madonna. We are merchants."

Nicola put down her glass. "This is very nice. I will take a flagon of it––but a small one, please."

As she crossed the Piazza Navona with her purchase, Nicola saw Giulio de' Medici ahead of her, standing face–to–face with a henna–haired woman whom she recognized. Luisa, Giulio's favored whore, had refused to betray him when Nicola and Raphael spoke to her at the whorehouse where Cardinal Beccaria died.

Now, Luisa was begging de' Medici for something, and he was refusing her. Nicola stopped and watched as he pushed her away, turned his back to her, and hurried off.

Luisa walked slowly in the opposite direction, as though she were in pain. Nicola caught up with her and touched her on the shoulder. "I will still pay for more information about that man," she murmured. "You said you wouldn't talk about him before. But I think he has just hurt you."

The whore grimaced, as though she were about to cry. "I'll take your coin now––I need it. I'm pregnant and he refuses to help me. Says it isn't his."

"Is it?" Nicola asked, immediately regretting her question.

Luisa shrugged. "Probably. He couldn't get enough of me. I was with him more than anyone else."

Nicola nodded, realizing that life as a prostitute had hardened this woman to rude questions and far worse. She held out a silver coin. "You said he was with you the night before Cardinal Beccaria's body was discovered. All night. When did he arrive, and was he really there all night?"

Luisa took the coin, tears spilling from her eyes. "He usually came after dinner, but that night the sun set early, and he was with me before candlelight. And yes, he was with me all night. I woke once, though, and he was gone. I thought perhaps he went to visit the jakes––there is a chamber pot in every room, but sometimes men want privacy and a seat when they have to do their business. He was back when I awoke again. That's all I can tell you."

"Was Cardinal Beccaria there? As a customer?"

"I don't know, Madonna. No one does. We didn't know him; didn't know what he looked like. Still don't. If he came, he came in disguise, not in cardinal's dress. And he was not a regular customer."

"What about Alfonso Zanna? Was he there? I know he was a regular customer."

"We talked about him after you left. He's a regular when he is in Rome, but he travels. He's a rough one. His usual bedmate specializes in such men and is not the brightest among us––too many knocks about the head, we think. She couldn't remember, or wouldn't try. That's all I can tell you. I must go."

They walked in silence for a few moments. "I can give you herbs to end your pregnancy, but they will make you very sick," Nicola ventured. "How far along are you?"

Luisa shook her head. "I know what to use. I just hoped I could avoid it this time. I wanted to be his mistress instead of a whore. But he just wants a whore."

"I'm sorry," Nicola said, watching as Luisa walked away.

When she turned to head home, Nicola saw Giulio de' Medici, and realized he had been following her and Luisa, watching them talk. They stared at each other for a long moment. Then he turned on his heel and walked back toward the Piazza Navona.

Ch. 35 - Hiding a Message

Woman writing a letter
by unknown Flemish artist, 16th century

Pavia,
Two days after Christmas

"I don't know if I can accept this letter, *Madonna*. It is highly irregular."

Caterina stared at the heavyset priest who had emerged to speak to her from the tall carved doors of Cardinal Alidosi's offices.

"But Alfonso Zanna promised me," she murmured, her voice low but insistent.

"Zanna is not here."

"I know. But if you disobey his directive, I will tell him. And what's the harm in carrying a letter for a widow?"

The monk looked at the letter, then at her, a frown on his face. "What manner of widow writes to the Captain of the Swiss Guard in Rome?"

"A Roman widow. I came here under safe conduct from the Compte de Chaumont, the governor of Milan. Who is an old friend. And I know Cardinal Alidosi too, because my firm does business with the pope. I need to get word back to Rome, to my business and to my kin."

His frown deepened. "I'll ask. Wait here." Turning, he disappeared through the doorway.

Caterina had spent agonized hours writing those letters, knowing they would likely be unsealed and read by Cardinal Alidosi's staff. The one to Francesco begged him to assure the pope and Cardinal

Alidosi of her undying loyalty, when next he saw them. Though she longed to address Francesco as a lover, she settled for a stiffly formal closing that thanked him for his many kindnesses and services, confident he would read between the lines. She prayed that letter would not fall into the hands of the French, since she had promised their *Générale* her undying loyalty, as well.

The letter for Nicola, tucked inside Francesco's for him to deliver, was even harder to write. Voicing a confidence she did not feel, Caterina assured her "niece" that the last leg of her journey would be safe and comfortable. Amidst lighthearted gossip and descriptions of her new clothes, she worked to hide what was most important. She wanted confirmation that Nicola had received the bill of exchange and paid the Roman armorers. And she wanted Nicola to know that Cardinal Beccaria had murdered his wife, and that someone had murdered a Roman guard in Count Beccaria's *palazzo* in November.

The priest returned. "May we read the letter? To ensure it is church business?"

Caterina blinked. She had expected them to read the letters, but not to be honest about it. "If you must. There is an enclosure for my niece. Bring them back to me to reseal."

"Of course."

The priest was soon back, still frowning, and bearing a candle and wax along with the opened letters. "The bishop says he is happy to deliver your letters," he said, his tone suggesting that he himself was not happy at all.

"Thank him for me," Caterina said. Nicola's letter had not been opened. Melting the wax, she re-sealed the one to Francesco with her signet ring. "When will your courier leave?"

"I don't know. Soon, maybe."

It was the best she could do. Caterina hurried from Cardinal Alidosi's palace to find Salai, who had escorted her and was waiting outside. He looked like a giant insect, in a bright green tunic under his black wool cloak, a darker green *beretta* pulled down over his ears, and tall brown boots. Sweeping off his *beretta*, he bowed as she approached.

She smiled. "They took the letters."

"I'm happy for you," Salai smiled back. "When does the merchant convoy leave?"

"It seems to be delayed and delayed. I am thinking of going alone. With my new maid, of course. The merchant I met at Christmas dinner mentioned a convent where we could stay in comfort an easy ride from here."

Salai offered his arm, and they began walking down the snowy cobbled street towards Caterina's rented house. "Going alone would not be wise. You are in French territory now, *Madonna,* but the roads are not as safe as they once were. I'll speak to Leonardo about whether Francesco and I could accompany you."

I'd be grateful, Salai. But if Leonardo needs you here—"

"*Maestro* Leonardo should check on the property he owns in Milan. Or ask us to do it for him. Really, you would be doing him a favor."

"I suspect Leonardo would rather stay by the fire. Is he well, Salai?"

"He is almost sixty, *Madonna*. And he feels his age. But yes, he is well, and concerned for your safety. I'll let you know what he says. Meanwhile, don't do anything rash."

Ch. 36 - Martin Luther Needs More Time

The Cloisters
by Christoffer Wilhelm Eckersberg

**Rome,
Two days later**

Frate Anton spotted Martin Luther at the opposite end of the *dormitorium* corridor, emerging from the chapel with his rosary in hand. "Martin, have you heard the news?" he called out. "The Prior General is on his way back from Bologna, now that the pope has gone into battle. We will be able to complete our business in Rome and go home!"

Frate Anton had hoped to bring a smile to Martin Luther's solemn face with this news. Instead, the young monk halted abruptly, looking dismayed. Anton hurried to his side.

"How much time do I have before we go home?" Luther asked, clutching his rosary. "I have not completed any of the tasks the prior assigned me. I have not caught the cardinal's murderer. I have not even completed the penances you assigned me."

They began walking down the corridor together. "I don't know how much time we have," *Frate* Anton responded. "Which of your penances remains to be done?"

"I have written to *Fraulein* Nicola's father about her dowry, but I have not spoken to *Meister* Raphael about marrying her. I was hoping to get a response from her father first—hoping that the dowry would make *Meister* Raphael do the right thing. Obviously, I can no longer wait. I will seek him out soon. For all the good it will do."

"Well, do what you can. That is all God can ask of you. Are you making any progress at finding the murderer?"

Luther shook his head, his face still despondent. "*Fraulein* Nicola is very busy in her bakery, but she keeps sending notes about things she has learned. I myself am spending time in the parish where the murder occurred. Watching. Searching. I think the killer may live there, or return there. No more time for that, now."

They paused outside the refectory to finish their conversation. "The only task I have completed is that I have prayed at all of Rome's holy relics. The major ones, anyway," Luther murmured as the other monks filed past them to sit down to breakfast. "But no one assigned me that task. It is my own vanity and ambition. And I am beginning to think it was useless."

"Useless? What do you mean?"

"I am losing my faith in relics, Anton. You'll recall the passages in Mark, where Jesus heals a man's blindness and a woman is cured by touching His robe? He says to them both, 'It is your faith that cured you.' As if to deny that His robe had any intrinsic power, you see. Even though it belonged to Him."

"Be careful, Martin. What you say verges on heresy. If faith alone heals, what need is there for relics? Or even for the Church? Come, let's break our fast."

Ch. 37 - Luther Performs His Penance

Psyche, at the Chigi villa,
now called Villa Farnesina,
By Raphael

Across the Tiber from Rome
The following day

"*Maestro* Raphael, I need to speak with you. Could you come down from there, please?"

Raphael could not resist a downward glance at Martin Luther, whose face was frozen into a comic mixture of horror and disgust, like an ancient Greek theatrical mask. If he had time later, he would sketch that face from memory--it was priceless. Twitching with suppressed laughter that he did not want Luther to see, Raphael turned to face his latest *fresco*. Currently he was painting Pysche's ample breasts, which likely explained Luther's expression.

"*Frate* Martin, how nice to see you," he said, when he had mastered his impulse to laugh. "I'm afraid I can't come down right now. A *fresco* is painted on fresh plaster--I must work quickly."

He applied a few more strokes of paint. "You will have to wait, or come again later. I'd rather you didn't shout at me from down there. I need to concentrate."

Luther stomped out of the room, and Raphael promptly forgot about him.

When he climbed down from the scaffold later in the afternoon, he was surprised to find the young monk waiting for him. Knowing what was likely in store, Raphael wished he could flee. Good manners forbade it, so he bowed instead. "How can I help you, *Frate* Martin?"

"It is I who wish to help you, *Maestro* Raphael. And also *Fraulein* Nicola. You are both in danger of being swallowed up in sin and beyond redemption," Luther began.

Raphael nodded politely and stopped listening. Words about dowry floated by––had the monk really written to Nicola's father? Luther's Latin was odd. He clicked and buzzed, like an angry bird. Hard to understand; easy to ignore.

Raphael was thirsty so he grabbed his cup and sipped watered wine. He was hungry, so he sampled dried figs from a bowl on the table in the reception room where Luther had waited for him. Still, the monk went on and on, scarcely pausing to catch his breath. Regrettably, he was sincere and articulate. He had evidently frightened Nicola, and was beginning to upset even Raphael.

Finally, Martin Luther paused. Raphael hastened to fill the silence, before the voluble monk could start up again. "I thank you for your concern, and all your efforts," Raphael said. "I'm sure Nicola does, too. But we simply do not share your beliefs, and neither do most of your fellow churchmen. Every priest in Rome who can afford it keeps a concubine. Unless he prefers boys. They are not worried about Hell."

"They should be." Luther's face was grim. "Anyway, they cannot marry. You can."

"No, we can't. Marriage in Italy is about money and property and family alliances, *Frate* Martin. Her father will not give me her dowry. He does not want me in his family. And her aunt doesn't like me, either."

Raphael sipped his wine, considering what to say next. "Nicola and I actually considered defying her family," he continued. "But she also values her independence and does not want to cede control of her funds to me. Which I, as a man, feel is my due. So we cannot marry, nor do we want to. We are happy the way things are. I appreciate your concern, but you cannot force this. You have done all you can."

"If I bring word from her father that he is releasing her dowry to you, would that change your mind?"

Raphael chuckled. "If you brought me word that the world was ending, I would quickly repent and marry Nicola, if she would have me. That is more likely than her father changing his mind."

***

Martin Luther clutched his rosary. "I tell you, Anton, I have never felt so low," he said. "I have failed at every task I have been given. I did not persuade *Meister* Raphael to marry *Fraulein* Nicola. I still have not found Cardinal Beccaria's murderer. I can't even teach the kitchen help how to do anything but write their names. Being praised for my scholarship has simply fed my sinful vanity."

Frate Anton pitied his young charge, who knelt beside him in the *dormitorium* chapel. Bowing his head, Anton asked God to help him guide Martin Luther from despair.

"Do not dismiss your scholarship, Martin. You know the Bible in ways most scholars do not. That is unique and important. If you have not succeeded with other tasks, God forgives you."

Luther shook his head. "I am a failure. My scholarship is meaningless. When I try to do something to help a fellow human–– which God put us on earth to do–– I fail."

Frate Anton looked up at the bleeding figure of Jesus on the chapel cross, and prayed that the words about to flow from his mouth would help his friend. "You did not fail at the tasks I gave you, Martin," he said. "I only required you to try, not to succeed. You did your best. You have planted seeds. Seeds can grow. If that damned woman's father releases her dowry, maybe the artist will marry her."

Luther's face brightened. "Jesus compared faith to a mustard seed," he said. "Several times, in fact. The tiny seed that grows into a huge plant. Maybe I have not acted in vain."

Relieved, *Frate* Anton smiled. "You must place this problem in God's hands. And the same with the murder of Cardinal Beccaria. You have asked all the questions you know to ask. Now you must pray that God will send you answers."

Ch. 38 - An Incriminating Admission

Baker, from the 16th Century book,
Housebook of the Landauerschen Twelve Brotherhood Foundation

Rome,
Eve of the Feast of Epiphany,
January 5, 1511

Exhausted from days of baking from sunrise until far into the night, Nicola found selling the easy part. Snaking around the interior of her bakery, a line of servants and clerics clamored for *pannetone* for the upcoming Feast of Epiphany. The next batch, fragrant of yeast, anise and dried fruit, waited to be punched down and kneaded at the back of the shop. Both Nicola and her baker Luigi were selling warm loaves as quickly as they could.

Under her apron, Nicola wore the emerald necklace Raphael had sent her for Christmas. She had finally written to him to thank him for it, and tell him about Giulio de' Medici's invitation to the masked ball for the Feast of Epiphany. She was not clear how she felt about Raphael, but she knew one thing: she wanted to go to that *ballo*. Raphael was now sending daily love notes claiming he was her slave and would do her bidding––but telling her that going to the Medici *palazzo* was not a good idea. Probably because he wanted to be in her bed instead, though he did not say so.

A tall, gaunt man with a wolf–like face and a long red cloak shoved his way through the motley crowd of customers, the look on his face and sword at his side silencing those who started to object. "Are you Nicola Machiavelli?" he demanded.

Nicola saw Caterina's handwriting on the sealed letter he held in his hand. "I am. And I see you have a letter from my aunt," she exclaimed. "Have you seen her?" He nodded. "Come behind the counter and warm yourself by the ovens. I'll be with you in a moment. There is fresh–baked *pannetone* and hot mulled wine on the bench there."

Despite the clamor around her, Nicola stopped to read Caterina's letter, noticing that it had been opened and clumsily resealed. It said she was near Milan with an old friend, the Compte de Chaumont, then added, "I am well but write in haste. Perhaps the bearer can answer your questions. His name is Alfonso Zanna."

Nicola was stunned. While relieved that Caterina was safe, it seemed impossible that the man in the red cloak was Alfonso Zanna, Cardinal Alidosi's hired assassin. Somehow, Caterina had managed to send him to answer questions about Cardinal Beccaria's death, without admitting in her letter that she even knew of the cardinal's existence. This, more than the letter itself, told Nicola that Caterina was alert and cautious; that all was well. She murmured a prayer of thanks.

"You saw her when she was with the French count? Was she well?" she asked, glancing at Zanna for affirmation. He nodded and grinned, exposing enormous crooked canines and more yellow teeth than seemed human.

"There is honey for the bread," she told him, gesturing. "I'll be with you as soon as I can. I want to hear how she does."

Nicola returned to selling *pannetone* as she thought about how to question Zanna, without exposing her suspicions that he had murdered Cardinal Beccaria. It's gone," Nicola called out when she had sold the last loaf, "but there will be more just after the *Nones* bells. Those of you at the head of the line––don't worry. I'll remember you, and let you have the first loaves."

After ushering the last customers out the door, Nicola distributed hot brown bread to the beggars who waited outside. Finally, she returned to Zanna, who was happily eating *pannetone* slathered in honey.

"So you saw Caterina. Did she look well? Where was she?"

"South of Pavia, where the French count had set up camp. She was muddy from riding, but otherwise looked very well."

"You have come a long way! Surely you live in Rome, if you serve a cardinal. What were you doing so close to Milan?"

Zanna fished a cinnamon stick from his wine and sucked it. "The cardinal's principal benefice is the See of Pavia. I was returning to Rome from there. Next I am bound for Bologna."

Nicola put a hand to her breast, as if surprised. "Bologna? Poor man. You can't even be at home for the holy days? How many places have you been since the beginning of Advent?"

He laughed. "As God is my witness, I don't remember. It has been a busy month."

"And such terrible weather! No one should travel during the holy days. Where were you for the Feast of Santa Lucia?"

"I believe I was in Rome for that." His face darkened. "Why are you asking me about that day, in particular?"

Nicola took a sip of wine, giving him the look of practiced innocence she had used on the nuns when growing up. "I just thought you would remember it, is all. It's a special celebration in so many places, and the beginning of the Advent season. Will you be able to spend the Feast of Epiphany here with your family? Or do you have to travel again, even on a feast day?"

"Even on a feast day."

"Alas for you. But how do you like Bologna?"

He scowled. "Not much. I spend as little time there as possible."

Nicola realized she had blundered. According to Francesco, Zanna had been responsible for assassinating the elite of Bologna, on orders from Cardinal Alidosi. Little wonder he avoided the place. Forcing a smile, she poured him more mulled wine and excused herself to help the baker assemble the next batch of *pannetone*. She gave Zanna the first of the new loaves when Luigi pulled them out of the oven.

"Safe journey to Bologna," she told him.

He bowed, and left.

As Nicola prepared to welcome her customers, she reflected on what she had learned. Alfonso Zanna had been in Rome on Santa Lucia's day, the day Cardinal Beccaria's body was discovered. He had just admitted it. And the prostitutes had hinted that he was one of their customers. He had probably travelled immediately from Rome to Venice, where Caterina first saw him, and from there to Pavia. That did not prove that he killed Cardinal Beccaria, of course; much less that he did it at Cardinal Alidosi's behest. But he could have done so.

As soon as she found time, she would send a note to Martin Luther.

Ch. 39 - At the Court of the French King

Niccolò Machiavelli
By Santi di Tito

The royal chateau at Blois, France
The same day

Niccolò Machiavelli settled into his chair, toasting his feet at the hearth of his bedchamber. By the firelight, he once again studied the letter he had received from Rome two days earlier, from a monk named Martin Luther.

It was a rhetorical masterpiece. The Latin was fluent, persuasive, and laced with religious platitudes that miraculously sounded sincere. Machiavelli had never seen the like of it from a diplomat, much less from a monk. He decided he would keep it to study the monk's prose, and perhaps even to steal a phrase or two, here and there. He recognized, though, that even if he copied the monk's wording exactly, no one would believe that he, Machiavelli, was a pious man.

Aside from admiring the letter, he did not know what to make of it. The substance was clear. Martin Luther wanted him to grant Nicola her dowry so she could marry Raphael, the upstart artist she had fallen in love with, years ago in Florence.§§ Otherwise, Martin Luther said, Nicola was bound for Hell. And her reputation would be forever sullied. And so forth and so on.

"Jean? Bring wine," Machiavelli said. Jean promptly poured him a cup, and left him the flagon. He took an appreciative sip.

The stratagem he had used years ago to keep Nicola's dowry had saved him money, but cost him dearly in other ways. He had sorely offended both Nicola and Caterina. Privately, he'd promised himself that he would dower Nicola if she got pregnant––provided Raphael married her, of course. There was no mention of a child in Martin Luther's letter. So, there was no obvious reason for Nicola and Raphael to marry. That much seemed clear.

But why was there no mention of Caterina? That worried him greatly. If this monk knew the intimate details of Nicola's life, surely he knew about her mother––or her aunt, or whatever Caterina was calling herself these days. Had Caterina died? Was Nicola still so angry with him over her dowry that she'd refused to write and tell him so? She had been such a sweet, considerate child––stubborn like her mother, yes, but courteous to a fault, from those years of being schooled by nuns. Surely she would have written, if Caterina had died.

Could Nicola have spent her fortune? Could Caterina have lost hers? Or had there been a rift between mother and daughter? What had happened, to make this monk so frantic?

The room was growing cold. Machiavelli rose and put another log on the fire. After poking it a bit, he returned to his chair and his thoughts.

---

§§ Read about it in *Da Vinci Detects*

From the monk's letter, it was evident that Raphael had risen in the world--just as Machiavelli himself had, in the years after Caterina's father had refused to dower her despite her pregnancy with Nicola. It was a relief that the painter had become a better marriage candidate for Nicola.

On the other hand, if Caterina was dead, then Nicola was not merely rich herself, from the money she had inherited from Caterina's father. She was spectacularly rich, as sole heir to Caterina. And if Raphael was rich as well, he had no real need of the dowry that the monk Martin Luther demanded.

And yet, despite their wealth, Nicola and Raphael had not married.

Machiavelli poured himself more wine and sipped it, considering. He himself was not rich. Best he keep the money for his legitimate children. Unless Nicola became pregnant. At least he, Machiavelli, was prepared to dower his daughter if she had a child-- unlike Caterina's villain of a father.

Caterina hadn't liked Raphael, either, back when he was just another young artist. Where was Caterina? She had not written in more than a year--or if she had, the letter had gone astray. Had she married again, and thrown over their daughter? Or perhaps her new husband took control of her funds, and was interfering?

Obviously, he was missing information. Should he write to Caterina? To his daughter? To this monk, Martin Luther? To all of them, perhaps? Or even to Raphael? *Mal fortuna,* his contacts in Rome were surely in Bologna with the pope.

As the fire died, he sipped his wine and thought. He had spent decades as a diplomat, playing one person off another. A stratagem occurred to him, that would cost him nothing but time. No one but the monk seemed in any hurry.

He rose again. The rain that had been beating on the leaded glass windows had turned to quiet snow that glittered in the moonlight. The muddy hoof and footmarks in the courtyard below were now outlined with snow, like a woodblock print. It was very late.

He placed Martin Luther's letter in the middle of his bedside table. It could wait for the morrow.

Ch. 40 - Conspiracy at the Medici Palazzo

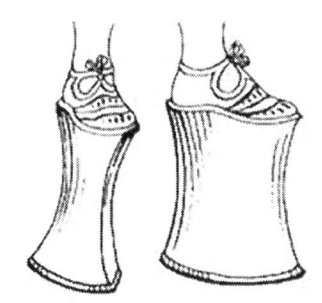

Pattens, or chopines, of various heights
were worn to keep feet out of mud

**Rome,
The Feast of the Epiphany,
January 6, 1511**

Pleased with how perfectly her mask matched her blue *gammura*, Nicola wore it to answer the door. Raphael's eyes widened when he saw her. Under the floppy black velvet *beretta* on his head, he was resplendent in a black velvet tunic trimmed with gold braid, a solid gold medallion, and tall black boots.

"You are exquisite," he pronounced as they climbed the stairs to fetch her cloak. "I chose the emerald necklace for you because I knew it would set off the blue of the *gammura*. I like how you have matched it with the velvet trim of those new sleeves."

As they reached the top of the stairs, he took her gently by the shoulders, turning her to face him. "I will do this because you wish it, *carina*. But it is not a good idea. The only women at this *ballo* will be courtesans, operating out of the upstairs bedrooms. Men will make assumptions about you. You will become notorious."

Though she badly wanted to kiss him, Nicola stepped back. "I have thought about this, Raphael. I want to go. Partly because I may see something that will help reveal Cardinal Beccaria's killer. Partly to celebrate after so many days of hard work in the bakery. And partly to be at a *ballo in maschero* in a *palazzo*, for the first time in my life. "

She smiled, and took his hands. "As I see it, I am already notorious. You and I have been seen together too often–– Giulio de'

Medici remembered you when he invited me. The masks will protect me from becoming even more notorious. If I hold tight to your arm, surely no one will approach me."

Raphael stepped closer. "Why are you so determined to do this? Wouldn't you rather stay here? We haven't seen each other for a fortnight."

Nicola pushed him away. "I am upset about some things, Raphael. You have some explaining to do. You hired a litter, as I asked? It can take you back across the river, if need be."

Raphael frowned as he placed her cloak around her shoulders. "We have gotten on so well, lately. Has that monk ruined things for us?"

Nicola lead him down the stairs, candle in hand. "It's not *Frate* Martin, Raphael. It's the same thing it's always been. It's your other women, and the lies you tell about them. I'm jealous, of course. You know that. But it goes beyond that. How can I trust you when you lie to me like that? "

The bakery was dark, the ovens cold for the first time in weeks. "I didn't lie to you," Raphael responded as they opened the front door. "Not this time."

Outside the door she picked her way through the snow in her wooden pattens, the slippers she would wear to the ball in hand. "You've been living across the river with a gaggle of courtesans, and you didn't tell me until Christmas. That isn't honesty."

He handed her into the litter, then joined her inside it. The bearers hoisted them up and began the walk across town. "It was a new commission. I don't tell you every time I have a new commission. And I swear, Nicola. I have resisted temptation."

She watched his face in the dark. The guilt she thought she saw brought tears, which she brushed aside. "I have trouble believing you. I think you know why."

He met her glance, then looked down. "And I begged you to join me as soon as you could. Please don't cry."

He touched her wet cheek with his hand, and she pushed him away. "What's wrong, Nicola? You aren't pregnant, are you?"

Now, she was angry as well. "What if I were? What would you do? I don't want to take that poison again. It nearly killed me, last time."

"I don't want you to do that either. You know that. If you are pregnant, we should marry. Are you?"

"Why would I marry you if you can't be honest with me? It wouldn't keep you faithful. You would be constantly breaking your vows, besides breaking my heart. And I've watched how you spend money--"

"Let's not get into that. Are you pregnant? Is that what this is about? Tell me, Nicola."

She took a handkerchief from her sleeve and wiped her eyes. "No. I'm not pregnant."

Raphael's relief was obvious, and hurtful. "*Dio grazie. Frate* Martin found me at Chigi's villa and lectured me about sin and marriage. Is he making you feel guilty? You never were before."

"He is making me feel confused. Adulterers and priests with mistresses are everywhere, so I never felt really sinful in the past--not compared to them. I ignored those parts of the Bible that said otherwise, until *Frate* Martin pointed them out. But I knew they were there."

"Please don't turn religious on me again," Raphael said. "Didn't we agree that love is a gift from God? That we should enjoy the pleasures He has given us? And if we need to, we can repent later?"

"True. We agree there. But Raphael--"

The litter lurched downwards. They had arrived. Raphael clambered out, then helped Nicola to her feet. The windows of the Medici palazzo glittered with candles and torches, the stonework glowing against Rome's dark night sky. *Magnifico!* Grateful that her mask would hide her tears, Nicola adjusted it, and took Raphael's proffered arm.

Guards stood at either side of the entrance, and Nicola recognized one of them: Heinrich, the bearded Teutonic knight who had fled the whorehouse when Cardinal Beccaria was murdered. Since she was wearing a mask, she knew she could study him unreservedly, and she did.

"*Maestro* Raphael Sanzio and a lady," the footman announced.

As they stepped into the grand marble entry, Nicola recognized Giulio de' Medici, standing with his corpulent cousin, Cardinal de' Medici. Nearby she saw Pompeo Colonna, chatting with the cardinal who had officiated at Cardinal Beccaria's funeral.

Heinrich strode over to Giulio de' Medici and whispered in his ear. They both turned to stare at her. Cardinal de' Medici listened, and raised his monocle to look at her as well.

"They all know each other," Nicola whispered to Raphael. "That's not what that bearded knight told Martin Luther."

"Did they see you when they ran out of the whorehouse, Nicola? After the murder? Because they seem to know you, too. You were wearing the blue *gammura* that day ––it's very distinctive."

In her mind's eye, Nicola pictured Heinrich and Giulio, fleeing from the whorehouse. Both had looked briefly towards Cardinal Beccaria's body, so they had seen her standing beside it. Little wonder Giulio de' Medici had stared at her when she appeared in Biondi's wine shop in the same *gammura*. And followed her when she left the Piazza Navona with his mistress.

"See how they stare at me. They're coming towards us, Raphael. I don't like it."

A cardinal stumbled into Nicola, sloshing wine onto her *gammura*. Then he squeezed her breast, as if he were sampling a melon at a market stand. Startled, she cried out in pain and rage.

"How dare you," Raphael said, hand on his dagger.

Fearful for Raphael, Nicola punched the cardinal hard in the face. He stumbled into a servant, shattering a trayful of crockery as he fell. The racket stunned the room into silence.

When the laughter began, Nicola was already on her way out the door, pulling Raphael with her. "Get me away from here," she said loudly, happy for an excuse to flee not only the drunken cardinal, but also Giulio de' Medici and Heinrich von Marburg.

When they arrived at the litter, Raphael helped her inside. "I told you this was not a good idea, Nicola. I'm sending you home. Much as I want to go with you, I need to apologize and make excuses to our host."

"I thought you were going to knife that cardinal, Raphael. Many a man would. Whatever you do, don't do that."

"I'll ignore him, I promise. I have no desire to start a *vendetta*, and you already gave him what he deserved. Cardinal de' Medici is one of my patrons, though. I need to calm the waters. I'm very sorry this happened, Nicola."

"You warned me repeatedly. Still, I'm happy I went. I saw exactly what I needed to see. I can't wait to tell *Frate* Martin."

*****

While she waited for Raphael, Nicola wrote a note to Martin Luther for Maria to deliver the next day, telling him what she had seen at the Medici *palazzo*. Increasingly fearful that she had cost Raphael an important patron, she busied herself preparing food and drink for him.

An hour later, she heard Raphael trudging up the stairs to her *appartaménto*. "Would you like some mulled wine?" she asked him. Then she sneezed. "I was fine until I got home, but I think––" She sneezed again.

"*Salute.*" Raphael raised a goblet of the hot, spicy wine to her, his face weary. "Cardinal and Giulio de' Medici send you most profuse apologies. And the cardinal who molested you is still unconscious. From drink––not from you hitting him. I doubt he will remember anything in the morning. Still, I am worried. You had best come across the river with me, Nicola, for your own safety."

Nicola coughed. "But surely he won't bother me here––"

"It's not the cardinal who concerns me. It's Giulio de' Medici and that bearded fellow. They were full of questions about you. They wanted to know where you live."

She gasped, which set off a fit of coughing. "What did you tell them?" she finally managed.

Raphael smiled. "That a gentleman does not disclose a lady's residence. They wanted to know if you knew Cardinal Beccaria and I said, 'I don't know this cardinal. Who is he?' But they will find you, Nicola. I don't want to leave you here alone. Please come with me."

Ch. 41 - A Sensual Interlude

Sketch of a young woman, by Raphael

Rome,
The Chigi villa
Three days later

Nicola felt a gentle touch on her shoulder. "Awake, *carina mia,*" said Raphael's voice. "It is nearly midday. Do you feel well enough to get dressed? Agostino Chigi will be here soon. He is eager to meet you. The cook has sent a hot *tisana* for your cough."

Smiling, Nicola willed herself out of the drowsing euphoria that Raphael's lovemaking always induced. She sat up in bed, coughed, and took the proffered cup. "Where is Maria?"

Raphael stroked her back. "I'll send her. Are you sure you feel well enough to dress?"

She gulped the hot *tisana* and nodded. "From what you have said, Agostino Chigi is likely to come see me in my nightdress if I don't." She stood. "A kiss?"

Raphael gave her a long, languorous kiss. "It's good to see you on your feet," he said, when she tucked her head under his chin.

"I thought you preferred me on my back."

Raphael chuckled. "Obviously your cold is better. The long sleep has made you more beautiful than ever. You will outshine your emeralds––but wear them anyway. I'll summon you when it's time. Now, I really must go."

Still stunned with sleep, Nicola watched him leave. Then she grabbed her shawl and went to the washstand.

She could never resist Raphael when he insisted on taking care of her. She'd never had that as a child. The nuns who raised her had been kind but distant, and she could not remember Caterina's mothering from when she was an infant. But Raphael always caressed her with words as well as kisses. And she always responded like a starving person sitting down to a feast. Craving his solicitude made her crave his body even more. Though she never completely trusted him, she could not stay away from him--and he knew it.

On this occasion, as her cold worsened, she had taken shivering pleasure in his cool, gentle hands. Her hot skin, in turn, had fed his ecstasy. They made love repeatedly, murmuring about her fever, and fires--his, hers, and the one crackling in the grate of their chamber. At intervals, she slept more deeply than she had in many weeks.

Maria brought breakfast and helped Nicola to dress. As she attached Nicola's best sleeves to her blue *gammura*, a servant brought a letter from Caterina. It was uncharacteristically chatty--so much so, that Nicola read it very carefully, wondering what Caterina had hidden in all the talk about parties and new *gammuras*. Two things stood out.

"Caterina spent Christmas in Pavia. She says a guard at the Beccaria *palazzo* there was murdered--garroted-- a month before the murder of Cardinal Beccaria in Rome," she told Maria.

Maria gasped. "You think the murders are related?"

"Probably not," Nicola said. "But it is something to think about. Maybe I should tell *Frate* Martin."

She thought about the murdered guard as she lay half asleep atop the bed's counterpane, waiting for Raphael to summon her; careful not to wrinkle her skirt. Though she could see no connection between the murders, she wrote a note to *Frate* Martin and asked Maria to see to its delivery.

"No courtesans here today?" she asked.

"Not so far," Maria replied.

As soon as she arrived at the Chigi villa, Nicola had inspected Raphael's unfinished *frescoes* by torchlight, searching for a portrait of the courtesan she had seen in the Vatican. As Raphael had promised, Imperia's face was not among those he had painted. He had foresworn her, he claimed. And perhaps it was so. Still, Nicola was jealous. While she was sick, Maria had been keeping an eye on Raphael. Agostino Chigi's mistress was the only female she had seen, aside from the kitchen staff.

After what seemed like hours, a servant led Nicola to the high-ceilinged, half-painted *sala grande* that ran the length of the house. Agostino Chigi sat on a bench next to his mistress Francesca while their small daughter played with a rag doll at their feet. Their sons, a little older, ran circles among the scaffolds, attended by a nervous nurse. Once a Venetian courtesan, Francesca wore a low-cut *camicia* and a pink *gammura* laced down to her pubic bone, a design that allowed the garment to be shed quickly. From the looks the two exchanged, she had done so earlier for Chigi.

He rose to greet Nicola, bowing as she curtseyed. A barrel-chested man with thick lips and wavy gray hair, he was comfortably dressed in a soft blue tunic and embroidered slippers. He looked her up and down. "You are the image of your aunt when she was younger," he said, finally. "Together the two of you would dazzle the sun. Have you heard whether she has arrived in Milan?"

Surprised, Nicola blurted, "Who told you she was going to Milan?"

Chigi laughed. "She told me nothing. But I was in the papal audience room last week, when the pope suddenly shouts, "She has grandchildren in Milan?" Everyone stopped and stared. We all wondered if he had heard something from an old mistress, perhaps. Then he shouts, "Send gifts!" And he waves away a very frightened Swiss guardsman. Of course, before the next bells rang, the guardsman told everyone his story. And everyone was talking about Caterina."

One of Chigi's sons skidded into his father's knees, followed by his brother. Chigi embraced them both, kissing their heads. As they squirmed away to hug their laughing mother, he pulled his little daughter onto his lap.

"It's amazing how calling Caterina a grandmother changed the feeling about her," he continued. "Men who called her a witch when she tended the pope were suddenly defending her. Everyone was talking about their grandmothers. Now the rumor is that Caterina's magic *tisana* was meant for her daughter-in-law, to help her through delivery––Caterina gave it to the pope because she found him in need, people say. And instead of appearing as if from the sky, on a broomstick, she came to Bologna as a good grandmother, on her way to help her family."

"So the pope is no longer angry at her?"

Chigi dandled his daughter's doll in front of her face and received a radiant, tiny-toothed smile as his reward. "Pope Julius is too busy being angry at his nephew to spare any choler for Caterina. The nephew is in charge of the papal armies, and Julius thinks he's incompetent. So he himself is marching on the Duke of Ferrara's *castello* at Mirandola. Accompanied by his bed. In case he gets sick again, six soldiers are carrying it to the siege."

A servant announced the midday meal. Chigi handed his daughter to the nurse and offered Nicola his arm as Raphael did the same for Francesca. *Pranzo* would be served in the formal dining room, at the opposite end of the soon-to-be magnificent *sala* where they had been sitting.

"I am wondering who the pope will appoint to replace Cardinal Beccaria," Nicola said as they strolled.

"No one," Chigi responded. "Cardinal Alidosi is taking over all Beccaria's northern benefices. The Prior General of the Augustinians will take over those in Rome."

"Were these wealthy benefices? Everyone seems to think that Beccaria lived very modestly."

"Very wealthy indeed."

Nicola watched Chigi's sons run the length of the room, followed by their little sister, waddling and swaying like a drunk on her stubby legs. "So, Alidosi benefitted from Cardinal Beccaria's death," she mused. "I hope he is not mad at Caterina."

Chigi pursed his lips. "She has made an enemy there, I'm afraid," he responded. "Before she left for Venice, Caterina confided to me that she suspected Alidosi of poisoning the pope. I felt it my duty to pass this on to the pope, very discreetly. He had already fired the doctors Alidosi hired for him. He immediately got better."

Chigi looked around, as if afraid someone might overhear him. "The obvious conclusion––well, people said it came from her mouth," he continued. "There were rumors she had accused Cardinal Alidosi of poisoning Pope Julius. I didn't start the rumors and tried to avoid them, but you know how people are. I'm sure Alidosi heard the rumors, and hates her for it."

Ahead of them, Chigi's daughter swayed, plopped down on her buttocks, and howled. The nurse swept her up and hurried away.

"So Caterina was accused of saying what everyone was thinking," Nicola said, once it was again blessedly quiet. She had rarely been around children, and felt about them as the nuns who raised her did: though vaguely endearing--like puppies--they were smelly, bothersome, hard to train, and loud.

"Exactly," Chigi said. "And she was not there to defend herself. Unlike Pope Julius, Cardinal Alidosi knows how to bear a grudge. The pope is like a thunderstorm--he blows over. Alidosi, never. The pope's nephew once accused him of treason with the French and he has been quietly revenging himself ever since, poisoning Pope Julius against his own flesh and blood."

"Alidosi has never liked Caterina. She thinks we will lose the papal account if Pope Julius dies."

"It's worse than that," Chigi continued, as he pulled out a dining chair for Nicola and helped her into it. The room, lit by heavy silver candelabras, had been hung with tapestries of harvest scenes to hide the bare plaster walls until they could be frescoed.

Seating himself, Chigi bent close to Nicola. "If Alidosi becomes pope, Caterina should stay away from Rome," he murmured. "If he is capable of poisoning Pope Julius--and I believe he is--you can imagine what he might do to a woman who has accused him of poisoning his predecessor. You didn't hear me say that, understand?"

Nicola swallowed. "Do you think she will be safe in Milan?"

"Her French connections will protect her in Milan. Probably."

A servant stepped forward to help Nicola to soup. She nodded her thanks, then leaned toward Chigi again. "Will you help me get word to her, to get to Milan as quickly as possible? She's in Pavia now, but I don't think she is getting my letters, now that she has crossed into French territory. She needs to know that she is in danger. Do you send couriers there? Will you help me?"

Chigi smiled. "Of course."

Ch. 42 - Hiding from the Swiss Guard

16th Century Swiss Guard

South of Milan
Several days later

Leonardo da Vinci watched as Caterina and her maid galloped towards the convent hidden behind tall brown brick walls, next to the road to Milan. A nun in white pushed the iron–studded gate open, then closed it hurriedly behind them.

"Why do you suppose Caterina is hiding from the Swiss Guard?" Salai asked, his voice puzzled. He and Francesco had halted their horses on either side of da Vinci, then grabbed his reins. As if he, da Vinci, could not handle his own mount. Which in truth was becoming more difficult as he got older.

"I don't know why she is so afraid of them. And once she saw them, she had no time to tell us. She asked us to keep her secret, and we will," da Vinci replied.

The hoof beats behind them were getting louder. Soon three Swiss guardsmen galloped past them, then swiveled their mounts to block their way. Young, tall and blond, they had faces like the angels in some of da Vinci's early paintings. Though they wore blue and yellow striped uniforms and swords, rather than wings.

"Do you know the name of that woman, the one who just went into the convent?" their *capitano* demanded.

"Of course," da Vinci said. "She is my sister Elisabetta. Why do you ask?"

The *capitano's* horse pawed the ground and he patted its neck. "We are looking for a woman named Caterina Biaggi. You haven't seen her, have you?"

"Not that I know of."

"What has she done?" Salai asked.

The three guardsmen looked at each other. "Nothing. We are bringing her letters and gifts from the pope, is all. We hoped to catch her before she gets all the way to Milan."

Salai raised an eyebrow. "Letters and gifts from the pope? For a woman? Really?"

"They are for her grandchildren."

"I see," Salai responded, grinning.

"It's not what you think," the *capitano* protested. But he grinned as well.

"If her grandchildren are in Milan, you had best go there, then," da Vinci said.

"We are headed to the next monastery for the night," Francesco said. "May we ride with you?"

"Of course," the *capitano* replied. "But we ride fast."

"Well, I don't. In fact, my old bones would like to get off this horse and have a bite to eat under that tree before we go any further," da Vinci said. "Don't worry, Francesco. We'll get to the monastery before nightfall. Safe travels to Milan, gentlemen."

After Cecco and Salai helped him dismount and handed him his cane, da Vinci made his way over to a solitary chestnut tree. The flat plain of the Po River Valley, covered in graying hay stubble, stretched out on all sides of them. He suppressed a groan as he lowered himself onto a rock next to the tree. The ride had indeed tired him, and made him feel old.

They watched as the *capitano* banged on the convent gate, then conferred with someone inside through a small grate. "Not here. Let's go," he called to his men as he mounted his horse. Soon, they were specks in the distance.

"Pope Julius is sending letters and gifts to Caterina," Salai said. "*Maestro,* do you suppose she and Pope Julius––" He raised his brows and cocked his head, the annoying expression he always wore when discussing salacious gossip.

Da Vinci grimaced. "Nicola's father helped her get a contract to manufacture weapons for Pope Julius.*** It's possible that she ended up in the pope's bed." He felt a stab of jealousy, despite all the years gone by. "But I still don't understand why she would run like that from the Swiss Guard."

He took a bite of the pork *salume* Salai had just handed him and a sip of the water. The *salume* was dry and hard to chew.

"Do you really have a sister Elisabetta?" Francesco asked.

"Half sister," da Vinci replied. "There were eleven of them and they all despised me because I was their illegitimate older brother. We don't speak."

Stiff and sore from the ride, Da Vinci shifted his body on his hard rock seat, suppressing a grunt. "Francesco, I need you to write a note to *Madonna* Caterina. Tell her what just happened and suggest that she stay at the convent a day or two. And say that, if necessary, we could go into Milan and make sure she will be safe at her stepson's armory."

"Going to Milan and coming back here to fetch her will greatly lengthen your journey. Are you sure you are up to it?" Cecco asked him.

"I am going to rest at that monastery ahead of us," da Vinci said. "You boys are going to do whatever is needful. For all we know she truly is expecting letters and gifts from Pope Julius."

"But she seemed so frightened of his men," Salai said.

Da Vinci grabbed his cane, and with help from Salai, pushed himself to his feet. "Women are never consistent or logical. We'll give the note to the nuns, and see what Caterina says in the morning."

*** Read about it in *Da Vinci Detects*.

Ch. 43 - Martin Luther Has an Epiphany

Detail from *Job and His Wife* by
Albrecht Dürer

**Rome,
The next day**

Frate Anton watched as Martin Luther strode towards him across the large courtyard containing the monks' herb garden, green with new growth in places despite the winter cold. The young friar had an uncharacteristically happy look on his face.

Frate Anton fell into step with him. "Well met, Martin. I have worried about you. But you seem to be feeling better."

Luther nodded. "I was in despair after my last confession. But I prayed humbly for God's forgiveness and turned the problem over to Him, as you told me to do. Then I meditated on the Book of Job, and was at last able to fall asleep."

Frate Anton could not help but smile. "The Book of Job has made you happy, Martin? How extraordinary. Few people could say that."

Luther chuckled. "Job was rewarded for his faith, remember? I have received new information concerning Cardinal Beccaria's murder."

"You have seen that damned woman again?"

"She keeps sending notes with information. And I received an answer to my letter to Pavia. It is all falling together, finally. God answered my prayer. I think I know who the murderer is, Anton."

Frate Anton looked at Luther in astonishment. "You have found the murderer? "

"I think I know who it is."

Ch. 44 - A Murderer is Revealed

Detail from engraving, from *The Large Passion* by Albrecht Dürer, 1511

Rome,
The following day

Nicola sat in the prior's office, with Martin Luther and Francesco Tedesco of the Swiss Guard. She felt embarrassed. "I should have seen it. I can't believe I didn't see it, even after I heard about the third murder," she said.

Martin Luther smiled, obviously pleased with himself. "You have been exposed to so much corruption and evil that you no longer see the good in people, *Fraulein*. Whereas I––when I first came here, at least––could not believe the evil around me. That allowed me to see what you did not. If I had known Rome as I do now, I might have been as blind as you."

Nicola felt a sudden stab of grief for lost innocence, Luther's and her own. "Everyone said Cardinal Beccaria died a saintly man, and I did not believe them," she said. "Isn't that sad?"

"You need to repent and change your ways, *Fraulein*. But you know that."

Francesco made a noise, his mouth twitching as if he were suppressing a laugh. "You have an interesting theory," he said to Luther. "But how do we prove it?"

"The blood," Nicola responded. "There had to be an enormous amount of blood, spilled on the floor. That's always been the problem with every theory but yours, *Frate* Martin. What happened to all that blood?"

"You know where to find it?" Francesco asked.

"Yes, of course," Luther responded. "But how do we get in?"

Francesco laughed. "How strong is the door?"

Martin Luther pursed his lips as he considered this question. "The two of us might be able to break it down, if that is what you are proposing."

"Francesco, I think we need more guardsmen," Nicola interrupted. "We are dealing with someone armed and dangerous."

"I'll bring a whole squad. Let's go."

It was late afternoon by the time they emerged from the Vatican, accompanied by four burly, fully-armed Swiss guardsmen. Martin Luther led them to the top *appartaménto* in a crumbling building near the Campo de' Fiori. The guardsmen ripped the door from its hinges with little effort.

Tiny and painfully neat, the room contained a bed, stool and chamber pot. In a corner sat a small chest that evidently held the occupant's belongings. Despite its tidiness, the room smelled like a butcher shop.

"The bed is in an odd place," Nicola said. "Let's move it."

A large, dark stain had soaked the wooden floor beneath the bed. Nicola borrowed Francesco's dagger and used the tip to scrape along the wood grain. "It's blood," she announced, after tasting the scraping. "You can smell it, too. And the flies know. See them?"

Luther, meanwhile, was looking through the wooden chest. "See. Here are documents, bearing Cardinal Beccaria's name. They are very old, from when he was Count. Some have to do with a land dispute. Another is a purchase agreement."

Nicola looked over his shoulder. "These documents come from Pavia. So they link him to the murder of the guardsman in Pavia. He could not read the Latin in any of them, or he would not have taken them."

Francesco smiled, fingering his moustache. "Proof enough for me. Let's go find him."

"He is armed and dangerous. Perhaps we should wait and take him when he is asleep?" Luther asked.

Francesco laughed. "A dagger is no match for four halberds, *Frate* Martin. If we waited, our comrades would call us cowards. Let's go."

"She should not come," Luther insisted, nodding at Nicola. "It is not safe."

Nicola was outraged. "You can't exclude me––I have the final proof and I will not give it to you. I want to see how it ends. I'll hang back, I promise. I will be safe."

Francesco looked at Luther, shaking his head. "There is no use trying to stop her. Let's *go*."

Martin Luther led the way, nodding to several puzzled friars as they descended into the corridors below the monastery. Motioning to the others to stay back, he peered around a corner. Then he hastened back to speak to them.

"His back is to you, but he is holding a knife," Luther whispered. "Perhaps you should wait."

Francesco handed his halberd to Nicola, startling her. "I'll take the knife hand. Let's go," he said. With a roar, the Swiss guardsmen rushed through the door.

Nicola stepped inside the room to watch as Francesco grabbed the murderer's wrist and struggled for the knife flailing between their heads. Two Swiss guards circled them, halberds pointed, searching for a way to kill the criminal without hurting Francesco. The guard holding the murderer's other arm yanked and kicked him. The whole group bellowed, circled and swayed in a hellish dance.

With a roar, Martin Luther grabbed the halberd from Nicola and headed for the murderer. "Don't," she shouted to him. She heard Francesco yell, but could not see him. The knife appeared overhead, then sank. She heard it hit flesh with a thud, a sound she knew she would remember for the rest of her life.

The murderer was still struggling, though someone had pinned his arms. Martin Luther threw aside the halberd, grabbed him from behind, and threw him to the ground. A guard jumped on him and punched him repeatedly in the face. Finally, he was still.

Cardinal Beccaria's body was brought into the brothel from outside. The others could not believe this––and indeed, it seems impossible. As *Fraulein* Nicola said, who could possibly bring a bloody dead body into a busy whorehouse? But I believed him to be a good and holy man. And despite the sinfulness of Rome, everyone I spoke to confirmed his goodness. So this idea persisted."

The prior reached for the poker he had heated in the fireplace, and plunged it into a flagon of spiced wine. It hissed and steamed, infusing the dark room with the odors of alcohol, fruit and cloves. He poured a cup for each of them, then nodded for Luther to continue.

Luther sipped his wine. "The strength of the blow and the risky decision to throw his body into the streets from a whorehouse window––like Jezebel thrown to the dogs––convinced me it was a crime of passion. The killer wanted to disgrace him. He wanted revenge. A cardinal who wanted to eliminate a rival for the papal throne would not want to disgrace the Church at the same time. No cardinal, good or bad, has any interest in disgracing the Church. For this reason, and because I hated to believe them anyway, *Fraulein* Nicola's theories about papal politics made no sense to me."

Luther shifted his stool away from the heat of the fire. "When she and Raphael visited the whorehouse, I went with them, you'll recall. And stayed outside. But I looked inside the back entry and saw the huge laundry baskets, filled with dirty sheets. Cardinal Beccaria was a small, thin man, with no blood in him by the time we found his corpse. He had stiffened into a tiny ball, like a babe in its mother's womb––except he seemed to be praying, which was horrifying. You cannot imagine."

"I can," the prior said. "He was repenting his sins and praying that we would find his killer. I am convinced of it."

Martin Luther nodded. "I hope that is how he spent his last moments."

"Go on," the prior said. "I did not mean to interrupt."

"When I saw that back entrance, I immediately pictured his body in one of those big baskets. I was sure it would have fit. And I thought immediately of the laundress––the big woman with large breasts and heavy arms, who left the whorehouse carrying a basket and a large bundle of linens. I never saw her myself, but that is how she was described. No one seemed to know where she was. It eventually occurred to me: why assume she was a "she?" A man in possession of women's clothing and a basket of sheets could pad himself out to appear as if he had breasts––close enough, anyway, if he was hunched over the basket. If he shaved himself well, downcast eyes and a veil would hide everything but a man's big arms. Which were strong enough to carry the bloodless body of a small man in a basket. But I said nothing to *Fraulein* Machiavelli. I thought she would mock me. I spent many hours in prayer, Reverend Father, asking God to show me the truth."

Luther set aside his cup. "And I began watching the streets near the whorehouse, because the Cardinal's body could not have been carried far in that basket. And the killer had to be familiar with the whorehouse and the back entrance to know he could leave the body there. So, I reasoned that he lived in the area. Somehow he induced the Cardinal to visit him. There had to be some kind of personal relationship between them––probably evidenced in those burned letters I found in the Cardinal's cell."

He paused for another sip of wine. "I also watched the women doing their laundry at the riverside below the whorehouse, hoping to see one that met the description of the missing laundress. Missing, because she never came forward to receive the coins *Fraulein* Nicola promised for her story."

"But you never saw her––"

"Because she was already dead. I believe now that she was the drowned corpse *Fraulein* Nicola found with the prostitute's body. The large corpse, wrapped only in a winding sheet because she was pulled naked from the Tiber. When Madonna Nicola told me about the line of corpses, all clothed but one, I asked myself: who strips naked to drown themselves, especially in winter? Later, I decided the killer had drowned her. Either she caught him washing the blood from his clothing, or he killed her simply to steal her garments and laundry basket. Or perhaps both. Once he stripped her naked, he had a disguise, and a way to get the corpse out of his chamber, and into the brothel."

Luther took another sip of wine. "Then, of course, I learned that the Cardinal had murdered his wife, who had presented him with a child that was not his. At first, I did not see any connection."

"How early did you realize there was one?" the prior asked.

"I began to piece it together at the Christmas *festa* when the men were talking about the Cardinal's murder of his wife. Roberto said, "I heard the boy was his." And it suddenly occurred to me—the baby that Cardinal Beccaria almost murdered would have been his heir, and the next Count Beccaria. Assuming the baby was a boy. And assuming, of course, that Cardinal Beccaria was actually the baby's father."

The prior refilled his cup. "Thank you," Luther said. "Then I remembered Roberto serving me sausage in your office the day of the murder. And the way he wielded that wicked knife of his, cutting bread at the Christmas *festa*. He was used to butchering animals. I thought to myself, 'It can't be him. He is such a good student.' But then I asked myself, 'Why is he trying so hard to learn Latin?'"

Luther paused to take another sip of wine. "Then I saw Roberto the street near the brothel. Luckily, he did not see me! I followed him to the building where he lived––and where the Cardinal was killed––and realized I could picture him, disguised as a woman. He has very muscular arms but barely the hint of a beard.

The prior poured more mulled wine for himself. "So you were beginning to suspect that your own special student—the one you were so proud of—was the murderer."

"It explained why he, alone of all my students, was so eager to learn Latin. He wanted to find evidence of his patrimony. Cardinal Beccaria, you remember, gave up his title to become a monk. Roberto believed he was the legitimate son of the true Count. To claim his place, he needed to find proof of his paternity. And to be an educated man."

"So you kept teaching him."

"Of course! And eyeing that big knife of his. Then I got the response to my letter, from your old friend in Pavia."

"*Frate* Giorgio," the prior said, raising his cup in salute. "A good man."

"*Frate* Giorgio knew nothing of what happened to the missing child," he explained, "but was able to look up his baptismal records, and gather a little information about him. His mother had him christened before she was murdered, you see. Her son was the same age as my student Roberto. And his *name* was Roberto. His mother claimed Cardinal Beccaria––her husband, back before he was a monk––as the boy's father. As you would expect. Finally, I began to piece together the story."

Prior Piccolimini set aside his wine and settled back in his chair. "Tell it again."

Martin Luther nodded. "It's the story of a young man named Roberto, who grew up very angry. He was convinced by the nursemaid who raised him that his father had murdered his innocent mother and deprived him of his birthright. He also grew up poor. And was trained as a butcher."

Luther took a sip of wine. "Last fall, Roberto broke into the current Count's document room, seeking proof that he was the true Count Beccaria, and killing a guard in the process. He found nothing, though he stole some documents he could not read. Then he journeyed to Rome, and took a job in the kitchens of this monastery, so he could be close to the man he thought was his father."

"I remember meeting him when he was hired," the prior mused. "He had a good reference and nice manners. If only I had known."

"You could not possibly have known, Reverend Father. At any rate, he contacted the Cardinal, and somehow arranged a meeting in his rented room. It did not go well. He may not have meant to kill the Cardinal––he knew how to use a garrote, since he killed the soldier in Pavia with one. It is a much less messy weapon. But when the Cardinal continued to deny him as a son, he reacted violently and with great force. The wound would have covered them both in blood."

"I remember *Madonna* Nicola, talking about the missing blood," the prior said.

"That's the crux of it––the blood. There was none in the brothel, except a smear on the sill from pushing the body out the window. The maids attested to this, and the place was scrupulously clean, according to *Fraulein* Machiavelli. There were no bloody clothes either. Why? Because the Cardinal bled out in Roberto's apartment. He probably used the Cardinal's clothing to mop up as best he could, and then sat there with a bloody corpse in his room, wondering what to do next. When it was dark, I think he went down to the river to wash himself and his clothing––as a poor young man, he would not have had spare clothing. There the laundress saw him and he drowned her, stole her clothing, basket and sheets, and dumped her body in the river."

The prior rose, and offered to refill Martin Luther's cup. Luther declined, and he filled his own. "I think I see where this is going," he said, as he sat down again. "Now, Roberto had a disguise and the means to get the corpse out of his room."

"Exactly. I suspect he went back to his room dressed as a woman, with his wet clothes in the laundress' basket, under the sheets from the whorehouse that she had washed herself. The Cardinal's corpse might have been stiffening by then, but he managed to get it cleaned off, and into the laundry basket."

"And then he hung his own clothes to dry, and shaved," the prior added.

"And put on women's clothing again, when he was sure the whorehouse would be quiet and empty, the next day. Because he had to get rid of the corpse, as far away from where he lived as possible."

"I see," the prior said.

"He took the body up the back stairs of the brothel. Perhaps he intended to leave it under a bed. Maybe he had trouble getting it out of the basket, because it was so stiff. But the prostitute in the yellow dress saw him going into the room. He could hear her, coming down the hallway. So he panicked, tipped the corpse out the window, and ducked into the closet with the basket. That is why none of the people who peered into the room saw anything. But the prostitute saw the open window with the blood on the sill, looked out, and saw the corpse. I can still see her face looking down at us, poor woman."

"And so she began screaming," the prior added.

"What could he do? He stayed in the closet and heard people leaving. Including, finally, the screaming woman herself. And he needed to leave, obviously. So he rearranged the sheets in the basket to hide any bloodstains left by Cardinal Beccaria's body, plumped up his false breasts, and went down the stairs himself, hunched over the laundry basket. People were too panicked to notice him."

"But the whore in yellow had seen him at some point, so he had to kill her."

Luther nodded. "Yes. And he had other things to do. In his room, he put on his own clothes--dry now. Then he rushed to the Cardinal's cell, and burned any letters to his 'father.' After that, he went to work in the monastery kitchen, as if nothing had happened. When he finished work, it would have been dark. Then he could hunt the streets for the prostitute who saw him and the Cardinal's body. With her, he was smart enough to use a garrote. At some point he got rid of the basket with the cardinal's clothing and bloody sheets--probably filled it with rocks and threw it in the river. But he couldn't wash the blood out of the floorboards."

Prior Piccolimini rose from his chair and stirred the fire. "Did you ever feel threatened by Roberto? He must have heard you were asking questions about Cardinal Beccaria's death."

"If he did, he never said a word about it, nor I to him. We spoke only of his lessons. I kept praising him for his efforts to learn Latin, which he liked. He was proud of himself. But I kept myself away from that knife of his."

"I wonder if he will confess."

"Likely. Francesco, the *capitano* of the Swiss Guard, told me they will torture him if he doesn't. They have enough evidence to do that."

The prior crossed himself. "And if he does confess?"

"He will be hanged immediately. But it is a merciful death, compared to death by torture. Do you know what he said to me, when they took him away? He said, 'How did you know?' I told him, 'There are no secrets from God.' "

The prior crossed himself again. "None. But I pray He will have mercy on that poor lost soul."

Ch. 46 - Martin Luther Begins His Journey Home

Raphael's "La Velata"
believed to be his mistress "La Fornarina"
with blue gammura

Rome
Mid-January, 1511

"Wait, *Frate* Martin. Wait."

Frate Anton was surprised to hear a woman's voice calling to his traveling companion. Low and sultry, but unmistakably female.

Frate Anton turned, and saw a slender young woman, modestly dressed in the blue of the Virgin Mary and veiled in white, holding a large basket. She was smiling, and so beautiful that it moved even his old man's heart. This had to be that damned woman, *Fraulein* Nicola.

The two friars had just left the monastery of Santa Maria del Popolo, to begin their long journey back to Erfurt, in Saxony. *Frate* Martin had avoided that damned woman since solving the murders, for the sake of his immortal soul. Yet here she was, walking beside them on the ancient Tiber River Road that led north, out of the city.

"I heard the Augustinians finally decided to reform themselves, so I knew you would be leaving," she said. "I'm glad I caught up with you. I came to say *'Addiò.'* And to make you a gift of food for your journey––a special bread from my bakery, and cheese."

She held the basket out for Martin Luther. "And to make sure you learned that Roberto confessed, even to the murder of the laundress. And was executed, without being tortured. And to tell you that I forgive you for interfering in my life," she added.

Frate Anton was incensed. "Forgive him? You should be grateful. He was trying to save you from eternal damnation, woman."

She nodded, her face solemn. "I know. That is why I forgive him."

Martin Luther stared at the basket she had thrust at him, as if it contained a poisonous snake. He swallowed hard, then looked up at her. "I heard about Roberto, yes. I am sorry I failed you, *Fraulein*."

She smiled at him. The smile of an angel, *Frate* Anton thought, on the face of a *succubus* devil. "Raphael and I will never marry, so you did not fail me. Be easier on yourself, *Frate* Martin. Jesus certainly forgives a man as good as you, for failings as small as yours."

Frate Anton wanted to slap her. "Who do you think you are, lecturing a scholar on religion? Your place is to follow the Word of God as explained by men such as Martin."

"And so I am doing," she responded, mischief in her eyes. "I am feeding the poor and hungry, and practicing forgiveness. As Jesus, a man, taught me to do."

Frowning, Martin Luther made the sign of the cross in front of her face as he backed away. "God bless you for your many good works, *Fraulein*. Offering two friars provisions for a long journey is certainly one of them. Understand, your good works will not save you."

"I will be saved by my indulgence," she responded, looking up at Luther through long eyelashes.

"Which you do not believe in," Martin Luther said.

She smiled. "But I try hard to believe in it, and other Church doctrine that makes no sense to me. I am a mere woman, and God surely forgives me for my confusion."

"We pray it is so, *Madonna*. Now, we must go. Good day to you," *Frate* Anton said. "Come, Martin."

"Addiò, *Frate* Martin," she responded. Then she turned and walked away, hips swaying.

They watched her go. "Now I understand your struggle, Martin, as never before," *Frate* Anton said.

"She believes God will forgive her many sins if she performs good works," Luther responded, as he shouldered the basket Nicola had given them. "As if God weighs our sins against our good deeds on a pair of celestial scales."

They began to walk again. "Some of what the Church does gives that impression," *Frate* Anton responded. "People refuse to see that they also need to repent and be absolved by a priest. And stop sinning, of course."

Luther was silent for a moment. "She seems to think she doesn't need a priest at all," he concluded. "Just good works, and reading the Bible. And a very merciful God.'

"Heresy, Martin. From an enchantress. You need to forget her. Shall we say the 'Hail Mary' together as we walk?"

Martin Luther nodded. "Over and over. Let us say it over and over, Anton."

Ch. 47 - A Ghost from the Past

Portrait of Niccolò Machiavelli
by Rosso Fiorentino, early 16th century

Milan,
Two months later

Caterina sat on the bench outside the Biaggi armory, watching wagons go by on the cobbled street, and enjoying the surprising warmth of the late winter sunshine. She tucked away the gold rattle that Pope Julius had sent for the baby drowsing on her lap, and gave silent thanks to God for all His blessings. It had finally been possible to reconcile the armory books, thanks to the accounting in the letters the Swiss Guard had brought from Nicola. After eight years, she had finally received and banked her share of the Milan armory profits, less what she owed her stepson from the branch in Rome. She was enjoying her grandchildren, her old friends, and the capable woman her stepson Carlo had been lucky to marry. Thanks to her daughter-in-law, the armory in Milan was well-run, though Caterina thought she could help with improvements.

A gentleman cloaked and booted in black dismounted nearby. Caterina took little notice, until his shadow fell across the baby on her lap. Looking up, she saw the startled face of Niccolò Machiavelli, whose close-cropped hair was now shot with gray. She felt her jaw drop, and her heart pound.

"Who is the lucky father?" Niccolò asked her, his voice strained.

"What? This is my grandchild. Don't be ridiculous."

Niccolò's brows shot up. "Nicola had a baby? Why did no one inform me?"

Caterina smiled at his confusion. "This is Carlo's baby. You remember my stepson Carlo? My late husband's son? The one who runs this armory? What are you doing here, Niccolò?"

His face relaxed into a smile. "I had reasons to stop in Milan on the way back from Paris. But really I was looking for you. I was worried about you."

Happiness bubbled up inside Caterina, to her surprise. She found herself smiling back. "Why? And how on earth did you know to find me here? And how is your wife?"

He grimaced. " My wife—regrettably—is fine, as far as I know. I was looking for you because I got a strange letter about Nicola from a monk named Martin Luther. The letter didn't mention you, which worried me. It seemed very strange that he left you out. I thought you might be here. And if not, I knew I could find out what happened to you at the Biaggi armory. Do you know this monk?"

How good it felt, to hear his concern. "Martin Luther? No. But I left Rome in November. As far as I know, though, Nicola is fine. I just got a batch of letters from her, in fact, assuring me that all is well. What did the monk say about her?"

Niccolò sat down beside her. "He demanded that I dower her so she can marry that painter Raphael. So I take it she and Raphael are still together?"

She stroked the baby's head, to keep herself from reaching out to touch Niccolò. "Most of the time. She loses patience with him, but always forgives him."

"How do you feel about him for a son-in-law? The monk says he has come up in the world."

She tucked the blankets around the sleeping baby while she considered Niccolò's question. "He has come up in the world," she said. "But Nicola has her own money, and mine too when I die. So she does not need a husband. And Raphael would spend it all. He would not be a good husband. If she marries him, she will live to regret it."

The worry on Machiavelli's face softened as they talked. He gave her the crooked, impish smile she remembered from their youth. "I wondered if you would feel differently about it now," he said.

They chatted companionably for a while, in the manner of old friends. Niccolò had heard about Pope Julius' latest miraculous recovery from a deadly fever, but not about Pompeo Colonna's failed rebellion against the papacy while the city waited for Julius to die.

"Our firm sold Pompeo the weapons for the rebellion, though Rodolfo didn't know it," Caterina said. "Fortunately, Nicola reported it immediately to the Swiss Guard, who sent a spy to follow the wagons from the armory to where they cached the weapons. The Swiss Guard broke in and spiked them, then spied until Pompeo and his men came to fetch them. Caught them all in the act. Pompeo had tried to set all of Rome against Julius, who by that time had recovered from fever. Again."

"I wonder how many times Julius will be at death's door before he finally steps through it."

Caterina laughed. "So do I. Anyway, the rebellion collapsed when the city heard of the pope's miraculous recovery. Pompeo and his followers were arrested, and that was the end of it. The pope was very, very grateful to us. He immediately placed a large order for *arquebuses*. And paid for them."

"So now that you're back in the pope's favor, you're selling weapons to both sides in this war?" Niccolò asked, with a teasing smile.

Caterina smiled back. "That's right. Maybe I learned a lesson from you. You always worked both sides."

Niccolò squeezed her hand. "All sides. But I don't make much money at it. Maybe I should learn some lessons from you."

The touch of his hand stirred old desires, though she was careful not to show it. She had not told him that Francesco, the man most instrumental in quelling the Colonna rebellion, was her lover. She felt no guilt about keeping secrets from Niccolò—he had plenty of his own—but what of Francesco? Did he expect her to be faithful? Would he forgive her if she reconnected with the father of her child?

"When will you return to Rome?" Niccolò asked.

"Maybe never," she answered. "Pope Julius is grateful for our help, and demands my return. But French soldiers captured me on the way here, and it is only by the grace of God that I escaped injury or worse. Even with escorts I would rather not pass through that war zone again. And Pope Julius cannot live forever. If Cardinal Alidosi becomes pope when Julius dies, it might actually be dangerous for me to return."

Niccolò covered her hand with his own, "Come to Florence with me, then."

She covered his hand with hers. "And be your mistress in the same town as your wife again? It's a miracle we kept that secret. My answer to you is the same one I gave the pope: I stay here, with my grandchildren, for now. For my own safety."

Niccolò's face fell, but he continued to rub her hand. "So we have only a little time together?"

"Only as long as you can stay."

"Then can you give this baby back to his nurse? I have traveled a long way today and need to find an inn and eat something. Will you come with me?"

"Yes, I will come with you. Don't I always? Give me a moment."

As she hurried inside the armory to hand the baby to her maid, Caterina thought about her off again, on again romance with Niccolò Machiavelli. They had spent more time apart than together, but he still made her heart beat fast, even after all these years. Seeing his crooked smile had made her want to fling herself into his arms. What would her stepson and friends in Milan think, if she suddenly took up with a man from Florence, after eight years as a widow? Did it matter what they thought?

And what of Francesco? She had not asked him to be faithful and doubted he had been. Was it fair for him to expect it of her? She might never see him again. And she could never confess her relationship with Niccolò to him, without also confessing that Nicola was her daughter, rather than her niece. That was a secret she had to maintain, for Nicola's sake as well as her own. If she kept another big secret from Francesco, what of it?

"It's too bad you missed Leonardo da Vinci," she told Machiavelli as she joined him outside. "He escorted me here. And took very good care of me, too. By now he's back in Pavia, drawing pictures of corpses. Again."

"I thought I cured him of that in Florence.[†††] Can you recommend an inn near here?"

"I can. I'll take you there, and see that you have a good meal. And then you and I, Niccolò, will have a good visit."

Ch. 48 - Cardinal Alidosi's Fate

Francesco Maria della Rovere,
Assassin of Cardinal Alidosi

Ravenna, Italy
May 24, 1511

Cardinal Francesco Alidosi, astride his donkey with Alfonso Zanna at his side, reflected on recent disasters as they rode to join Pope Julius for dinner. They had lost Bologna. The Bentivoglio family

---

[†††] Read about it in *Da Vinci Detects*.

was back in power and the pope had barely escaped capture. The fickle Bolognese--who had destroyed the Bentivoglio *palazzo* when the pope took the city--had welcomed back the former tyrants, and razed Pope's new *castello* to its foundations. The French had recaptured Mirandola and were making inroads everywhere. There was no end in sight.

The pope's nephew had once again accused Alidosi of treason with the French. Fortunately, Pope Julius once again believed him, rather than his own nephew. It had been small work to convince Julius of his nephew's incompetence, because his nephew *was* incompetent. Alidosi was back in power, but tired. Very tired.

So much rancor and venom--he, Alidosi, was getting too old for this. Once he was pope, he would swiftly end this war with the French. It was too bad the doctors in Bologna had been unable to dispatch Pope Julius, who seemed to thrive on bouts of temper that would kill most men his age. That, and the tisana he now drank to keep new doctors away. Damn that woman, Caterina Biaggi. Her time would come.

Ahead of him, Alidosi saw the pope's nephew, riding towards him with his armed retainers. He slowed his donkey so that he was surrounded by his own guards, then nodded politely to his adversary, and looked away.

Shouts erupted as he crashed to the ground, stung by the blow to his cheek. The pope's nephew and his men were above him, cursing and stabbing, their faces contorted with hate. He glimpsed his own guards skewering a screaming Alfonzo Zanna with their halberds, looks of savage joy on their faces. Pain ripped through his belly and chest; his own hot blood flowed through his fingers. He had been betrayed.

Ears ringing, Alidosi realized he was dying, his ambition pouring out with his lifeblood. He would never be pope. He would die without receiving extreme unction or absolution for his sins. As his eyesight dimmed, he turned his thoughts to prayer. And realized, as his last living thought, that he had spent so little time in honest prayer that he had forgotten how it was done.

Ch. 49 - Henry VIII Makes a Regal Offer

Earliest known portrait of Henry VIII as King
by unknown artist, 1509

Rome,
Two months later

Nicola stepped from Caterina's armory onto the cobbled street, and nearly ran into two blue-eyed noblemen as they handed their lathered horses to a manservant, who tied them to the rings on either side of the armory door. The noblemen wore foreign doublets striped in green and white, and foreign-looking swords.

The handsomer of the two blocked her passage. "*Salve, Madonna.* My name is Sir Piers Butler and this is my cousin, Sir Thomas Boleyn. Are you *Madonna* Caterina Biaggi?" he asked, in Latin.

"No. But she is within. Do you have business with her?" Nicola answered, stepping back into the doorway. He was one of the tallest men she had ever seen, with a physique that reminded her of Michelangelo's statue of David, in Florence. He smiled down at her.

"Are you, perhaps, her niece?" the other man asked, as he hoisted the saddlebags off his mount, and handed them to their manservant. He was older, shorter and not nearly as handsome.

"I am her niece, yes. May I help you?"

The servant shouldered the saddle bags from the horse, which were obviously heavy. The men looked her up and down, as if she were trade goods. "Take us to your aunt. We have business to discuss, but not in the street," said Sir Thomas.

Nicola curtseyed to them, glad she was wearing her new maroon *gammura* and best sleeves, with the garnet necklace Raphael had given her. She knew nothing of these men, so they were surely new customers. Their clothing was rich and their Latin excellent, so she did not fear them. But she wondered how they knew that Caterina had a niece.

"Follow me, please," she told them. They walked through the armory with her, conversing in a tongue she did not understand; pausing to watch the workmen making swords. Then one of them lapsed into French. "Do you think she will do?" he said.

"Very nicely. But be careful what you say––she may speak French."

She turned and gave them her best smile. "I do speak French. At least a little."

The tall man smiled back, displaying dimples and perfect teeth. "Excellent," he said.

Caterina, still bent over the ledgers they were examining earlier, raised an eyebrow when Nicola walked into the armory office with the two men. As always, Caterina had dressed to emphasize her position as a wealthy widow. Today she was in black Venetian *brocado,* with a silvery silk veil and sleeves.

"Here are foreigners who were looking for you," Nicola told her in Italian. "They speak Latin and French, and they know I am your niece. They say they have business with you."

"I am Sir Thomas Boleyn, and this is my cousin, Sir Piers Butler. We are emissaries from King Henry VIII of England," the taller man said, in Latin. Both men bowed deeply, doffing their floppy caps. "His Majesty has executed the contract you sent him. We have brought the first payment."

Nicola translated, wondering why she knew nothing about this contract. As she did so, the manservant dumped the saddlebags onto Caterina's desk. They jingled with coins. Many coins.

Caterina's jaw dropped. She swallowed, then looked at Nicola, brows raised as if asking for something. "Ask them if they have the contract," she told Nicola. She did so.

"Yes. Of course," the tall man said. "Signed by King Henry himself. Give it to her, Piers."

With a bow, Sir Piers produced a leather purse from beneath his doublet, and a sealed, beribboned document from the purse. Holding it in both hands, he looked at it as though it were holy writ, then handed it to Caterina with a smile. "We will also be the escorts for your niece and her maid." Nicola translated, wondering where these men expected to escort her.

Caterina broke the seals, eyes widening as she looked the contract over. She swallowed again. "I need to examine this more carefully. And count these coins," she said. "And speak to my niece, if you will excuse us?" She tugged at Nicola's sleeve. "Tell them to make themselves comfortable. And put out some wine and food for them. Then come with me."

Nicola did not recognize the document. "I didn't draft that contract," she murmured to Caterina. "And what do they mean when they say they will escort me?"

"I will explain. Just tell them what I said, then follow me. We need to talk."

Nicola translated Caterina's welcome as she removed food and drink from a wooden cupboard and placed it on a side table, gesturing for the gentlemen to help themselves.

Both men grinned as she poured them cups of wine. The tall one raised his cup to her while his companion chose a fig. "Thank your aunt for us," he said. "We are famished. But we cannot possibly let you take these coins from the room. We will count them together, when you have satisfied yourself about the contract."

"Of course. Of course," Nicola said. She explained quickly to Caterina, who curtseyed to the men and hurried from the room, gesturing to Nicola to follow.

"What is happening?" Nicola asked her. "Why didn't I know anything about this?"

"Because I never thought King Henry would sign it," Caterina said. "Come in here, so the men don't hear us."

They stepped inside a supply room, lined with ingots of pig iron and pallets of wood the correct size for making charcoal. Caterina pulled the door closed, shutting out the rhythmic clanging of hammer on anvil and the shouts and laughter of the armory workers.

"I'm charging the English king three times our usual price," Caterina began.

"But who drafted the contract? It's in Latin. You don't know Latin."

"Niccolò and I worked on it, when I was in Milan. I sent it off as an offer, and forgot about it."

Nicola was relieved. "If my father drafted it, I'm sure it's in order. I'll look it over, then let's go count the coins. Congratulations!"

"Wait," Caterina said, clutching the document. "Before you read it, there is something I need to explain."

Caterina looked as pale and frightened as she had as a new widow, years earlier. Nicola's elation turned to misgiving. "What is my father up to?" she demanded.

Caterina put a finger to her lips. "It was his idea, and I went along with it. I never dreamt it would actually work."

Nicola's misgivings were turning to alarm. "You never dreamt what would work?"

"Those coins they brought as our first payment? It is less than half the money, Nicola. This contract will make us a fortune. '

Nicola was losing patience. "For doing what?"

Caterina squeezed her arm. "Shhh. Try to listen, and not shout."

Nicola vowed to hold her temper, at least until she knew why she should be angry. "I will not shout," she promised, gritting her teeth. "What have you agreed to do?"

Caterina took both of Nicola's hands, and looked into her eyes. "I have agreed to send you to England," she said, clutching Nicola, who tried to wrestle her hands away.

"England? Send me to England? Why?"

Caterina squeezed Nicola's hands. "Shhh. To teach the English how to manufacture cannons and *arquebuses*. From start to finish. We fulfill half the order here, and you bring it with you. When the English workers have produced the other half under your supervision, we get our final payment. King Henry pays for your voyage, both ways, before you leave Italy. So even if they renege on the final payment, you get an ocean trip to England and back. And we will be so much richer—"

Nicola was angry, but she kept her voice low. "You did this to get me away from Raphael, didn't you?"

Caterina shook her head. "No. Well, partly, maybe. But in essence, we offered to send you because you know the business, and speak the language of the English court. We have no one else who does. And since you are not a man, we told him that you are also beautiful and accomplished. This new English king is young, and rich, and educated. He is besotted with his new Spanish wife, they say—but he likes beautiful women. You were an inducement."

Nicola's anger bubbled over. "An inducement. My father is trying to sell me abroad as a king's mistress, isn't he? Isn't he? So he won't have to pay my dowry. Why would you agree to prostitute me—"

Caterina put two fingers to Nicola's lips. Shhh. It's not like that at all, Nicola. The English king was not seeking women to warm his bed. There are plenty in England, including his new wife, to do that. He is seeking Italian craftsmen—crafts*men*—because he is trying to build a navy for England. He put out a general invitation, and your father thought I should compete for the business. But we agreed I should charge a premium, since we will lose the future business to the Englishmen we train."

"You've never done that before—give away our secrets."

"True. But we—your father and I—agreed that *someone* will teach the English. Or they will figure it out themselves, just as we did. So filling a large contract first is a good idea. No one was trying to prostitute you. How could you think such a thing?" Caterina patted her arm. "I know you love Raphael. But he is not good for you. So the thought did occur to us that it would be best for you to get away from him for a while. If you and Raphael truly love each other, the time apart will not matter. It never mattered to your father and me."

Nicola stamped her foot. She was right about her parents' motivation—and they were right about Raphael. He was *not* good for her. She *should* get away from him. "How long?" she asked. "How long will I be away?"

Caterina made a palms–down gesture that begged Nicola to calm herself. "However long it takes," she replied. "It depends on how primitive the English smelters are, and how good their local metals are. You have to teach them how to purify the ores, and make the amalgams. And how to mold and weld and case–harden cannons and *arquebuses,* so they don't blow up. You and Leonardo worked out local variations when we opened the operation in Florence, based on the materials available there.‡‡‡ You learned a great deal. I'm confident you can do the same in England."

Nicola thought for a moment. "It will take half a year, maybe."

Caterina's face brightened. "Maybe. The contract promises you private quarters in one of King Henry's castles, access to his library, and food and drink at his table. You can bring your own maid, or they will supply one. I never thought he would agree to all that, but he has."

She took Nicola's hands again. "My honor is at stake here, *cara.* The King has signed my contract. If his payment is short I could reject it, but his letter––charming letter; someone composed it in Italian–– says he is including a bonus. I have given my word. If you refuse to help, my reputation will be ruined."

Nicola thought about Raphael's betrayals. Then she considered the tall blue–eyed man who waited in the next room. The thought of a sea voyage––her first––to a royal court in a new land was attractive. Not just attractive––exciting. Her own quarters, maidservant, and access to a king's library, too?

"Tell my father to give me my dowry," she told Caterina. "If he does, I will go to England."

Caterina frowned and wrung her hands. "I can tell him. I can beg him. But I can't make him do it, Nicola. And transferring your dowry from Florence to Rome will take a long time to arrange. These men want an answer *now*, and I owe them one. Please, I beg you. I

---

‡‡‡ Read about it in *Da Vinci Detects*

know I should have told you, and I'm very sorry I didn't. But I didn't know the English were such. . . ."

"Such easy marks?" Nicola laughed. "*Va bene*. If you will make every effort to wrestle my dowry from my father, I'll see that King Henry gets what the contract specifies. Promise me, though."

Caterina kissed the silver cross hanging from her neck, threw back her head, and laughed. "*Dio grazie,*" she said. "I promise, with all my heart. And I also promise you a new wardrobe, in the latest fashion. Because King Henry's ladies will want to see how Italian ladies dress."

She rose from her chair. "Come, let's read the contract, and compare it with my copy. Then we will count the coins. You will have a great adventure in England, *carina*."

Nicola could feel her excitement mounting.

Author's Biography

Maryann Philip (a nom de plume) has sold thousands of e-books in the Nicola Machiavelli historical mystery series, consistently receiving 4 out of 5 stars on average, after more than 170 Amazon reviews. Maryann graduated with honors in "Renaissance Studies" (a self-created interdepartmental major) from Stanford University in 1975, having spent part of her junior year at Stanford's Florence campus, researching her honors thesis using original Italian texts in the Biblioteca Nazionale. She then went to law school (U. Chicago '78) and spent the next thirty years raising children and practicing law, with occasional time out to sing in small ensembles devoted to Renaissance music. She now lives in California, having retired from law practice to brush up on her Italian and devote herself to travel and her favorite period in history: the Italian Renaissance.

Afterword

As in earlier Nicola Machiavelli mysteries, historical characters appear only where and when they did in real life, doing what they did in real life. Exceptions and general observations on the history behind this mystery are noted below.

Cast of Characters:

As noted, real historical figures are *italicized*. The story that Raphael died from too much sex with his mistress, on whom Nicola is loosely modeled, comes from Giorgio Vasari's famous *Lives of the Artists*. Though only 9 years old when Raphael died, Vasari knew plenty of Raphael's contemporaries, who doubtless passed on salacious rumors concerning his early death. A plausible reading of Vasari's account (which is couched in medieval medical terminology) is that Raphael had a heart attack, and his doctors made the mistake of bleeding him.

Chapter 2:
Leonardo da Vinci's connection with Machiavelli, the basis for my second book, "Da Vinci Detects," is historic fact. And da Vinci was indeed working on a book on human anatomy with Marcantonio delle Torre in north Italy during the time Martin Luther was in Rome. Delle Torre's joke refers to the Church rule against dissections of Christians, except for executed felons (who were thought to be headed for Hell anyway). Delle Torre died suddenly in the middle of his joint project with da Vinci, which was never completed.

Chapter 3:
The story of Luther's disagreement with a chantry priest who mocked him for taking too long to recite Mass is from the historical record, though the original version does not involve a woman. I have no idea if Martin Luther had a distinctive spoken voice, though he was an amateur musician and an excellent writer. His voice is metaphorical here.

Chapter 4:
The recurrent fevers suffered by Pope Julius II are attributed either to secondary syphilis or malaria, both of which afflicted him. However, it was typical to suspect poison when any important person was ill.

The description of Pope Julius' short–lived castle, built as a defensive measure next to one of the city walls after he conquered Bologna in 1506, is entirely imaginary. It was razed by an angry mob when papal forces were ejected from Bologna in 1511.

Chapter 5:
Michelangelo had barely begun the ceiling of the Sistine Chapel when Martin Luther arrived in Rome, and spent much of this time journeying back and forth to Bologna for funds. His first endeavor, the Noah frescoes, are not his best works. His Sistine Chapel ceiling has nonetheless eclipsed the works of other famous artists, such as Botticelli, that adorn the Sistine Chapel walls.

Chapter 6:
    The bill of exchange was the Renaissance equivalent of a check, which revolutionized commerce by allowing merchants to travel from place to place without having to carry and guard vast quantities of gold. Banks were mercantile houses rather than modern institutions, however. The exchange system depended entirely on the acumen, power and sense of honor of wealthy individuals and their customers.

Chapter 12:
    By his own account, Martin Luther spent his time in Rome going from relic to relic to pray for blessings and absolution. The story about his visit to the Scala Sancta, when he half wished his parents dead so he could save them from Purgatory, is his own. The Church of San Sisto was on the pilgrim's route at the time and the saint's bones, now elsewhere, are still Catholic relics. "Pig knuckles" are my own addition.

Chapter 17:
    At this time, Rome's great families—most notably, the Orsini and Colonna—lived in large fortified compounds of which there are now only traces. One family actually occupied the Coliseum, having built guard towers along the top. And the entire city bristled with tall towers, because every influential family had built one for self-protection.
    Christopher Columbus brought tobacco back from the New World early on, but the tobacco habit had not yet become widespread.
    The rape and murder of women and children by the French in Fivizzano is historic fact, as is the decimation of the French army by virulent syphilis ("The French Disease"), newly-arrived from the New World on Columbus' ships. Whether Italians managed to avenge the atrocities at Fivizzano, however, I do not know.

Chapter 18:
    Though he was deeply religious and well-educated, Martin Luther never lost the coarseness he owed to his background as the son of an uneducated miner. And he did like his beer. He accelerated the secularization of the Teutonic Order many years after this book occurs,

when he advised them to abandon their monastic lives to start families. The head of the Order took Luther's advice and resigned his post.

Chapter 20:

My sources give varying names for the friar who accompanied Martin Luther to Rome. I chose one of them.

Scholars have speculated that Martin Luther's deep sense of his own sinfulness stemmed from sexual thoughts he could not control, since he was by all accounts a very virtuous man. Luther eventually married and fathered a number of children, after persuading himself that priestly chastity was not sanctioned by the Bible. So perhaps the speculations are correct.

Chapter 21:

Rome today looks little like it did in Martin Luther's time. Until the popes rebuilt the ancient aqueducts and forced the reigning families to tear down their defensive towers and arcades, the population was tiny and concentrated in medieval hovels near the Tiber River, its water source. The rest of Rome was a ghost town, the rubble-filled expanses around its ancient monuments used to graze cattle and sheep. One of the earliest fountains to be rebuilt—though not yet festooned with the baroque statues familiar to modern tourists—was the ancient fountain at Trevi.

Chapter 24:

Leonardo da Vinci's dalliance in early 1510 with a courtesan from Cremona, a town between Pavia and Milan, is documented in Charles Nicholl's excellent biography, *Leonardo da Vinci: Flights of the Mind*. It is thought that she was da Vinci's model for Leda, whom Zeus seduced in the guise of a swan. Da Vinci's "Leda and the Swan" exists only in copies by other artists because a French queen deemed the original obscene and ordered it burned, in the century after da Vinci's death.

Many scholars think Salai and perhaps Cecco were da Vinci's "boy toys," and not his adopted sons. As explained at greater length in my earlier book, *Da Vinci Detects*, there is no evidence that da Vinci was a homosexual, or of sexual relationships between da Vinci and any of his apprentices. Conversely, there is evidence consistent with a parent–child relationship with both of them, and in Cecco's case, even documentary evidence of his adoption (then a kind of sponsorship) by da Vinci.

Salai and Cecco stayed with da Vinci until he was elderly and they were middle aged, ultimately becoming his principal heirs. Cecco reverently preserved his notebooks. I choose to treat them as adopted sons because it is consistent with the circumstantial evidence and because I refuse to label da Vinci a pedophile where no such evidence exists. (Salai became his apprentice at 11 years old.)

Chapter 28:
Scholars are uncertain of the dates when Raphael worked on frescoes of beautiful women in the Chigi villa. The *Triumph of Galatea* is thought to have been completed at the villa before 1514.

Chapter 30:
So far, I have found no art historian who agrees with me that the "angelic boy" whose face is found in Raphael's famous "School of Athens" and two of the other wall frescoes in that room is, in fact, a woman. But the face and hair do bear a strong resemblance to Raphael's profile of Sappho, the only female poet shown in in his famous "Poets." According to art historians, the Roman courtesan Imperia was the model for Sappho. And Imperia was a close acquaintance of Raphael's, though perhaps not as close as his chief mistress, "La Fornarina."

Chapter 31:
Martin Luther was an amateur musician who wrote several of the the foundational Lutheran hymns, and knew how to play the lute. He, as much as anyone, is the source of the Protestant tradition of hymn singing. He apparently wrote one Christmas hymn, but it is obscure enough that I could not find it and no one would recognize it.

The story that Agostino Chigi invited Raphael's mistress, "La Fornarina," into the Chigi villa because Raphael was distracted by his longing for her comes from the historical record.

Chapter 32:

The meal, table decorations and entertainment described in this chapter duplicate that of an actual wedding banquet described in Cristoforo Messisbugo's 1557 book, *Banquets: Composition of Dishes and General Presentation*. Sugar, available only to the wealthy, was used in surprising ways at this time. Messisbugo also wrote the first known recipe for caviar.

Chapter 33:

While information regarding popes' sexuality is often speculative, as a youth in Florence Giulio de' Medici (later Pope Clement VII) sired a servant's child who was acknowledged and raised by the Medici family. He later supported the young man in his quest to become head of the Medici. Giulio was close to his cousin/guardian Cardinal de' Medici, who became, Pope Leo X, his papal predecessor. However, as far as I can tell, the rumors of homosexuality surrounding Leo X did not extend to their relationship.

Chapter 39:

Pope Julius himself performed the marriage ceremony for Agostino Chigi and the celebrated Venetian courtesan who was his mistress, after they had produced four children together.

Chapter 45:

To wrap up this book I have cheated a bit on some dates. Niccolò Machiavelli's 1510 sojourn in France actually ended a couple of months earlier than indicated here, and his side journey through Milan on his way back to Florence is plausible but fictional. Pompeo Colonna's failed rebellion against Pope Julius actually occurred the summer following Luther's journey back to Rome.

Chapter 46:

Cardinal Francesco Alidosi died as described in this chapter, for the reasons described. His evil reputation and scandalous death have obscured his papal ambitions in the histories. He may or may not have been engaged in treason with the French, as accused by the pope's nephew and others. But he was so loathed that, according to the histories of the time, no one but Pope Julius mourned his passing.

Partial Bibliography

Bainton, Roland H. *Here I Stand: A Life of Martin Luther* . Mentor Books, 1950.
Dillenberger, John. *Martin Luther: Selections from his writings edited and with an introduction. Doubleday & Co., 1961.*
Marty, Martin. *Martin Luther: A Life.* Penguin Books Ltd. 2004.
Wilson, Derek. *Out of the Storm: The Life and Legacy of Martin Luther* St Martin's Press , 2007.
Plass, Eward. *This is Luther.* Concordia Press, 1957.
Koestlin, Julius *The Life of Luther.* Kessinger Publishing, 2010.
Mee, Charles L.Jr. *White Robe, Black Robe: Pope Leo X, Martin Luther and the Birth of the Reformation* . J.P. Putnam & Sons, 1972.
King, Ross. *Michelangelo and the Pope's Ceiling.* Penguin Books, 2003.
Gilbert, Felix. *The Pope, His Banker and Venice.* Harvard University Press, 1980.
Murphy, Caroline P. *The Pope's Daughter : The Extraordinary Life of Felice della Rovere.* Oxford University Press, 2005.
LeRoque, Noel C. *Martin Luther's Friends* . Providence House, 1997.
Una Guerra d'Italia, Una Resistenza del Populo:Bologna 1506 Societa Editrice Il Molino, Bologna, Italia.
Partner, Peter. *Renaissance Rome 1500-1559: A Portrait of a Society. University of California Press 1976.*
Pietro Arentino. *The Secret Lives of Nuns*, trans. Maria Falus: Hesperus Press 2003.
Anne Willan and Mark Chemiavsky, The Cookbook library: Four Centuries of Cooks, Writers and Recipes that Made the Modern Cookbook; citing Cristofero Messibugo, *Banchetti, Composizione de Vivande e Apparecchio Générale (Banquets, Composition of Dishes and General Presentation)* at p. 79
Burckhardt, Jacob, *The Civilization of the Renaissance in Italy* ((Modern Library Edition, 2002)
Chamberlain, E.R. *Everyday Life in Renaissance Times.* Putnam, 1965

Chamberlain, E.R. *The Bad Popes*. Harold Ober & Associates 1969, reprinted by Barnes & Noble, 1993.
Viroli, Maurizio. *Niccolò's Smile* . Hill and Wang, 2002.
Cloulas, Ivan. *The Borgias*. Franklin,Watts Inc. 1989.
Borman, Tracy. *The private lives of the Tudors: uncovering the secrets of Britain's greatest dynasty*. Grove Press 2016.
Nicholl, Charles. *Leonardo da Vinci: Flights of the Mind, A Biography*. Penguin Books, 2004.

Made in the USA
Middletown, DE
13 December 2018